THE DEVIL DÉJÀ VU

ALSO BY H. BYRON EARHART

The Twin Destiny Series

No Pizza in Heaven

Faith Finds Forgiveness

Meeting the Devil

Devil Deja Vu

Canterbury Canticle

THE DEVIL DÉJÀ VU

BOOK 4 OF THE TWIN DESTINY SERIES

H. BYRON EARHART

iCrew
digita publishing
Chula Vista • Columbus

Printed in the United States of America

Published by iCrew Digital Publishing

Website: icrewdigitalpublishing.com

e-mail: icrewdigital@gmail.com

ISBN: 978-1-946739-08-7 (iCrew Digital Productions)

iCrew Digital Publishing is an independent publisher of digital works. We support the efforts of authors who wish to self- publish in the digital world.

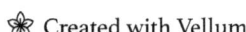 Created with Vellum

This book is dedicated to all the teachers who had the patience and persistence to nurture my appreciation for the diversity and richness of human life and culture.

PROLOGUE

L*ife is good*, Faith thought, as she sat in her condo overlooking placid Lake Michigan.

Saturday mornings she loved to slip on a robe and relax in her recliner, soaking up the sun's warmth while gazing at her beloved lake. On Saturdays Scott always left early, putting the final touches on Sunday's paper. Faith enjoyed the solitude, giving her a break from the hubbub of the office and time to herself when she could reflect on her situation and count her blessings.

Yes, she reminded herself, life *is* good. More than six months had passed since she and her clan had faced Doug and dealt with all of the problems he triggered. Doug had tried to barge into the family—as Scott put it, like the proverbial camel sticking its nose in the tent. Jeremy would have let Doug in the family, but Jonathan was dead set against it. Not only did this issue pit one twin against the other, it positioned Jeremy and Melanie on opposite sides. Even Faith and Scott had a serious disagreement about a family meeting with Doug, and how they should handle him.

Looking back on this thorny episode, Faith breathed a sigh of relief. In the end, they avoided serious confrontations with one another while keeping Doug outside the family circle. Her clan had survived, and in the process strengthened their family bond.

Lake Michigan could turn violent and send ships and sailors to its watery depths, but now its glassy surface was welcoming and peaceful. She hoped her clan would be able to weather the inevitable storms and enjoy a pleasant and serene future.

1

Whenever Faith reminisced, she couldn't help time-traveling back to her idyllic childhood in Canton, then the ill-fated meeting with Doug at Pappy's Pizza Parlor, the birth of the twins and the traumatic separation from her boys, followed by decades of lonely self-exile in Chicago. Reunion with her grown sons and their families was almost too good to be true.

She had been sipping chamomile tea, and felt like another cup. She went to the kitchen and microwaved water, taking a tea bag from the cupboard. Waiting for the water to heat, she wondered what she and Scott would do over the weekend. Some Saturdays when he got home from the office, they made love, and she looked forward to that.

As she walked with her tea back to the recliner, the phone rang. Sure it would be Scott, she picked up without looking at caller ID.

"Hi, hon."

"Hello, Faith."

Her surprise at not hearing Scott's voice turned to shock and fear as she recognized an unexpected intruder—*Doug*!

She hesitated, hoping she was wrong.

"Well, Faith, that was a nice greeting. You know who this is, don't you, your old friend Doug."

"Uh ... I thought my husband was calling."

"No, I guess we never made it to the altar, did we?"

Faith closed her eyes and gritted her teeth, shouting, "What do you want?"

"Hey, don't get all hot and bothered; this is just a social call, to see how you and the boys are doing."

"We're doing fine, thank you. I have to hang up now; I'm expecting a call."

"Well, give me a few minutes. Hubby can wait."

"If that's all you wanted, then—how did you get this number?"

"Oh, Faith, dear, I have my ways. You had your Chicago bloodhounds track me down, and us downstaters have our coon dogs and weasels to snoop around for us."

"You may have succeeded in finding my phone number, but I don't have to talk to you."

"I hope this doesn't get back to, 'My lawyer will talk to your lawyer.' You might want to hear that I have a new lawyer. My old lawyer, Stan, was a fraternity buddy, and a nice guy, but not that hot as a negotiator. One lousy half hour in a lawyer's office to talk with my boys, that's all, and then your stuffed shirt legal eagle threw me out, threatened to call the police."

Faith's voice became shrill. "Let me remind you, Mr. Parinello, the only reason they met with you is that you withheld family histories crucial for the medical treatment of my sons."

"Hell, they are *my* sons, too."

"You certainly didn't act like it, not handing over the medical papers."

"Well, they're okay now, aren't they?"

"Uh, you know, my lawyer told me several times I don't have to give you any information, so we can consider this call over."

"Not so fast, Miss high-powered executive. My lawyer says I have the right to know about my sons."

"You never bothered for thirty years."

"No, and you never told me about them for thirty years."

"Mr. Parinello, we settled all that in the Chicago meeting in the lawyer's office, so it's over. Done. Finished."

"You're wrong; it's just starting."

Faith tried to laugh. "Hah. What do you think is starting?"

"You may not want to recognize it, but the twins are my sons, too, my flesh and blood, and I want to meet them."

"No way. Never."

"You may have to rethink that. And you Chicago hotshots don't realize it, but when you put me behind the eight ball for the medical records, you made a mistake."

"What do you mean?" Faith's tone turned sharp. "I think you're bluffing."

Doug chuckled. "I thought you wouldn't like to hear how my lawyer and I outsmarted you. See, it's like this. Somehow you got my DNA and proved that I am the father of the twins. That's what my attorney called a legal boomerang. You gave me proof of paternity, my key to access to them."

Faith raised her voice. "Being a father may be a biological fact, but you never paid a penny to support them, and you never did a thing to *father* them."

"True, true, but I'm still one up on you. My attorney gave me an education about 'parental rights.' Ever hear of that fancy term? When you gave up the twins for adoption, you signed away all parental rights, so you stopped being their parent. Me, I never signed any such papers, so I never gave up my rights to being a parent. And my attorney says that means I have the right to contact my sons."

Faith was hyperventilating. "You can't ... you can't ...."

"Honey, I can and I will. The only question is whether you're going to help me get in touch with them, or if the courts are going to order you to do it."

Faith gasped, struggling to breathe. "Why ... why don't you just leave us alone?"

"Now that's not nice. Just be a good girl and help out an old friend."

"No! I'll never ...."

"My lawyer says never say never."

"I'm hanging up, and never ... don't ever call again."

She slammed the phone down, held her hands over her face and cried, sobbing as she tried to catch her breath. Her heart pounded like it might jump out of her chest. She tried to get up out of the lounger, but felt so dizzy she slumped back down. Her heart raced even faster, and sharp pains accompanied each beat.

The phone rang, startling her. She reached for the receiver, dropped it, then picked it up again and shouted into the phone, "I thought I told you never to call again!"

"Uh, dear, what are you talking about? Get an obscene call?"

"Yeah, Scott, a really obscene call. From Doug."

"That perverse bastard!"

"Scott, forget about him. He scared me so much I can't get my breath, and my heart is racing out of control. It hurts real bad."

"Listen to me carefully. Is the pain only in your chest? Does the pain move down your arm, or up to your chin?"

"No ... I don't think so. I'm so woozy I couldn't get up from the lounger. Get home as soon as you can."

"I will, but first I'm going to call 911. Now let's see if you can get up slowly, holding the side of the lounger, and unlock the door for the paramedics."

"Oh, Scott, I'll be alright; just get home right away."

"I'm sure you'll be fine, and I'll rush home, but let's play it safe with a trip to the hospital."

"I'll have to get dressed."

"No! Just get back to the lounger, and stay there."

2

Scott made the call to 911, then ran to his car. Using blue tooth, he called Bill Ludwig.

"Bill, this is Scott Henderson. Faith may be having a heart attack. I called 911 and told them to take her to Michael Reese. What's the name of your cardiologist there?"

"Harry Hancock. Top notch."

"I want you to contact him or the on-call cardiologist and have them meet Faith in ER. I'm leaving the office now, on the way to the condo, and will probably be able to ride to the hospital in the ambulance."

"Scott, will do. Don't want to hold you up. Minutes are precious. Call me for anything."

Scott got to his car and raced home, running some lights. At the condo parking garage, he punched the elevator button several times, then squeezed between the doors as they opened, and jumped out when the elevator reached their floor. The condo door was open, paramedics surrounding Faith, asking her questions while administering oxygen and hooking up an IV.

Scott reached across a gurney and held Faith's shaking hand. "You'll be okay." Then he turned to the team leader. "I asked for her to be taken to Michael Reese. Can you do that?"

"I can probably clear it with dispatch." He turned away and made the call.

IN A FEW MINUTES, they were out of the condo and in the ambulance, whose sirens announced their trip to the hospital.

Scott stared in disbelief at Faith's ashen face. She tried to smile. Scott said, "Take it easy, dear, we're almost there, and Bill Ludwig has called ahead to have a cardiologist examine you."

The paramedics efficiently brought Faith into ER, where nurses rechecked her vitals and hooked her up to an EKG monitor. Soon a doctor entered the examining room. "You're Scott Henderson, the husband? I'm Kent Cunningham, the on-call cardiologist for Dr. Hancock. Fill me in. Were you with her when this started?"

"No, she received a troubling call, and then phoned me—hyperventilation, rapid heartbeat, dizziness, some shaking."

"Happen before?"

"No. Excellent health."

Dr. Cunningham examined Faith and ran her through a battery of questions. Then he motioned Scott into the hallway.

"EKG is normal. Her pulse and blood pressure are a little high, but not dangerous. We should keep her here today for observation, probably overnight to see if she settles down."

"Diagnosis?"

"Too soon for a diagnosis. You said she got a troubling call. Could be what is commonly called a panic attack. If nothing shows up in twenty-four hours, that would be good news."

"I'll stay with her."

"Your presence would probably help her."

. . .

SCOTT SAT on a chair by her bed, holding her hand. A sedative made Faith drowsy. She napped off and on. When Faith woke and saw Scott by her side, she smiled.

By late afternoon Faith was more alert and wanted to go home. The nurse laid down the law. "Doctor's orders are for you to be here overnight. If you're better when they make rounds tomorrow, they may release you."

Faith called Bill Ludwig. "I'm fine; sorry to trouble you."

"Young lady, you scared the hell out of us. I won't keep you on the line. Get some rest, mind the doctors, and get well."

THE NEXT MORNING Dr. Cunningham signed Faith's discharge papers, with instructions to see her family physician within two weeks.

Scott had slept at the hospital in a lounge chair, checking on Faith several times during the night. They took a taxi home.

"Scott, thanks for being so good to me. I guess it was nothing, and I put you and the doctors through all that commotion for nothing."

"Dear, we never know. Better to let the doctors decide what is serious."

"Well, we have to talk about Doug. The gist of what he said is that he has a new lawyer who claims he can force us to give him contact information for the twins. He quoted his attorney that our paternity test proves he is the father and that gives him 'parental rights.'"

"He's a little late to play daddy."

"Scott, you should have heard him. He's determined. And as Bill once told us, he's smart. The new lawyer seems to be brighter than the fraternity brother who used to represent him."

"Sooner or later we'll have to talk about this, but right now I want you to set this aside, get some rest, watch TV, read a book. Your system has been on overload, so don't work yourself up into another spell."

After Scott fixed a light lunch, he asked, "How about a short walk along the lakefront?"

"Nothing would please me more. I feel like an invalid."

When they left the building, the doorman asked, "You okay, Miss A? You gave us a scare."

"Yeah, I'm fine. Just a routine checkup."

Scott held her hand as they enjoyed the brisk fall breeze off the lake. After ten minutes he said, "Let's head back."

When they returned to the condo, Scott led her to her recliner. "How about a cup of tea?"

"You're a mind reader."

When he returned from the kitchen with two steaming cups, he asked, "Do you feel up to talking about it now? I don't want you to get upset and have another episode."

Faith looked down at the floor, shaking her head. "Well, before we talk about Doug, let's talk about me. I'm ashamed of myself for going out of control over his call. I pride myself on being a high level, high-stress manager and negotiator, and then go off the deep end over a simple phone conversation. The difference, you know, is that as a business executive, I'm in control. But when it comes to our family, and negotiating with Doug, it's personal, and I'm not in control, so it's threatening."

"You always were good at self-analysis. Now the question is what you're going to do. Correction—what we're going to do."

"Let me ask you, Scott, do you think Doug and his lawyer can force us to give contact information for Jeremy and Jonathan? That's the question I'd like answered before moving on to the decision of what to do. And maybe you can't answer that."

"No, and I shouldn't try to give you an answer. I've heard lots of stories of adoptions that went bad, and then the birth parents tried to back out. Doug is certainly right on one point; he was never a party to the original adoption. But that was all more than thirty years ago, and I don't know about the statute of limitations for such things. Did Doug say why he wanted to contact the twins?"

"He pulled the 'flesh and blood' card, and wants to connect with his offspring."

"Sounds fishy, hokey, to me, and I would imagine it would play out the same for a judge, but you never know. That's an angle Bill Ludwig will have to handle. Why don't you set up a meeting with him? Hell, who knows, maybe Parinello is just being nasty, calling to needle you, and he's bluffing about a court case."

"He sounded dead serious, and seems to know a lot about parental rights."

"Set up a meeting with Ludwig tomorrow, and he can help us decipher the legal mumbo jumbo."

3

The next week Faith and Scott met with Bill Ludwig in his office.

"Faith, good to see you, but first I want to hear about your health. Are you sure you want to tackle heavy-duty legal issues? I don't want to upset you. If you feel uncomfortable, you can walk out that door any time. And if I see any stress on your part, I'll usher you out myself."

"Bill, that hospital trip was a wakeup call for me. I have to learn to deal with Doug, using my brain, not my emotions."

"Alright, what can you tell me about this nonsense of Parinello wanting to contact his sons? I thought we settled that in my office with Jeremy and Jonathan."

"Saturday I got a surprise phone call from Doug, and he says he has the right—he called it the parental right—to see his children. He has a new lawyer who claims the proof of paternity we used in the medical records negotiation proves he is the father, and that means he has the right to see them. He needled me that when I signed the adoption papers I gave up my right as a parent, but he had no part of the adoption proceedings, so he never gave up his right as a parent. Well, that's what the call amounted to. It shocked me so much I went into an emotional tailspin. What do you think, Bill?"

"Well, I'll be damned to hell and back. He's smart and clever, and apparently, he has upgraded his legal representation."

"Bill, what I want to know is—can he force us to give him contact information for Jeremy and Jon?"

"Is that what he asked for?"

"Yes. He said if we didn't cooperate with him, the courts would force us to get him in touch with the boys."

Bill looked at Scott. "And you two don't want that?"

Scott chimed in. "Neither of us wants that."

"What about the twins? What do they think?"

"We haven't told them or anyone else about this. We wanted to hear your legal advice first."

"Well, my dear friends, the first thing I have to admit is I've never handled a case like this. In fact, I've never heard of a situation that matches it. Most of the time, messy family situations involve bitter divorces. And there are plenty of cases of unmarried couples who have a kid, then split, and the guy either wants custody or at least visitation provisions."

Faith frowned. "So what happens now?"

"That's a good question. I don't handle many divorce cases, so I'll have to check with some of my colleagues to see what they think. But frankly, I doubt if there's ever been this kind of litigation in Illinois Family Court."

"Is that where it would be handled?"

"Yes. Each party would present their argument to a judge who would hand down a ruling."

"How does the judge decide?"

"There are no hard and fast rules, but a number of soft principles. The judge usually instructs each side to present an argument of 'what is best for the child.' By the way, notice the language of 'the child,' because most of the time the sad fact is that offspring get caught in the crossfire between mother and father. If the 'child' is an infant or toddler, he or she has no say. If the child or children are old enough to understand the situation, the judge may gingerly ask a kid if they are happy in their living arrangement, and which parent they want to live with."

Faith stifled a laugh. "Hah! Jeremy and Jon are long past childhood, with their own children."

"Of course, and that's what makes this case unique. Unless we have a time machine to transport us back several decades, Parinello can never change a diaper, hold a baby bottle, take kids to kindergarten, teach them to ride a bicycle—you know, the standard parenting things."

"Bill, even when I was on the phone with Doug, and couldn't think straight, I told him something along those lines. I said he has proof of paternity, which gives him *biological* credentials as a father, but he never actually fathered them, took care of them. And he didn't provide a cent to support them."

"Faith, we know that story. His side will argue that you didn't tell him you were pregnant and had twins. And you didn't ask for any support."

Scott blurted out, "And he didn't bother to find out if his pleasure resulted in pregnancy, did he?"

Bill said, "No, and this is the kind of exchange we'd have to deal with in court."

Faith edged forward in her seat. "Bill, what else do they consider?"

"Faith, are you sure you want to talk about this today? You seem to be upset."

"Don't worry about me; I'm just concerned for my kids. Oh, and grandkids."

Bill bit his lip, then continued. "Yes, grandkids. That's another wrinkle of divorce. Even if, say a divorced husband is a louse, an alcoholic, and never contributes support, the guy's own parents may petition the court for visitation as grandparents."

Faith covered her face with her hands, choking back a sob. "That's what I was afraid of."

Bill looked at Scott, and they exchanged nods. "Well, Faith

we've covered a lot, and I think that's enough for today. Let me just give you some tips. Whatever you two think, *don't contact Parinello!* Keep the ball in his court. Until he calls you, just wait him out. He may be bluffing. It could be he's just getting his revenge on you and the rest of us."

Faith dabbed her eyes with a handkerchief. "I understand."

"And if he does give you a call, don't concede or admit anything. Tell him the matter will have to be handled by your attorney. Just give him my phone number and address." He paused, looking back and forth at Scott and Faith. "Uh, you said you hadn't mentioned this to the twins. This is up to you, but my judgment is that it's better not to bother them. Maybe Parinello is just blowing smoke, and this will all go away. No point in involving them unless Parinello forces the issue."

Scott said, "Thanks for meeting with us today and for that good advice."

Bill gave Faith a hug. "One more thing, young lady. Take it easy. Remember that Horton Hotels got along before you were around, and will do fine if you take some time off. I've cut back on my schedule, and think you should consider the same."

BEFORE SCOTT WENT to the newspaper office, he took Faith to a nearby coffee shop to talk over their meeting with Bill.

"Scott, what do you think?"

"Short and sweet. He's a smart lawyer, gave you the basics, and ended with sound advice. You're in good hands, and have to follow his script if and when Doug calls."

"If it goes to court, it won't be easy."

"No, of course not. And just like the fight over medical records for Jeremy, there'll be a lot of back and forth, and it may never see the inside of a courthouse."

"I hope not."

"Hon, I've got to run to the office. I have a suggestion to add to what Ludwig offered. We've got the ball rolling with our legal eagle.

Why don't you make an appointment with your father confessor? He'll help you sort out the personal, emotional issues."

"You're right. When I get home, I'll call Father Whitmore. He was a big help when we were fighting the battle over the medical records, and I'm sure he'll be able to see this mess more clearly than me."

4

Faith called Church of the Redeemer and set up an appointment with Father Whitmore several days later. Just arranging a time to meet with him made her feel better. She went to the hotel, glad to have plenty of work to keep her busy while waiting to have a session with her priest.

TOWARD THE END of the week, driving to the south side for the meeting, she remembered earlier trips there to discuss the medical, legal, and ethical concerns about Jeremy's kidney problems. Father Whitmore had offered sage advice.

When she climbed the steps to Church of the Redeemer, she walked past the priest's office, glad he was on the phone. She entered the sanctuary and stepped in front of the stained glass window of Madonna and child she had commissioned. Bowing her head, she placed her hands together and prayed, "Mother Mary, thank you for helping me in times past. Please help me through this difficulty. I know that you and Saint Harriet will be with me as we face our decisions."

Faith didn't care what theologians might say about her promotion of Harriet Beecher Stowe to the status of saint. Harriet was sister, mother, and saint combined.

Faith left the sanctuary for Father Whitmore's office. She started to knock on his door when he saw her and called out, "Come on in. Good to see you."

Taking a seat, Faith smiled. "I paid my respects first to Mary and Harriet, who have been my spiritual support."

"A lot of parishioners appreciate the window. I don't tell them about Harriet; that's between you and me."

"Good." Faith's smile disappeared as she thought about Doug.

"Hmm, what's on your mind? You seem seriously concerned about something."

"You always have been able to psych me out. To joke about it, it's SOS, the same old stuff, but with a new twist. Somehow Doug found my phone number and called, threatening to take us to court if we don't help him get in touch with the twins."

"Ouch! That must have thrown you for a loop."

"Worse than that. I was so discombobulated, I went through what the doctor called a panic attack, and had to go to the ER and stay overnight in the hospital."

"Sorry to hear that. You're better now?"

"Yeah, I got over the hyperventilation and heart palpitations, but still don't know how to deal with the emotional turmoil of Doug and his ultimatum."

"He hasn't had any papers served on you, has he?"

"No, we're in the waiting process now. Scott thinks Doug may be bluffing, just wanting to pester us and get revenge for outsmarting him in the medical records negotiation. We've seen our lawyer, Bill Ludwig, to find out what Doug can and cannot do, in Family Court. Bill, like Scott, thinks Doug may be bluffing, but I sense that Doug is hell-bent—excuse the phrase—on getting his way."

"Faith, I don't understand this new wrinkle. Last year, the standoff with Doug was you trying to force him to hand over medical records. Now he's the one pushing the legal buttons, trying to force you to get him in touch with Jeremy and Jon. Is that it?"

"Yeah, doesn't make much sense, does it?"

"Well, to put it bluntly, what does he expect to get out of a meeting?"

"He wants to connect ... reconnect ... with his sons. It's some kind of personal mission he's on. Scott and I, and even our attorney, Ludwig, don't fully understand it either. All we know is that Doug is clever, has teamed up with a smart lawyer, and seems determined to push the matter."

"Can he do that? I mean, require you to bring him together with your sons?"

"We discussed the legalities with Ludwig. Usually, such matters revolve around custody provisions for minors, and what is in the best interest of the children. Whether or not Doug, as a parent, can require us to introduce him to the twins, is something Ludwig is exploring."

"It's one thing if you have small kids, but this is a different ball game."

"Right. And what is a fifty-plus old man going to do if he is successful in making two thirty-plus guys meet with him?"

"As adults, they have rights, too."

"Yes, and I'm not worried about the twins. They can take care of themselves. The scary part is grandchildren. As you must know, Family Court does handle cases of visitation for grandparents if a divorced daughter-in-law—or son-in-law—refuses them access to grandchildren. In that situation, Jeremy and Jon might have to introduce their children to 'Grandpa Doug.'" Faith closed her eyes tight, clenching her jaw. "My grandkids should not be pawns in this mess."

"I remember all too well, the last time you faced legal hassles with Doug, you were more concerned about grandkids than the twins." He paused, hand in chin, then said, "I don't want to rub salt into the wound, but doesn't Doug have other children?"

"You're right."

"How many?"

"Who knows? At least there's two with his first wife, another two with his second wife, one with a live-in, and one that we found out from a paternity suit in southern Illinois. That's six, not counting Jeremy and Jonathan. So that makes eight we know of, maybe others waiting in the wings."

The priest let out a low whistle. "He should be busy enough just relating to his own brood without bothering your family."

"There's the rub. He's been shut out by the two ex-wives, who remarried and apparently turned the kids against their Casanova father who each time was caught cheating on the kids' mother. The live-in moved away, and his out of court lump sum payment in the paternity case probably cut off ties with that woman and her child. So he's spoiled each chance he had for being a 'father,' and I use that word loosely. Now he finds out about us, totally by accident, and wants to use our family for therapy and rehabilitation, so that he can qualify as an authentic male parent."

"You don't think it's possible for Doug to turn over a new leaf?"

"I was considering this, Father, how I could explain it to Doug, rationally and logically, in construction terms. If an earthquake badly damaged a house, you couldn't try to repair it if it had a bad foundation. Doug's marital history is like a combination of earth-quakes, tornadoes, and floods. He doesn't have a sound foundation to develop parental character."

"You have a colorful way of describing a personal character calamity."

"He's a walking disaster, and I don't want this catastrophe waltzing into our household."

"Not being a lawyer, I can't foresee how this might play out in court. But I hope you and your lawyer are keeping all this back-ground information close at hand as you prepare to argue before a judge."

"Yes, Bill Ludwig did a great job in the last legal wrangling, and I'm sure he'll do his best to represent our side in Family Court."

"Uh, Faith, I know you don't like me beating around the bush, so let me come right out with it. I sense there's something else both-ering you, but don't know what it is. Do you want to talk about it?"

"You're spot on! What's bugging me is something I came to realize this past week, thinking about Doug's call and how it disturbed me. And the only way I can bring it up is to tell you again what you already know of my past." Faith forced a grin, and said, "Maybe I should start with, 'Bless me, Father, for I have sinned.'"

He made the sign of the cross and said, "Go and sin no more."

"Now I have to retreat into the darkest days of my life when I was pregnant, and my parents said I had to give the babies up for adoption, and then after I held my sons for a few precious minutes, they were taken from me. To be honest, Father, although I finally managed to forgive Mom and Dad for that cruel separation, I have never completely forgotten it. The split from my children is a scar I will live with the rest of my life." She sighed. "For thirty years, while climbing the ladder of business success, I was drowning in a pool of loneliness and sorrow."

Faith paused, collecting her thoughts. "Okay, that you know. Here's what you haven't heard, and no one in my family knows. I hate to admit it, hate myself for acknowledging it, but I can see where Doug's coming from. It's because I suffered through decades of separation, I can feel for his desire to reconnect with what he calls his own 'flesh and blood.'

"It's still hard for me to come to terms with my feelings. I'm different from Jeremy, who argued that we're all sinners and should accept Doug back into our family as a redeemed soul. Maybe he's not the Bible's prodigal son, but a prodigal father. Anyway, my view is not so much religious, it's flesh and blood, skin and bones. I will never forget that one beautiful moment when I first held my twins, cradling each one against my cheeks."

Faith grabbed a tissue and dabbed at her eyes. "Much as I despise myself for saying it out loud, I can understand what is behind Doug's request. He doesn't deserve sympathy, but I still can't help pitying him, because I lived so long in the valley of isolation and melancholy. Well, that's part of my confession, and although I can talk about it with you, I don't dare mention it to the family or the lawyer. You can see I'm torn between feelings of compassion—

my softheartedness, and my recognition that Doug could ruin our family harmony—that's my hardheartedness. The reason I haven't mentioned this even to Scott, or the rest of the family, is that the sharp differences of opinion on how to handle Doug almost tore our family apart, and bringing it up again would threaten to divide us."

Faith cried for a few minutes. Father Whitmore waited until she stopped and looked up.

"You're a brave soul for looking into your heart, and balancing compassion with your head and common sense. I can't predict how you will resolve this difficult situation but know you'll find a solution. Mary and Harriet will help guide you, and my prayers will be with you."

He ended the session with a prayer, asking, "Lord, help us to see what is right, and do what is best."

WHEN FAITH LEFT Church of the Redeemer, she went straight to the condo. She needed several hours to regain her composure before Scott got home from work.

She would have liked a glass of wine, but would wait to share one with Scott if he was in the mood. She grabbed a soda from the fridge and relaxed in her recliner. Taking stock of her spiritual consultation, she made mental notes.

Mary is with me.
Harriet is with me.
Father Whitmore is with me.
I have backup with Scott and Bill.
Doug and his lawyer are my opponents.
That's five to two odds, pretty good.

SITTING IN HER RECLINER, reflecting on her problem, reminded her of the times she had sat there writing in her journal. She got up and rummaged through the back of her underwear drawer until she retrieved the little notebook. She carried it back to the lounger and opened it to a new page. She wrote in it

Trouble!

Revolving in her head were Doug's phone call, the session with Bill, and the confession/consultation with Father Whitmore. She was too confused to write more, so she got up and returned the journal to its undergarment hiding place.

WHEN SCOTT CAME HOME, he asked Faith, "How did it go with the good father?"

"He always helps me calm down. Well, I said prayers to Mary and Harriet, too. That was good."

"The more help, the better."

Faith hugged him tightly.

"Hey, what's that about?"

"Scott, no matter what happens, we're in this together. I need you now more than ever."

"Sure, babe, I'm on your team right along with Mary and Harriet."

5

The next weekend the clan gathered at the Goodman's new house in Downer's Grove. Because Jeremy had become head of the Chicago-based Mothers and Kids Foundation, the Goodman family moved from Springfield to a Chicago suburb. This reunion marked the first get-together at their new home.

On the drive from downtown to Downer's Grove, Faith and Scott agreed they wouldn't mention Doug's call to the others.

When Faith and Scott arrived, the kids burst out of the house and surrounded Scott, who had a gym bag full of goodies.

"What's in the bag?"

"Grandpa Scott, we gonna do a newspaper?"

Scott humored them. "Hey, let's ask your moms and dads what they want to do. Let's see when they want to eat, and if we have time for fun and games first."

The kids yelled in unison, "Fun and games!"

Melanie and Rachel chimed in. "They're too excited to eat." "Let them have their fun."

Scott said slowly, "Well, I don't know if we can do a newspaper, do you kids have any news, anything new, for a newspaper?"

Beth perked up. "Well, we *moved*. From Springfield to here!"

Big brother Mark added, "We have a new *house!*"

Scott snapped his fingers. "Well, we can do better than a newspaper, we can do a live newscast, and call it 'The Goodman New House Newscast.'"

The kids ran around in circles, excited about the project.

Scott assigned reporters.

"Beth, you tell us what your old house was like. Mark, you tell us about the new house. Stephie, your job is to ask Uncle Jeremy what he likes about the new house, and Jeb, you ask Aunt Melanie what she likes about the new house. You kids will be the interviewers, and I'll be the cameraman. After we have recorded all the interviews, we'll play it back on the television."

The children proudly carried out their assignments, with prompting of questions from Scott. In a half hour, they had the rough video ready and played it back on the television. The kids giggled at their own and others' bumbling interviews. The parents, as always, ate up the attention to their children.

Faith was the matriarch, mostly silent, but beaming with joy at this wonderful expression of love and sharing.

Then they sat down to a meal Melanie had prepared. Faith's cell phone rang. "Darn, I meant to turn that off." She picked it up.

"Hi Faith, it's Doug again. Thought I'd give you a call to see when we can get together with our sons."

"I can't take this call now. I'm in the middle of a meal."

"Hmm, you're always busy when I call. Well, I'll text you my phone number, and expect to hear from you by mid-week about a meeting with my sons. Remember, you can run, but you can't hide."

"Sorry, I'll get back to you later."

The rest of the family ignored the interruption, but Scott's long glance at Faith indicated he guessed who it was.

After the meal, the kids ran outside to play in the large yard with a nice lawn. At first, they just played tag, then Jeremy got out a bean bag toss game, and they took turns seeing who could score the most points. The children egged on Jeremy and Jon to see which twin would win. Then they had to have a competition between Melanie and Rachel. These ladies urged Scott and Faith to try their hand at the game.

Faith said, "Oh, I'm not good at sports. I'm having a good time just watching the rest of you."

While the others played, Scott asked Faith, "Are you okay?"

"Sure. I'll be fine."

Scott joined Jeremy and Jon for a three-way contest.

As the afternoon wore on, Melanie ushered everyone inside for drinks and a snack. Faith helped Melanie clear up. Melanie and Faith were alone in the kitchen.

Melanie asked, "Mom, are you not feeling well? You don't seem to be your usual cheerful self."

Faith turned to her, started to say something, then reached out and gave her a tight bear-hug. "I should never play poker because I can't hide my feelings. Thanks for asking. You and Rachel are so good to me."

"Uh, Mom, you want to talk about it?"

"Oh, dear. I want to talk about it, but can't."

"Not you and Scott?"

Faith chuckled. "No, we're fine. It's just something I agreed not to talk about. Before long I'll be able to tell you what it is."

At that point the kids interrupted. "Mom, can we watch cartoons?"

SCOTT AND FAITH stayed until late afternoon, then took their leave and headed for the condo.

Scott asked, "Do you want to talk about it now?"

"Not really. It's a shame to ruin a lovely day with the family by bringing up the call from that skunk."

"The gist?"

"He insists on meeting the twins, will give me til mid-week to reply. No real threat, just a time deadline. Oh—he did add that famous line, 'You can run, but you can't hide.'"

"Not very original."

"No, Scott, but he does seem to be determined."

"Well, dear, I guess we'll have to make a return trip to Bill."

"Much as I hate it. Tonight I'll send an email to Bill, ask him how soon he can meet with us."

"Doug must be a basket case."

"Scott, you know, we just had a glorious day with our kinfolk, and there's no reason Doug couldn't have spent a nice Sunday afternoon with his offspring. It's a shame he alienated himself from the ones he should be closest to."

"He's his own worst enemy."

"Such a shame."

"Faith, you're not feeling sorry for him, are you?"

"I used to hate him, but he's so pathetic I can't even muster up my anger."

"He's gotten what he deserved."

When they made it to the condo, they had a glass of wine while viewing the colors of the sunset over the lake.

Then Faith got on her computer and brought Bill Ludwig up to date, asking for a meeting as soon as he was free.

TUESDAY MORNING SCOTT and Faith sat in the reception area waiting for their appointment with Bill. He hurried out of his office, said a quick hello, then went down the hall to get one of his colleagues. He returned with a forty-ish woman, plump, and salt and pepper hair cut short. Her horn-rimmed glasses and charcoal pantsuit added to her appearance that would qualify her description as mature and matronly.

"Scott and Faith, this is Miriam Dugan, my colleague, and arguably the best family lawyer in Chicago. I want her to be part of our team. If we have to go to court, she'll be the lead lawyer, because she has handled a ton of cases there, and is respected as a tough but fair litigator."

Miriam reached out for a firm handshake.

"I've already briefed Miriam on your past dealings with Mr. Parinello, and this latest speedbump, including his call over the weekend."

They walked into Bill's office, Faith and Bill taking the client chairs, Miriam pulling up a chair next to Bill. Miriam sat back in her chair, making herself comfortable.

Bill said, "Miriam why don't you take over?"

Miriam smiled. "Scott and Faith, like Bill, I'm here to serve your best interests, first to listen to your concerns, and gather all the facts, and then give you the best possible advice. What brings you to us today?"

Faith looked to Scott, who spoke up. "You know Doug Parinello and Faith had a one-time meeting thirty years ago. He never knew of the pregnancy or twin sons who were the issue of that meeting. A year ago, the kidney problems of one twin forced us to contact him for medical records. He was very uncooperative. Bill was very good at securing the medical records, and we thought we were done with him. Now he calls Faith and insists he wants to meet with his sons. We want to avoid a meeting between Parinello and his sons. And for that matter, we want to keep grandchildren out of the picture. Parinello claims he can assert 'parental rights' and legally compel us to introduce him to the twins. Uh, well, Bill, did I leave anything out?"

Bill said, "Well done, Scott. You know Miriam, he's a crack reporter for the *Trib*.

Miriam had nodded as she listened to Scott, taking notes on a legal pad.

"Good. Bill gave me much of the key information, but I wanted to hear it from you, to make sure we're all on the same page. Let me begin by dividing the issue into short term and long term strategies. Bill advised you not to initiate any conversation with Parinello. I concur with that advice, and in the short term, suggest that you text —not call—Parinello our firm's address and phone number. Because Bill dealt with Parinello before and actually met him in our conference room, it's best not to surprise him with any new faces. That leaves it up to Parinello to tell us what he's up to. We don't ask about his lawyer but expect him to tell us who his lawyer is when he replies. How does that sound to you?"

Faith turned to Scott, and said, "Yes, that's about what we expected, but we don't know much about Family Law, and would appreciate your take on how we stand if this goes to court."

Miriam wrinkled her brow. "The short term strategy is short and sweet. The long term strategy is lengthy and complicated. Family law is more fuzzy and ambiguous than business contracts, wills, and estates. A great deal depends on the situation, how well each side presents their arguments, and how the judge interprets the best interests of all parties. Most focus, as you know, is "the best interests of the child." An unusual aspect of his situation is that the child, or children, have already become adults, and have their own legal rights. Without raising the facts of the case, I'd go out on a limb and say the particulars of the age of the twins, the family history of the plaintiff, and the thirty-year time lag all indicate we have a strong basis for persuading a judge not to grant any kind of 'visitation' order."

Faith, sitting on the edge of her chair, leaned back and let out a sigh of relief.

Miriam continued. "Mind you, there are no guarantees in legal proceedings. The back and forth could be extensive, messy, even vicious. That's why you have Bill and me to handle the negotiations."

Scott asked, "Do we have to wait until Parinello files a petition to the court?"

Miriam laughed. "Oh, no, like in most legal cases, much of the give and take happens before the court appearances. From past experience, I would anticipate an overture from Parinello's attorney, saying they have a simple, reasonable request, and don't see why our side will not agree to it. We respond that we see no reason for this bizarre request. The back and forth continues until the other side actually files a petition, and then—if that happens—we respond in court."

Scott asked, "What are the important considerations the judge will look at?"

"Well, first and foremost, the argument each side presents. And I mentioned the 'best interests of the child,' which in itself is a stretch. Then, very important is the character of the plaintiff and defendant. They look for any bad apple features such as alcoholism, drugs, abuse, arrest record."

Scott asked, "Do you know enough about us and Parinello to give an idea of how a judge might evaluate the situation?"

Miriam let out a belly laugh. "In a few words, you two are Eagle scouts and model citizens, Parinello is a low down dirty scoundrel. The defendants are successful in their careers, have a harmonious family unit. Parinello has an on-and-off business record, he's gone through two bitter divorces, then a live-in situation that soured, and an old paternity suit. By my count, he has 'fathered' about eight children but has not been a good father to any of them. This will make it very difficult for him and his lawyer to make the argument that, thirty years after the fact, he wants to do the right thing, and be a father to the twins. If we get into court, I'll slice and dice him into mincemeat."

Scott said, "That's about what we understood from talking to Bill, but there's something we haven't raised yet. Each twin has two children, and that would bring up the visitation issue for Parinello as a grandparent wanting to see his grandchildren. How do you see that?"

Miriam frowned. "I've never heard of a case like this, so it's hard to answer. The same factors I mentioned would be important. I mean, if he couldn't win the argument to meet his sons, then it would be an uphill battle to ask to see his grandchildren."

Bill said, "Well, we've covered the basics. The next step is for you to text our firm's info to Parinello, and see if he's bluffing or if he wants to go ahead with this. Here's your script for the text: 'Please contact our lawyer, who will be handling this matter.'"

Scott and Faith thanked Bill and Miriam, then headed for the elevator.

Faith said, "I really like Miriam. She's knowledgeable, articulate, and to the point. I think we can work with her."

"Babe, I've dealt with a lot of legal types, and can't remember meeting a better lawyer."

When she got to the hotel, she texted Doug, telling him to contact Ludwig.

6

Faith hated the waiting game. She and Scott were in limbo until Doug contacted Ludwig. Scott kept reminding her that if he was bluffing, he might not call or write. Faith felt that was out of the question. She had heard the resolve in his voice, the urgency in his request.

They made it through the week, dancing around the subject on their minds, but didn't discuss it.

Saturday morning Scott left for the newspaper and Faith was enjoying her routine of a cup of tea in her recliner. She realized it was just a week ago that Doug had called and wondered if he would make a repeat performance. She had rehearsed her lines, just in case.

When the phone rang, the caller ID listing Parinello Construction, and she picked up the phone.

"Faith, I thought I'd find you at home again on a Saturday morning. So, hear me out; don't let the lawyers get in between us."

"I told you in my text that our attorney Bill Ludwig will be handling this matter. He has instructed me not to talk to you, so I'm going to hang up."

"No, No! I want to—"

Faith told herself to be calm, even as she noticed her heart racing. She welcomed the silence. A few minutes later the phone rang again. She saw the caller ID and Parinello Construction, so she did not pick up. The call eventually went to the message machine, which beeped after it had recorded for five minutes.

Faith knew she would have to relay Doug's message to Bill, so she got pen and paper to jot down the gist of it.

"Well, Faith, you won't take my call, so I'm leaving this message. The bottom line is that you and I can arrange something without any lawyers. All you have to do is give me the information for my sons—their legal names and phone numbers. I can call them, ask to get together with them. Hey, it's up to them. If they say, 'Thanks but no thanks,' then that's the end of the story. I hope they'll give me a chance—a second chance—to show that I want to be a part of their lives. You know, hear how they grew up, what they're doing now. They probably got married, had kids. It would be great to hear about my grandkids.

"You know I'm a businessman, and I do drive a pretty hard bargain. I can be rough and tough, but now I'm trying to live up to my born again commitment and do the right thing. If you ask people in Peoria, they'll tell you that I don't beg. As they say in business, I bargain from strength. But now I'm weak and you hold all the cards. So, I'm not begging, but I'm asking you as nice as I can, to give me this chance. You and your lawyers know I messed up with my wives and kids, and they won't have anything to do with me. These twins are my last chance. I'm past fifty, and I don't want to grow old being on the outs with all my kids. Please, give me a chance."

He rambled for a few more minutes until the message machine cut him off.

Faith felt drained. Her heart raced, and she was short of breath. Yes, his plea was moving. Yes, she did feel sorry for him. At the same time, she could hear the voices of Scott and Bill saying this was classic Doug—a con to make her feel sorry for him and give in.

Doug's message made such an impassioned plea that she

couldn't concentrate on taking notes. She knew what to do, get her mini recorder from her purse and playback the message again, recording it for Bill and Miriam. She went into the bedroom and found her little recorder, then thought again. She could record Doug's remarks later when she played it for Scott.

She opened her underwear drawer and got out her journal, taking it to her lounger and opening it to the last entry, the single word, *Trouble.*

Underneath that entry, she wrote:

Yes, I'm in trouble. Because I can't help it, I feel pity for Doug. Even though he doesn't deserve sympathy from me or anyone else.

Scott and Bill are right, he's a slick con man, and I have to be careful.

Why do I feel pity for him? Maybe it's because I'm so happy surrounded by our beautiful family, and he's so wretched in his isolation and loneliness.

It's the contrast, the difference, almost like a rich person giving a dollar to a homeless man on a street corner.

That's it! I feel guilty being so happy when he is so miserable. Maybe that helps me understand my feeling of compassion for him.

But that doesn't help the lawyers and our family figure out how to deal with Doug. And when our family discusses this, if I go soft on Doug, probably Jeremy will want to rescue his soul, and that will cause problems with the others who want nothing to do with Doug.

Yes, "pity" is something I will have to consider very carefully.

SHE KNEW Scott would be coming home soon, so she returned the journal to its safe place, and waited for him.

As soon as he opened the door, she said, "Well, Doug called, he—"

"You didn't talk to him, did you?"

"Oh, no, I told him again that he'd have to contact Ludwig."

"Good!"

"But he didn't give up. He called back and left a long message. We can play it now, and I'll record it for the lawyers to hear it when we meet with them."

Scott scowled as he listened, muttering expletives. "That message can be summed up in two words: 'Poor me.' He's a narcissistic creep. All he can think about is me-me-me. 'Look at me; I'm a victim.' He doesn't mention all the people—especially women—he's mistreated. He made the mess he's wallowing in."

Faith nodded.

"You're right, Faith, Bill, and Miriam need to hear this, so they'll know what he's up to. They won't fall for his con, because they've dealt with lots of perps like him."

"Well, I'll go ahead and call Ludwig's office and leave a message. We don't need to talk to lawyers until he makes a move to take us to court."

Calling lawyers was easy. When Scott went out for some groceries, Faith made a more difficult call, to Church of Redeemer. She didn't reach Father Whitmore and was glad the secretary could give her a Tuesday morning appointment.

Both Scott and Faith felt the tension of waiting for Doug's next move, but they got through the weekend, doing some shopping and watching old movies.

TUESDAY MORNING FAITH drove to Church of the Redeemer, entering and quickly stepping into the sanctuary to commune with Mother Mary and Saint Harriet in a silent prayer.

Thanks for your support in the past. Now please help me with my present problem. Lead me to do the right thing. Protect me from myself, so I don't do something foolish with Doug that disturbs our family.

WHEN FAITH WENT to Father Whitmore's office, he joked with her. "I saw you making a beeline for Mary and Harriet. It looks like I'm playing second fiddle in the spiritual resource department."

"Don't blame them or me because you steered me to them."

"Okay, let me know what's on the docket today. The secretary stacked up some appointments, so I don't have a lot of time."

"Well, Father, my problem today can be summed up in one word: guilt. I already told you about Doug threatening to take us to court to get in contact with the twins. But over the weekend, he changed tactics, and left a sad message, almost begging us to help him develop a relationship with the twins. Doug admits he screwed up all his relationships with his wives and live-in, and their kids. He found God and wants to be the good guy reuniting with his sons. Well, he made such an emotional, heartrending appeal that I began to feel sorry for him. Here I am, reunited with my boys, and I have a loving husband, a wonderful family—and he's like the cheese standing alone. I pity him, even though he doesn't deserve my pity."

"Well, you pity him because you're a caring person, what's wrong with that?"

"As I told you, it makes me feel guilty like I should help him."

"And you can't do that?"

"When we had the big fight with Doug over medical records, Jeremy felt sorry for Doug and wanted us to help him with his born-again rehabilitation. The rest of the family, even his wife, objected to Doug having anything to do with our family. So now I'm fighting a kind of double battle. My heart says to feel sorry for Doug and help him. My head says that is not wise and might tear the family apart. That's one battle. The other battle is tension in the family. Scott was super, guiding and supporting me in the past conflict with Doug, and if I mention any pity or feeling sorry, he's not going to like it one bit."

"I see. That's what people call being between a rock and a hard place."

"Yeah, and I don't expect you to perform a miracle and make this problem disappear, but if you have any advice at all, I'd be glad to hear it."

"Hmm. In the past year, we helped you with the recognition that, although usually, you are strong, sometimes you are weak. Also, although most of the time you are tough, you admit that you can also be vulnerable. Today we seem to run into another quandary. You see yourself as very capable, and that's how you became a successful executive. However, some conflicts in life you may not be able to solve. Tough conflicts or differences may be too problematic for any human to overcome. So, don't set yourself up with an impossible mission and then blame yourself for not accomplishing it. Look at it this way; guilt is what you feel when you can do something but don't. It's when you do something you shouldn't. I don't think you should feel guilty for not taking care of an impossible dilemma."

"Father, that's not absolution, but it's very helpful. It's like the bromide of accepting what you can't change."

"Your heart and head will talk to each other, and reach some middle ground, a compromise."

"That gives me hope."

Father Whitmore ended the session with a prayer asking divine help for Faith as she navigated her way through a delicate situation.

FAITH HAD FOLLOWED Bill Ludwig's advice about taking more time off. She left Church of the Redeemer and headed for the condo. She could use some solitude to digest her priest's comments and see if she could develop a dialog between her heart and her head.

When she opened the condo door, the answering machine's beep interrupted her plans for reflection. Seeing it came from Doug, she thought she might as well listen to it.

"Faith, I'm disappointed that you didn't take my call, and didn't ring me back. Actually, I'm not that hard to get along with. And since I was saved, I've stopped using bad language and am trying to be a better person. That's why I'm calling today, to make one last request for you to help me contact the twins. I imagine the lawyers are telling you to ignore me and wait until I go to the court. I don't want to do that but will if I have to.

"I'm serious about this. My situation has changed since we took care of the medical records. Then I was head over heels busy with my business. A national company came in and bought my business. That means I have plenty of time and money. I can choose to free-lance with construction consulting when I want to, but my priority is to get my life straightened out, and I want to start by recon-necting with the twins.

"As I said before, I don't like to beg, and I don't want to threaten. Please help me find my sons. If you don't, you leave me no other choice than to go to my lawyer."

Doug's call made her head spin and her heart thump. Faith sat in the lounger for a while before retrieving her journal and opening it. Maybe writing would help organize her thoughts.

Heart.
Head.
Softhearted.
Hardheaded.
Pity.
Reason.
Where is the balance, the halfway point, the compromise,
between these opposites?
Mary, Saint Harriet, Father Whitmore, help me!

SHE PUT the pen down and returned the journal to its usual resting place.

She called Scott and left a message to bring a pizza when he returned from work.

7

Scott barged in with his square box. "Okay, here's the pizza, now what's the problem?"

Faith shrugged. "When I got back from talking to Father Whitmore, Doug had left a message."

They listened to it as they attacked the pizza.

"Faith, we ought to talk to Ludwig about a restraining order, something like that."

"Is that necessary?"

"He's bothering you, and it bothers me if he keeps pestering you."

"He didn't threaten me, anything like that."

"We should inform Ludwig and let him make the decision. After all, you told Doug to contact our lawyer, but he insisted on calling you."

"Okay, I'll tell Ludwig tomorrow when I mention the gist of the call."

. . .

THE NEXT MORNING, Faith phoned Ludwig from her office, summing up the message, and mentioning Scott's suggestion about a restraining order.

"Well, Faith, you say he didn't openly threaten you, claiming he'd kill you. And he didn't threaten damage to property, like burning your house down. So, we'd have a weak case, which might be dismissed as a frivolous accusation. And we don't want that in the background when we go before a judge."

Faith relayed Ludwig's advice to Scott, which he did not take kindly. "I wonder what he'd say if some nut kept bugging his wife with phone calls."

Faith and Scott had always gotten along well, and she didn't like it when he became cool and distant. They did not make love that week, and Faith hoped they could have a makeup meeting in bed Saturday morning when Scott returned from the office. She got up, showered, put on a lovely negligee and used her best perfume, then donned her robe.

Mid-morning the front desk called her. "Flowers for Miss A. Want me to bring them up? The delivery man says he can run them up."

"Just have him bring them up."

"Hey, what's the occasion?"

Faith figured the flowers were Scott's way of making up. He was always so thoughtful. She remembered, the very first time he visited the condo, he came armed with a single rose.

Faith was ready for the knock on the door. Looking through the peephole, she saw a bouquet hiding the face of the delivery man. Opening the door wide, the delivery man handed her the flowers. Deprived of his mask of flowers, the delivery man was revealed as Doug.

She blurted out, "What ...?"

"Just to show you how nice I can be, I brought these flowers for you." He moved forward, stepped across the threshold and put a foot on the condo rug, as Faith fumbled with the flowers and at the same time trying to close the door.

"Now is that nice? Is that the thanks I get for giving you flowers? You're not going to ask me in? You won't take my calls, but Hell, I drove several hours to Chicago to deliver flowers, so you can at least give me a few minutes."

Faith dropped the flowers and tried to slam the door shut, but he had placed his foot between the door and the door jam.

Doug laughed. "Hey, you forget, I ran a construction company. These are steel toe shoes; you can't hurt them."

"If you don't leave now, I'll ... I'll...."

Doug smiled. "You'll what?"

"Call the police."

"With what? You don't have a phone with you, and by the time you run to get it, I'll be in your place and take the phone from you. Then, whether you like it or not, we'll have our talk. A nice *friendly* talk. Just like old times." His eyes moved up and down her robe, and he had a wide grin on his face.

Faith wanted to scream, but she was hyperventilating and couldn't find her breath.

At that moment an elderly couple from down the hall opened their door, and asked, "Faith, do you have a problem?"

"Yes! Call the police!"

Doug quickly drew his foot back and shut the door, and walked over to the couple, smiling. "Sorry, you had to hear that. Just a little lovers' quarrel. Sometimes she says those things, never means it." He hurried to the elevator and got on it while the couple knocked on Faith's door.

Faith had put the security chain on the door, checked the peephole to see that just her elderly neighbors were there and opened the door a few inches. "I'm okay, thanks for asking. I'll take care of everything."

She called the front desk, told them the guy with the flowers was not a delivery man, and never to let that guy up.

"Sorry, Miss A, he knew your name, had it written on the slip with the flowers, and presented the business card from the flower shop."

"I should have had you bring them up."

THERE WAS no point in calling Scott, who would be home soon. Waiting for Scott, she got out of the negligee and robe, putting on clothes. She was not in the mood for love. What was on her mind was hate and anger.

As soon as Scott opened the door, Faith ran to him, hugging him and crying.

"Hey, babe, what's the matter?"

Breathlessly, she murmured, "Doug."

"The bastard called again?"

"No, he was here!"

Faith tried as best she could to describe the brief encounter with Doug and being saved from a confrontation with him when her neighbors appeared at just the right moment.

Scott insisted on a restraining order, and Faith had to agree. Scott put in an emergency call to Ludwig. Scott did all the talking because Faith was still too shaken to think straight.

Bill said, "I won't be able to get a judge to sign a restraining order this weekend, but it would be good for Faith to call the police and file a report. If the neighbors will back up her statement that a man tried to force his way into your condo, that would probably be sufficient. The deception of pretending to be a florist delivery man is also important." Bill hesitated. "I might as well mention this to you now, to think about over the weekend. With a restraining order and a police report, from here on we'll probably be playing hard-ball. I'll call Parinello Monday and talk directly to him. The first requirement, of course, is to ask whether he wants to hide behind his lawyer. If he does, then I have to wait until his lawyer contacts me."

Scott talked with the front desk, telling them to be more careful, and never to send someone up, even a pizza delivery if he or Faith did not okay it.

Faith was still unnerved by the encounter with Doug. Scott asked, "Do you want a drink? I can get out my Seagram's."

"Oh, no, not this early in the day. Just hold me and tell me you love me."

He wrapped his arms around her. "I love ya, babe, and will take care of you."

She sniffled a little, wiping away tears.

Scott insisted she take a nap in the afternoon. She relented but asked him to lie down next to her.

That evening, to get her out of the condo, he took her to Boccaccio's, the restaurant where they first met.

"Oh, Scott, that's so thoughtful of you. This place brings back good memories."

After a nice meal, they went home and passed the time watching television. When they went to bed, Faith was still too tense to make love but snuggled close to Scott. She dozed off and on, then woke with a start, in the middle of a nightmare trying to get away from Doug. The bedside clock said 1:15. She couldn't get back to sleep, so she tiptoed across the room and got out her journal.

Sitting in her lounger, she replayed the scene of the fake delivery man. The flowers were the enticement. He wanted to get in the apartment, and then get "friendly" with her. The look on his face was more than a grin; it was a leer. Faith realized that if her neighbors hadn't come along, he could have forced his way in and forced himself on her. She would have been no match for him.

She had put on a robe, but still, a cold shiver ran down her spine.

Opening the journal, she drew a large X through the last page she had written. On the next page she wrote:

Anger

Hate
Justice
Doug = guilty
Faith = innocent
Those who are innocent do not need to feel guilty.
The guilty should not escape punishment.
Doug = The Devil déjà vu.

SHE WENT BACK to bed and snuggled close to Scott.

8

J ust as Ludwig had predicted, the Saturday episode with
Doug, the restraining order, and the police report brought
a lot of swift action. The following Monday, Ludwig called
Doug and formally notified him that their firm would be
handling all legal matters for Faith. At first, Doug tried to sweet talk
Ludwig, saying he was just trying to be nice bringing flowers to
Faith. Ludwig reminded Doug that in a previous phone call, Faith
had told Doug to deal with her lawyer, and not to contact her again.

As Bill had expected, Doug chose to hide behind his lawyer,
Luciano Garibaldi.

"Fine, Mr. Parinello, I will be in contact with him, confirming
the restraining order that you will in no way contact Faith
Armstrong, by phone, email, U.S. mail, or in person at her residence or her workplace."

Doug didn't acknowledge this shot over the bow, ending the call
with, "See you in court."

"Mr. Parinello, that is your prerogative."

The next day Bill received a fax from Luciano Garibaldi which
included unctuous statements: "We hope to reach an amicable
agreement to a simple request for Mr. Parinello to meet with his

twin sons," and "We regret that you and your client saw fit to issue a restraining order because Mr. Parinello made the friendly gesture of giving flowers to the mother of his sons."

Bill returned his saccharin sweet letter stating that he surely wanted this, like all negotiations, to end amicably. But he reminded Garibaldi that in the past, Parinello had not been reliable, and had to be ushered out of their offices by security.

Bill called Faith and Scott into the office for a consultation with him and Miriam.

Bill led off. "Folks, we don't know if, when, or what legal proceedings Parinello and his attorney Garibaldi will set in motion. But we're not waiting for court papers. We're preparing our case, and Miriam has some questions for you. She may repeat some of the queries I put to you, but she wants to be double sure she is on the right track."

"Faith, we need to be very precise about all our information, and I have to ask tough questions now, so you'll be prepared for them in court. An embarrassing but necessary particular is when you got pregnant. I understand you only had sexual relations with Mr. Parinello once, your first time."

Faith looked down at the floor. "Yes, that's right."

"Do you remember the exact date?"

"Yes, the last day of March 1969."

"And your birthday is in April?"

"Yes."

"So, you were sixteen at the time."

"That's right, a few weeks before my seventeenth birthday."

Scott chimed in. "I see what you're driving at, technically, she was below the Illinois 'age of consent' of seventeen, but the statute of limitations for statutory rape would be long past."

Miriam nodded. "Yes, but we're not building a case for statutory rape. We're developing a profile of two people: one a sixteen-year-old minor high school student, the other a twenty-one-year-old adult college student. We want a judge to look back at an innocent girl and a grown man taking advantage of her. The five-year difference between sixteen and twenty-one is much more significant than between these two people at fifty and fifty-five."

Scott nodded. "Smart thinking."

Miriam added, "I won't give you the entire set of factual particulars but want to demonstrate a pattern of behavior that goes back more than three decades. We string the beads of evidence together, including the old paternity case against Parinello in southern Illinois, two marriages, each ending in divorce that involved infidelity. And then a common-law wife. As we said the other day, including your twins, that's eight children we know of. This necklace of evidence we will hang around Parinello's neck, and ask him sticky questions—when did he last see the other six children, etc.?

"Bill has filled me in on Parinello's poor performance in the medical records case, first denying paternity, until your side proved it. And he delayed handing over the records, even though he had doctors' statements that the records were crucial for Jeremy's diagnosis and treatment. He didn't show concern for the well-being of his twins.

"And we end up with the latest episode of him trying to force his way into your apartment when he was told to deal only with our firm. The restraining order and the police report will probably be the drum roll that marks the collapse of his desperate case."

Faith asked, "How do you see our position?"

"Very strong. You two are upright, reliable people. I've seen a lot of deadbeats, cads, and con men in my time, and Doug ranks among the lowest of the low. A real scumbag. He's clever and daring, like his ploy to get to you by pretending to deliver flowers. He's a man-size rat, and we need to prepare a man-sized rat trap for him."

Scott sat back in his chair. "I'm impressed with your preparations so far. Now we need for Doug and his lawyer to make his move?"

Bill spoke up. "Yes, and I want to assure you that Miriam and I will do our best to keep this out of court. Litigation before a judge can be very ugly, and we want to spare you that. However, I'd be remiss if I didn't ask you where your sons are on this."

Scott looked at Faith. She said, "We were waiting to inform them about this latest action by Doug until he petitioned the court. We didn't want to bother them if Doug was bluffing and didn't petition the court. Maybe now we have to let them in on the situation."

"Yes, I think so, because it looks like he's dead-set on court, and the judge might insist on input from them."

Faith groaned, "Oh, no."

Bill said, "We'll try to keep them out of court, and handle their input, if necessary, in a deposition."

When they left the office, Miriam walked over to Faith and hugged her. "I want you to know that we're much more than legal angles and formal papers. Bill and I are looking out for your best interests. You didn't say it in so many words, but you've been under tremendous stress, and we wish you the best. Hang in there."

"Thanks, Miriam, I appreciate that."

In the elevator, Scott said, "Well, the good news and the bad news. On the positive side, we're in good hands, and the case is already stacking up in our favor. On the negative side, court will be ugly."

"Yeah, and now we have to let the family know about this. I hate that."

"Listen, honey, as Miriam said, you've been through an emotional stress test, so today let me type out a draft of an email we can send. I have an idea of how to handle this but have to get to the office now. I can tell you about it over dinner. Shall I bring home a pizza?"

"You're giving pizza a bad name. I'll fix us sandwiches."

9

S cott arrived home with a manila folder containing two copies of his draft email.

Faith grabbed her copy. "I have to read this first; then we can talk it over while we eat.

Scott's draft:

Guys and Gals,

Your mother and I have been juggling a delicate issue for some time and didn't want to bother you with it, but now we have no choice and must inform you of what our family faces.

Doug Parinello called with a request that he be provided contact information so he could connect with his sons and threatens to go to court if this request is not honored. We tried, with Bill Ludwig's help, to deflect this request, but recently it has become more likely that Doug will file a petition to Family Court. Although your mother will be served the papers, this is a matter that involves the entire family, especially Jeremy and Jon, and we want input from all of you before we have to face a judge.

We propose a family gathering at our condo on a Sunday convenient for everyone. Faith will fix a picnic-style lunch; afterward, Scott will take the children on an outing, probably to the Shedd Aquarium. That will provide the adults some kid-free time to discuss the issues.

Please let us know when you would be available for a gathering.

Love to you all,

Faith and Scott

FAITH SHRUGGED. "Well, Mr. *Trib* reporter, that's to the point, and better than what I could put together. We might as well send it out."

Faith picked up her sandwich, took a bite, then put it down on her plate and looked Scott in the eyes. "Scott, I'm tired. We've gone through so much with Doug; I just want to be done with him."

"Faith, baby, that's life. Whether it's a hotel or a newspaper, there's always something. It's the same with cars and families. Cars need oil changes and new tires. Our family requires maintenance. You love our clan's good times, so we have to pay for them."

"You're right; I should quit complaining. I'd much rather have a family to fuss over than be a lonely old maid."

Scott's email elicited the response that both twins and families would be available the following Sunday.

Faith called Father Whitmore, and he was able to squeeze her in for a Friday appointment.

DRIVING TO CHURCH OF REDEEMER, Faith tried to organize her thoughts, realizing full well that her priest could not do anything to change the situation.

When she arrived at the church, she made her regular pilgrimage to Mary and Harriet.

Thank you, holy saints, for allowing us to have such a wonderful family. Help us, we pray, to do the right thing and keep the family together, safe and sound.

Entering Father Whitmore's office, she received his teasing. "Paying your respects first where it counts most, huh?"

"Oh, father, I can't thank you and the church enough. You for introducing me to Harriet, and the church for agreeing to the Madonna window. These two have become my spiritual compass, helping me steer a steady course."

"Well, what's up? Again, today I'm on a tight schedule, so I need to hear what's on your mind."

"It's Doug, and we'll probably be seeing him in Family Court because he insists on meeting his sons."

"That's what you expected, isn't it?"

"Yes, but the needle on my softhearted and hardhearted gauge has swung sharply from the soft toward the hard side." She quickly brought him up to date on Doug's deceptive flower delivery. "Father, I didn't tell Scott, but the way he looked—leered—at me when he was pushing the door open, and how he said we would have a *friendly* conversation, I could tell he was intent on more than friendship."

"Well, the restraining order should keep him away, right?"

"I think so. What bothers me now is the family meeting next Sunday—we'll have to miss church."

"I understand. How will you handle the situation?"

"I have to be careful. I haven't told Scott and don't want to let on to the twins that Doug seemed about ready to rape me. That might stir some unhelpful machismo and violence against Doug."

"I see what you mean, but that doesn't make it any easier for you."

"One thing is obvious, Jeremy and Jonathan are adults, and they have to have a say in this. But we can't leave out Melanie and Rachel, who want to protect their children from this delayed adolescent. On the soft-hard scale, Jeremy will lean toward soft pity, and Jonathan will be hard as nails. The last time I talked to you, my heart was softening, but Doug's bad behavior playing flower boy diminished my reservoir of pity and compassion."

"Well, Faith, how can I help you?"

"Just listening to me blather on is a big help, because it helps me to verbalize my inner turmoil. Well, one thing you can help me with. I remember from the Bible passages like, 'Vengeance is mine, saith the Lord.' God is love and compassion, but also judgment and even punishment. My problem is how to be firm with Doug and protective of the grandchildren without losing sight of compassion."

"That's a tough balancing act, and every parent has to learn how to be firm in a loving, not in a mean way."

"Hmm. Tough love, huh?"

"If you boil it down to two words, that's it."

The next appointment showed up, so Father Whitmore and Faith ended their session with his prayer asking for divine guidance in the family council.

ON THE DRIVE back to the condo, Faith slowed down, crying softly. She expressed her emotions in a monolog.

Thank you, Father Whitmore, for patiently listening to me. Thank you, Scott, for supporting me. Thank you, Jeremy and Jon, for letting us into your lives. Thank you, Melanie and Rachel, for granting us the gift of new life. Thank you, God, for giving Mary and Harriet as faithful guides.

Faith felt better. Somehow, with such a strong support network, she would make it through the difficult Sunday session.

ON SUNDAY, Faith had the lunch ready, and the kitchen table lengthened by two card tables so that they could all squeeze around. The kids were almost too excited to eat.

"Grandpa Scott, what're we gonna do?"

"How would you like to go fishing?"

"Yeah!" "Alright!"

"Well, kids, the last time you came here for lunch, we went by the Aquarium but didn't have time to stop. Today let's go look at the fish. We won't catch them, but I have an idea. We'll go through the whole building, and you can pick out your favorite fish. Then I'll take a picture of you and the fish you like most. Later—not today—I can send you a digital scrapbook of your trip to the Aquarium."

The kids wanted to hurry and eat so they could go to the "fish house."

Before they left the condo, Scott ordered them all to the bathroom; then they formed a family prayer circle. He led the prayer. "God, we thank you for the blessing of these wonderful children. We pray for your help today in keeping them safe and sound. Amen."

The kids shouted out their "Amen."

"Now children, when we're at the Aquarium, we want to stay together. No one goes off alone. Beth and Stephie, you stay together. Mark and Jeb, you're best buddies."

Scott and the kids left the condo for a taxi ride to the Aquarium, leaving Faith to handle the meeting with the twins and their wives.

With the lunch dishes cleared away, Faith took a seat at the end of the table, the two couples on each side.

"Before we begin, let's join hands for prayer. God, we are weak; you are strong. Hold us up, shed light on our path, show us the way."

With the amens to that prayer, the meeting began.

10

"Let me start with an apology for not telling you about this sooner. Some time ago Doug called me and insisted that I introduce him to his sons, and if I didn't, he would take us to court. Scott and I remembered how difficult Doug was when we desperately requested his family medical records and didn't want a replay of those messy negotiations. We hoped that Doug would give up on this request, but hehas persisted, even when we told him to contact Bill Ludwig's office. He called again, almost begging to see his twins. He admits he's alienated himself from all of his other children and sees old age staring him in the face, a lonely man.

"Scott and I wanted to handle this request through Ludwig because he was terrific the last time we dealt with Doug. Then, two Saturdays ago, Doug showed up at my door. He told the front desk he was a delivery man from the florists. When I looked through the peephole, he had the flowers in front of his face so that I couldn't see who it was. I opened the door, and he tried to come in. I told him to leave, but he stuck his foot between the door and the door jam, and I couldn't close it. When I told him, I would call the police, he laughed and said I didn't have a phone in my hand, and if I went to get one, he'd be in the condo."

Melanie blurted out, "What did he want?"

"Uh, well, he said he wanted a conversation—a *friendly* conversation."

At the words "friendly," Melanie and Rachel looked at each other, gasped, and together said, "No!"

Jeremy said, "He wanted to talk to you?"

Melanie snapped, "Jeremy, more than talk, he wanted to get *friendly*."

Faith held her hands up. "I shouldn't have told you that, but let me finish that part of the story, and then brief you on the legal stuff. Fortunately, my neighbors came into the hall, and Doug left. Scott came home soon after that. Ludwig had us file a police report on Doug trying to force his way in, and he drew up a restraining order preventing Doug from contacting or approaching me. Well, naturally, we had a consultation with Ludwig, who called Doug, and it looks like Doug will file a petition to Family Court requiring us to hand over the names and addresses of the twins.

"This is where it gets very tricky, because usually such petitions are for custody cases in bitter divorces, and now the 'children' in our case are adults. We discussed this with Bill Ludwig and his colleague, Miriam Dugan, an experienced Family Lawyer. They think that because of Doug's bad history with his own families, his case is very shaky. But even so, the judge might ask for a deposition from you two guys. In talking with these two lawyers, we've learned two new legal phrases. The first is 'parental rights,' the basis for his request, and 'in the best interests of the children,' the guiding principle for Family Court decisions.

"Thanks for your patience in hearing me out. Now the floor is open for your questions and comments. Whatever you have to say will be what Scott and I take back to the lawyers."

When Rachel got up from her chair, Melanie followed her clue, and they walked behind Faith, hugging her in a clamshell.

Melanie said, "I knew when you were at our house, you were carrying a heavy load, but didn't know what it was."

"Sorry I couldn't tell you then, but our lawyer thought Doug was bluffing, and in that case, there was no need to bother you. Ludwig asked us to keep the matter to ourselves until Doug forced a court proceeding."

Rachel said, "Guys do you realize what strain your mother's been under? Having to fight off Doug?"

Jeremy asked, "Fight off? He brought flowers and wanted a conversation."

Melanie screamed, "A *friendly* conversation. Who knows what would have happened if those neighbors had not come along?"

Jonathan shook his head. "Not good. Not good at all."

Jeremy asked, "Well, what will you do?"

Faith closed her eyes, wadding a tissue into a small ball. "Right now, we have to wait. Wait for Doug to file papers, which the lawyers think he will. But Bill and Miriam have been developing character profiles of Scott and me, as well as of Doug. They think we're upstanding citizens, and Doug is an unreliable flake."

Jonathan snorted. "That's putting it mildly."

Melanie exchanged glances with Rachel, who spoke first. "Mom, we really appreciate the lengths to which you—and Scott—have gone to protect us. And by 'us' I mean especially the children."

"Oh, Rachel, thanks for reminding me of the children. Scott and I told Ludwig because Jeremy and Jonathan are adults, they have a major say in whatever we do, however we respond to the petition. But no matter what the twins decide, there's a strange provision in the 'parental rights' law that grandparents can petition to arrange for visitation with grandchildren. For example, grandparents whose son is divorced may have a nasty daughter-in-law who won't let the grandparents see their grandchildren. In that situation, even if the father is out of the picture, the grandparents can petition to visit the grandchildren. So, this is one reason we all have to be very careful about how we handle the request for access to the twins. Scott isn't here but remember his saying about the camel. Once it gets its nose in the tent, it's in the tent. I think the same applies to our family."

Melanie piped up, "Well, I said it before, and I'll repeat it, I don't want this camel ... or whatever animal Doug represents, in our family."

Rachel added, "The same is true for me."

Faith looked back at forth at her twins. "What do you guys think?"

Jon took his hand away from his chin. "I don't see Doug as an animal, more like poison. And I don't want him near our kids."

The group waited for Jeremy to speak. Faith said, "Jeremy, your turn."

Jeremy spoke slowly and deliberately. "Melanie repeated her opposition to Doug. I understand where everyone is coming from. At the last big family council, we agreed not to let Doug into the family, but to pray for him. I will continue to do that. And, to be honest, I have to be open to some change in my position in the future. I can't commit now to never having anything to do with my father, who is a human being. Flawed, and a sinner, but he claims he has been saved and is trying to start a new life."

Faith's brow wrinkled. "Yes, Jeremy, Doug mentioned that to me again. Just so you all know, he sold his business and is trying to make a new start in life. He's burned all the bridges to the rest of his offspring and sees our family as his last chance."

Jon clenched his jaw, then shouted, "He doesn't deserve a chance with us! He has fathered a half dozen other kids, so let him go on his hands and knees begging to be let into their families."

Jeremy asked, "Mother, what else can you tell us about the case?"

"Well, one fact you should know. Remember that Scott got Doug's DNA and confirmed he is your father. So, this establishes paternity, a key consideration for parental rights. Our side could not contest that. The argument that Miriam and Bill are developing is that it is not in the best interests of the children, and here we mean both the twins and grandchildren. And to document his poor character, they would refer to his long and contentious relationships with his other families.

"Miriam will be the lead lawyer in any proceeding. She's sharp.

She pried out of me some valuable information. That one time Doug and I were together, and I got pregnant, was while I was sixteen, a few weeks before my seventeenth birthday. Doug was twenty-one. So, I was a minor, just below the age of consent, and Doug was twenty-one, an adult. This is the way Miriam would introduce Doug to the court as an unreliable character, and from there run through his disastrous relationships."

Jonathan said, "Wow, this Miriam sounds good. I want to meet her."

Faith joked, "You may, sooner than you like."

Rachel and Melanie were giving eye signals to each other. Melanie asked, "Mom this has been a long, tough meeting for you. Is there anything else we need to discuss today?"

"Just one other important thing. In case this goes to Family Court, we will do our best to keep your names hidden. For Jeremy and Jonathan, we assume they would be anonymous, maybe twin one and twin two, but they might be asked to file a deposition. So, I would ask each of you guys to be thinking about, or even drafting, a brief statement of whether and why you want or do not want to meet Doug. If this does go to court, Bill and Miriam will certainly help you with your depositions."

Rachel and Melanie stood up. Melanie said, "Okay, the meeting's over. I'm going to get tea and coffee ready. Mom, we're in charge of the kitchen. You are under orders to go into the bedroom and lie down so you'll be fresh when the kids get back."

Tears trickled down her cheeks as she followed orders and went into the bedroom.

11

The stress of the meeting exhausted Faith. In spite of the scenes of the discussion whirling around in her head, she dozed off for about fifteen minutes.

She woke to the sound of excited children.

"You should have seen the sharks!"

"Some fish looked almost like butterflies."

"Grandpa Scott, show them the pictures."

Jeb said, "My favorite fish was an octopus." He ran around the room with his arms outstretched, wrists dangling down and waggling his fingers, trying to make like an octopus.

For the first time that afternoon, Faith laughed. Her lips curled upward in a smile. "So you boys and girls had a good time?"

"A great time."

"C'n we do it again?"

Scott beamed. "I told them if they were good and stayed with me, they'd get ice cream from the vendor outside the fish house. So we had a treat before coming home."

Melanie and Rachel said it was time for them to get home. The kids lifted Faith's spirits, but she knew Scott would want a rundown of the meeting, and it was good to see their company leave.

"Faith, a glass of wine?"

"Yes, I'm up to one glass. Just one, because I'm so bushed, a second glass would put me to sleep."

"Problems?"

"No, not really. Just tension."

"Jeremy presented a problem?"

"Not exactly. He went along with the consensus that it's not good to bring Doug into the family now, but he's in the 'never say never' camp."

"Well, that's not bad."

"I did the preliminary work for Bill and Miriam, asking the guys to draft deposition statements on why they would or wouldn't want to meet Doug. With Jon, it's no, no way, never. With Jeremy, it's more like no, not now, maybe in the future."

"You couldn't expect more than that, right?"

"Yeah, and again the gals gave me support, came over and put me in the daughter-in-law love press. That helped me get through the meeting. They understood, as women, the threat that Doug posed when he tried to barge into the condo. Jeremy didn't see the danger, but Jonathan was furious."

"Where does that leave us?"

"Good news: the family is alive and well. Bad news: we're all in the waiting game, with the ball in Doug's court."

SCOTT AND FAITH had a post-meeting confab with Bill and Miriam. Faith said, "Actually our meeting went rather well. Jeremy still wants to leave open the possibility of meeting Doug sometime in the future, but for the moment we all want to avoid letting Doug into the family."

Bill said, "You gave them the rundown on Family Court?"

"As well as I could. And at the end of the meeting, I suggested that the guys start drafting deposition statements about why they don't want to meet Doug."

Miriam spoke up. "Yes, it's important that the depositions be in their own words, not a fancy lawyer's document. A judge can smell a ghost-written statement a mile away. If the court asks Jeremy and Jonathan to weigh in with depositions, Bill and I can make suggestions, but we don't want to write anything."

"Here's our team strategy," Bill said. "I handle all negotiations with Doug and his lawyer. That's my forte. Then if we have to appear in Family Court, Miriam will take the lead, because that's her specialty."

Faith sighed. "So now all we can do is wait."

Bill laughed. "Nothing we can do about that. And we don't want to contact Doug or his attorney, because that would indicate weakness or willingness to make concessions."

The meeting ended with Miriam hugging Faith. "Honey, I'm supposed to be the Family Lawyer, but from what I hear about your gatherings, you are a superb family mediator."

They all had a good laugh.

SCOTT RAN TO THE OFFICE; Faith went to the hotel. When she got to her office, she told the secretary to hold her calls for a half hour.

Faith didn't like the waiting game. She had to keep busy and accomplish something. Looking back on her life, she figured she was the success others complimented her on. She had gone from high school grad and bottom of the totem pole green hire at Horton Hotel to an executive vice president position. She had solved several difficult labor disputes and managed the hotel efficiently to make money for the corporation. But she sensed something was missing, and couldn't put her finger on it.

The most important event of her adult life was the reunion with her twins, and she did nothing to bring that about. That was pure serendipity, manna from heaven. She wanted to do something useful with her life, something that made a difference. She decided to ask Scott about what she should do. He would be able to look into her soul better than she could.

. . .

THAT EVENING FAITH SUGGESTED, "How would you like to go out to Berghof's?"

"Sounds good to me. Special occasion?"

"I like to go back to places where we first met. It's romantic."

When they got to Berghof's, the maître 'd recognized the couple. "Ve haf not seen you, long time."

They asked to be seated in the little alcove where they had their first meal at this restaurant.

After they ordered, Scott said, "You've often admitted you should never play poker, because your face gives you away. Tonight, I know it's not about the mess with Doug—but something's on your mind. What's up?"

"Dear, I'm not sure and expect you to read what's on my mind. Lately, I'm tired and restless. Not sure what I want to do with the rest of my life."

"Ah-hah! Ms. Armstrong is going through mid-life crisis."

"You're probably right, but that still doesn't help me figure out what to *do*."

"Aren't you busy enough at work?"

"Sure, but it's not as satisfying as it used to be."

"Well, most of us most of the time are just taking care of business, answering the phone, handling the cash register, weeding the garden, delivering groceries. Me, sometimes I'm bored stiff listening to city council meetings and writing nothing articles about nothing meetings."

"You hit the nail on the head. I'm bored; don't know what to do."

"Hey Faith, I know you. You don't want to be tied up with humdrum busy work; you want to *do good*."

"You're on the right track, and I don't know what that do-good thing is."

"How about volunteer work. Not what you are told to do, have to do, but what you want to do. No pay, yet the reward is feel-good satisfaction."

"Uh-huh, but I'm so close to me that I can't see what would make me happy."

"Why not something at church?"

"Hmm, a possibility."

"Here's something from left field. You started the Mothers and Kids Foundation, and it's going great guns. Jeremy told me one thing keeping it going is a lot of volunteer workers. This is a cause you believe in, and you'd make a great contribution."

"Why didn't I think of that?"

"Because it was staring you in the face."

Faith put her fingers to her lips, then reached across the table and touched Scott's lips. "You are a mind reader and therapist all wrapped up in one package."

12

T he next morning Faith called Jeremy. She rehearsed her speech, almost as nervous as a teenager in a job interview.

"Jeremy, do you have a few minutes to talk?"

"Sure, Mom, is something up with the lawyers?"

"Hey, I don't always have to call you with serious stuff. This is just between you and me."

"Secret?"

"No, not really, it's just ....Well, let me get right to the point. I know you're doing such a good job with the Mothers and Kids Foundation, and wonder if I could help out."

"Uh, you want to volunteer?"

"Well, I guess that's what you'd call it. You don't sound too excited about it. If you don't think—"

"No, no, no, you just caught me by surprise. That' great. In fact, I've been holding off asking you for some assistance, but figured you were too busy with the hotel."

"The hotel will do fine without me, and what do you think, maybe I could, as you say, 'volunteer' one day a week? If I'm at the hotel Monday-Tuesday and Thursday-Friday, midweek Wednesday would be easiest to arrange."

"That would be super. You could participate in whatever aspect of the Foundation you want to. When you come, you'll see that we've tried to use the consultation suggestions you made for the One Way organization." He hesitated. "Well, we do have a couple of problems that I'd like to discuss with you."

"Sounds interesting, challenging. You know I'm committed to your project, and will contribute wherever you think I can make a difference."

"Can you start next Wednesday?"

"Sure, I look forward to it.

FAITH SHARED the exciting news with Scott that evening.

"Honey, you've got plenty of money so that you can afford a smaller paycheck. Now reward your inner spirit."

THE FOLLOWING WEDNESDAY, Faith drove to the Mothers and Kids Foundation, housed in a renovated small residential hotel on the West side, in a mixed residential and industrial area. In the parking lot next to the building, she squeezed her late-model shiny Lincoln between several dinged up older cars with faded paint. Walking across the lot, she recognized Jeremy's Toyota, and next to it a new Buick. She thought the old clunkers belonged to residents of the foundation, and the Buick probably was the car of a well-to-do volunteer.

Faith sized up quickly the building's faded brick façade, in need of tuckpointing. Entering the lobby, she had to dodge young children playing tag, running around dilapidated couches and easy chairs probably donated furniture. She glanced at young women seated here and there in the lobby, most wearing faded jeans and old T-shirts. And she noticed the women eyeing her stylish slacks and jacket over a blouse. One teenager seated in the corner, holding her baby, had on a cute dress and a matching cardigan. In another corner was a large TV, with kids sprawled on the floor watching cartoons.

Faith made a mental note that just as her Lincoln outclassed the other vehicles in the lot, her clothes upstaged the Foundation guests. She couldn't do anything about her vehicle, but next week she'd be more casual in dress.

She approached the front desk, which served as a catch-all of check-in, check-out, mail, and reception, and asked a lady for Jeremy. This woman ushered Faith into an office in an adjoining room.

Jeremy jumped up from an overloaded desk and hugged her. "Mom, it's great to see you here. Did you find a space in the parking lot? I forgot to warn you; sometimes it's full."

"Yes, I got the last spot."

"The parking lot, just like our facility, is overcrowded, but we do the best we can."

"Well, Jeremy do you have time to give me a tour? Show me what I can do."

"Uh, Mother, I don't want to insult you, but the state—you know, social services—requires information and a background check on all volunteers. They even do impromptu look-see visits, so you'd better fill out one of these volunteer applications. That way, if the investigators come in, we won't get in trouble."

He cleared away some of the mess on his desk and handed her a form and a pen, while he went to help settle a squabble in the lobby.

Faith felt humiliated by the barrage of offensive questions asking if she had ever been arrested, and if so the details; had she ever been in a mental institution; what was her history of recreational drugs; had she ever registered as a sex offender in this or any other state. She had to sign a statement that if a background check discovered a falsehood on any of these responses, she would be permanently barred from this facility.

"Sorry for that interruption, Mom. We have lots of little kids here, and the young mothers often are still adolescent. The kids disagree, and then the mothers side with their boy or girl."

Jeremy gave her a tour, starting with the large room next to the lobby that served as a dining area and meeting room, and beyond that the kitchen.

In the kitchen, he called out to a heavy-set Hispanic woman. "Maria, this is my mother Faith, who's going to help us one day a week."

"How do you do, Miss Faith. Your son, he a good boy. He help my daughter. I help cook, then he hire me to be regular cook."

Jeremy laughed. "She keeps us well fed."

Jeremy led her to a corner of the kitchen and a large washer and dryer. "Everyone has a different weekly window for laundry. The only way we can run the place is to assign duties for every resident —kitchen work, washing dishes, cleaning, front desk time."

"Your cook is full time."

"Yes, we have to have someone reliable for ordering, planning, and preparing meals. We have two other full-time salaried people, Jim Anderson, our financial officer, and Julia Kaminski, the social worker. Jim receives and processes donations and keeps the books for the required annual audit. Julia has regular appointments with each resident. Our goal is to 'transition' these young women and their children back into mainstream society. The women know when they enter that this is not a permanent home."

They climbed a back stairway to the second floor, which had a center hall and five rooms on each side. As they walked down the hall to the front of the building, women and children greeted Jeremy. A toddler blocked Faith's path and demanded, "Who are you? Are you a mommy?"

Faith answered, "Yes, I'm a mommy, and also a grandma."

They went down the front stairway and back to Jeremy's office.

"The third floor is the same as the second, so there's no need to look at it."

"So you can accommodate about twenty women, and about the same number of children."

"Right. When we first started, we were just accepting requests for financial aid and helping as many as we could. When we found this building, we jumped at the opportunity to be a kind of halfway house between young mothers in need, and facilitate their progression to independence. We realize that we can't deal with battered women who have school-age children. Other agencies handle that better than we can because we can't manage the school logistics. We do take in pregnant women and see women with preschool children through a few months of assistance. We don't expect any residents to be with us for more than six months. This way, we can cycle through seventy-five to a hundred young mothers each year."

"Jeremy, this is an impressive facility."

"When we have extra cash, we still give financial aid to women we don't have space for."

"I imagine there's more demand."

"We work with other agencies, and have a waiting list. If we had more rooms, we could easily help thirty or forty women."

"How would you do that?"

"Well, that's something I wanted to talk to you about. We've been keeping our eyes out for a larger facility. You know, something like a closed boarding school or seminary, a place with individual rooms, a dining area, and kitchen."

"You would want to purchase a place?"

"That would take a lot of money, in the millions. Maybe we could get in the door with a short term lease and maybe a lease-to-own agreement."

"How's your bank account?"

"Our cash flow is good, but we don't have money for a purchase."

"You have a building campaign fund?"

"No. Jim Anderson is a good financial officer, and efficient at receiving donations, but he's not a fundraiser."

"I see your situation. Well, you know your Mom, the instant analysis person. Although you could replace Jim Anderson with a fundraiser, I see a different scenario. Once you have a sketch of your long-term plans, hire a fundraiser for the building campaign, say for a six-month contract. Such a contract could always be extended or renewed. For stability, it's good to keep Jim Anderson on top of the day-to-day accounting."

"Mom, that's just the cut through the fog advice we need. Well, we've talked quite a while, and it's about time for our early lunch. I always eat here with the residents."

"I'd love to eat with these people. Now don't get me wrong, I appreciated your tour, but I'm much more interested in meeting and talking with the women and their children."

13

J eremy and Faith fell in line behind more than twenty adults and youngsters waiting for the cafeteria window to open for serving.

"Jeremy, if you don't mind, I'd like to eat with the people I'll be getting to know."

"Sure thing."

After Faith got her serving of Navy beans and cornbread, she looked around the hall and saw a woman and her baby sitting by themselves. She recognized the rather well-dressed woman she had noticed in the corner of the lobby when she arrived. Faith stood opposite her. "Mind if I join you?"

The woman shrugged. "Okay."

"I'm Faith, new here."

The woman asked, "Are you a social worker?"

"Oh, no."

"Of course not, you're dressed too nice."

"And you are ...."

"Amelia."

"What's the name of your baby?"

"Robby."

"How many months?

"Four."

"How long have you lived here?"

"Two months. If you're not a social worker, you're full of questions. Why are you volunteering?"

"You're right; I shouldn't be so nosey. To come right out with it, although I'm a lot older than the women here, I have something in common with you. When I was in high school, I got pregnant, and long story made short, my parents made me give up my twins for adoption. After many years I was reunited with my boys, and now I want to see if I can help young mothers keep and raise their children."

"I wouldn't believe you if my parents didn't put me through the same wringer. They told me, 'You made a mistake. Get an abortion, or if you insist on having the baby, let an adoption agency have it. Then you can go to college, and get on with your life.'"

"Amelia, you have a beautiful baby, big brown eyes. You must be glad you kept him."

"Yes, but it's not easy. My parents didn't throw me out, yet things got so bad that I moved out. Now I have to get my life back on track."

"Jeremy will help you."

"You know him?"

"Uh, yes ... he's my son."

"What? And your folks made you hand him over to an agency?"

"Yes, but we got back together, and he has children, and we have wonderful family gatherings."

They had finished their meal and were eating the canned sliced peaches in small dishes set at each place.

Amelia was feeding crumbs of cornbread to Robby. "Tell me, Faith, how did you get through the heartbreak of losing your twins? I know you're successful because you have good clothes."

"Amelia, we can talk about me some time, but one reason I'm volunteering is to help young women keep their children and make good. Did you graduate from high school?"

"Yeah, and I was accepted by several colleges, but my pregnancy got in the way."

"Have you thought of community colleges and online classes?"

"I wanted to do that, but my parents held out for giving up the baby and going to a fancy four-year college."

"Amelia, I have to be careful here, I don't want to argue against your parents, but—"

"Oh, don't worry about them. They've given up on me, 'washed their hands' of me."

"People say things like that, but don't always mean it. I think they'd be impressed if you started taking classes."

Jeremy had finished his meal and walked over. "Well, Mom, you and Amelia seemed to have a lively conversation."

"Yes, Jeremy, we were just at the point of her considering taking a community college or online course. You must have materials for that, don't you?"

"Sure, Amelia, stop by my office and we can talk it over."

"Uh, maybe I will."

WHEN THEY GOT BACK to the office, Jeremy asked, "Well, what's your take on the foundation?"

"Jeremy, you know I'm always using my radar, scoping out a place, and I found out two things about gender and age here. It's mostly women, and young, and no men except you. I saw a new Buick in the parking lot and an older woman in the kitchen. I figure no young woman would own an expensive car, and the older woman in the kitchen must be a volunteer like me, probably the one with the Buick."

"Bingo! You're right. Come on into the kitchen; I'll introduce you."

They walked to the kitchen.

"Mom, this is Maisie Bedford, Maria's sous chef."

Maisie said, "When I saw you come through the line, I didn't know if you were one of our resident's mother or a volunteer. I figure the best thing I can do is help put food on the table. Some of these youngsters have never cooked before, so it can be a culinary catastrophe asking them to help with a meal."

"You and Maria put out some of the best beans and cornbread I've had since I was a kid in Central Illinois."

"Not fancy, but filling and good for you."

Jeremy and Faith went back to his office.

"Mom, you're a miracle worker. Amelia came here a loner and hasn't opened up to anyone. How did you get her to talk?"

By chatting with her, finding out about her, complimenting her on her lovely baby. Jeremy, I'm glad to discuss financial and funding issues, but I would love to talk with Amelia and others like her, help them get ahead in life."

"Next week our social worker will be here, and you'll have to meet with her. Counseling is her territory, and she likes to screen the volunteers who go one-on-one with residents."

"Of course, I understand. Helping transform the lives of these young mothers is the heart of your project, and it's crucial that everyone work together to achieve that goal. I look forward to hearing her plan."

A woman stuck her head in the office. "Jeremy, I don't want to interrupt, but let me know when you have time to talk. I finished my interviews earlier than expected."

"Julia, you made your entrance right on cue. Take a seat. I was just talking about you."

"I hope it was favorable."

"It was. Julia, this is my mother, Faith Armstrong. I must have mentioned to you she's going to be coming one day a week as a volunteer. Mom, this is Julia Kaminski, our social worker. She splits her time between counseling current residents, and visiting our 'transitioned' former residents, helping them adjust to life on their own."

Faith said, "That must be rewarding work."

"It is, sometimes down and dirty tough, but today was very good. I met with three women who are doing well and helped another one who will need more assistance from us. Jeremy, I'll have more details in my case files."

"Good, Julia."

"By the way, Jeremy, another bit of good news. On my way through the lobby, Amelia stopped me, actually *spoke to me*, and asked about starting back to school. I don't know what came over her, but she's a changed person."

Jeremy and Faith laughed.

Julia looked back and forth to Jeremy and Faith, asking, "What's so funny about that?"

Jeremy smiled. "Well, just before you popped in, Mom and I were talking about Amelia. At lunch, Mom saw Amelia sitting alone, as she always does, and Mom asked to eat with her. One thing led to another, and Mom is the one who suggested Amelia kick start her new life by going back to school."

Julia jumped up from her chair and turned to Faith, hugging her. "I don't know how you got her to open up. Jeremy and I have joked that she's tighter than an oyster, and if we could only get inside her shell, we'd find a pearl. How did you do it, Faith?" Julia sat back down.

Faith shrugged. "I just talked to her, admired her baby, and wondered what she wanted to do with her life."

Jeremy said, "I told Mom that before she talks to any other residents, she should have the orientation session with you.

"Orientation, damnation. She has what it takes, and just proved it in spades. Jeremy, you've heard this a hundred times, but Faith hasn't. My two keywords for counseling are trust and rapport. You demonstrate those abilities by getting Amelia to come out of her shell. Our goals are to encourage self-confidence, build self-esteem, cultivate independence and initiative. In one conversation, you succeeded with Amelia in doing what we failed to achieve these past two months."

Jeremy smiled. "Do you want to talk more with Mom?"

"No. Orientation complete. The only thing I ask is that after you talk to a resident, be sure to leave a note in her file so that I know how that person is doing. You can read other files to see how we quickly draft a progress report."

"I can't wait to get started."

"Well, Faith, I share your excitement. I'll leave with Jeremy a list of residents you can contact the next time you volunteer—next Wednesday?

"Yes."

"Mom, let me suggest that you get an early start for home to beat the late afternoon rush. I need to get Julia's update on her interviews."

Faith was so elated she floated out of the office. In the lobby, she saw Amelia and Robby in her usual corner. Walking over to her, Faith said, "I have to get home now but wanted to say goodbye to you two. Uh, you know, my grandchildren are getting beyond the cuddling age. Do you mind if I hold Robby?"

Amelia took a deep breath, then handed Robby to Faith. Robby gurgled, then as Faith rocked him back and forth, he smiled and seemed to laugh.

"He likes you!"

"Not as much as I like him." She handed Robby back to Amelia, saying, "See you next week, and good luck with your school applications."

14

Caught up in replaying the day's events, Faith had to pay attention to the road as she drove home.

When Scott came in the door and looked at Faith, he said, "Turn the lights down! You're beaming like a hundred-watt bulb."

She regaled him with the details of the day, ending with, "Scott, I think today was a life-changing event. I've had a successful career at the hotel, but can't remember a day there as satisfying as helping a young mother start to turn her life around." She added, "You know what, not once did I think about that creep Doug and the mess he created. The Foundation is good therapy for me."

THURSDAY, working at the hotel, Faith's mind traveled back to the Foundation. She came up with an idea and called Jeremy. "Listen, it occurred to me that next Wednesday I could come in early, beat the morning rush traffic, and eat breakfast with the ladies. Would that be okay?"

"Well, sure. Maria and Maisie tell me the early birds are in line at seven-fifteen, waiting for the seven-thirty opening, and the sleepy heads show up at just before—sometimes after—the eight-thirty closing."

"Great! I'll plan to be there by seven-thirty."

"Uh, Mom, Julia scheduled you for two get-acquainted talks with residents next Wednesday. Since you're coming in that early, if it's not too much, you might go down the list, do two interviews in the morning, and two in the afternoon."

"Son, I have a much more rigorous schedule at the hotel. I'd be glad to do that."

USUALLY, Faith welcomed weekends, but after her glorious day with young mothers and kids, couldn't wait for Monday and was impatient for the calendar to advance to midweek.

On Wednesday she arrived at the Foundation a little before seven-thirty, falling in line with the early birds. She caught the eye of Amelia, asking, "Can we sit together?"

Amelia nodded.

Maria joked, "My cooking must be good for you to drive across town this early."

Faith chatted with several women while getting their food. "Why don't we sit with Amelia and Robby?"

The women looked at each other, then said, "Okay, I guess so."

The conversation, awkward at first, picked up when Faith asked Amelia about school, and she proudly announced she was filling out applications. The two other women immediately pumped Amelia for more information. Amelia and Faith had an impromptu session on completing your education. They lingered over break-fast until after eight-thirty.

Jeremy walked into the cafeteria. "I figured I'd find you here."

Amelia said, "Here's two more who would like information about school."

Jeremy and Faith walked to his office. "You never quit, do you?"

"Honestly, this is the most satisfying activity I've been involved in since I was a teenage counselor in church camp."

Jeremy showed her files of four residents. "Start with Barbara and Lillian. The files give you background information and notes of previous interviews. We don't expect miracles. On a first meeting, just get acquainted, and where possible, nudge them toward their transition to independence and self-sufficiency."

Jeremy introduced Faith to Barbara and Lillian, then let Faith and Barbara bond. After a half hour, Faith found Lillian, and they got to know each other. The interview was winding down when Jeremy rushed over to them.

"Mom, never a dull moment here. Our volunteer for morning playtime has an emergency, can't come in. Could you handle the kids for about forty-five minutes?"

"You need Scott, the official kid-wrangler, but I'll do my best."

She asked herself what Scott would do, and a bizarre idea came to her.

In her loudest voice, she yelled to the kids, "Who likes trains?" Shouts of approval filled the room.

"Okay, we're gonna take a train ride." She ushered about fifteen kids into the dining room and pulled out a chair. She picked the oldest boy, Leonard, announcing, "This is the locomotive, you're gonna be the engineer driving the train. Now, everyone pull out a chair and line up behind Leonard. You're the cars on the train." The kids grabbed chairs and formed a line behind the make-believe locomotive.

Faith spoke over the kids' chatter, "The train makes this sound, 'choo-choo-choo.' Let's hear you all make the train sound." She yelled, "A train makes a lot more noise than that." After a louder response, she told them, "A train has a whistle, and makes a loud toot! Let's hear you give a loud toot."

A few more kids showed up, got chairs and placed them behind the others. "Okay, kids, I'm gonna sing a song, and then you'll sing it with me. She sang "I've been workin' on the railroad," and at the point where Dinah blows her horn, she shouted out a loud "toot." She ran them through the song, then asked Leonard where he was taking the train.

"New York City!"

"Okay, boys and girls, we're heading for New York City as we sing our train song."

After Leonard's turn, he went back to the caboose, and every child moved forward, picking a new destination, and a new rendition of the song.

By the time every kid had a turn, more than a half hour passed. Faith realized that most of the mothers had gathered to watch, and joined in the singing and tooting. Even Jeremy came out of his office to see the hullabaloo.

Faith announced, "Okay, train ride's over, chairs back at the table."

The kids and mothers clapped and cheered. Leonard ran up to her. "You're fun!"

Jeremy joked, "Mom, you're dangerous. I think you could give Scott competition."

"Oh, I'm just an amateur; he's the professional entertainer."

FAITH ENJOYED HER LUNCH, receiving plenty of invitations for her to sit with kids and mothers.

Jeremy and Faith had a brief talk before her two afternoon interviews. "Mom, I guess you won't have any problem writing up notes for these meetings, will you?"

"No, the earlier notes give me a good pattern to follow. Why don't I wait until I get home and email you the notes?"

"Works for me."

AFTER HER TWO AFTERNOON INTERVIEWS, Jeremy saw her and told her, "You've had a full day. I'm ordering you to go home and get some rest. Kids and interviews are intense, hard work."

"You're right, but they also pump up your energy. My adrenalin gauge is on the full mark."

. . .

THAT EVENING, Faith bubbled over with enthusiasm telling Scott about the impromptu train ride.

"Hey, are you trying to horn in on Grandpa Scott's territory?"

"No, at least not in our household. But I'd like to borrow some of your tricks for future Wednesdays."

"Help yourself."

THE NEXT WEDNESDAY, Faith had Scott prepare a cardboard box theater and took it and thirty pairs of cotton gloves, and colored markers, to create glove-puppets. The response was even more enthusiastic than her train ride.

The kids learned quickly that Faith meant fun. As soon as she arrived at the Foundation, the kids mobbed her, wanting to know what they were going to do.

Faith enjoyed playing with the kids, but also met almost insurmountable challenges with the problems of some young mothers, especially those fighting depression and attempted or contemplated suicide.

She asked Jeremy, "How do you deal with this hopelessness and despair, day in and day out?"

Jeremy cocked his head. "It's the power of God, and the belief that no human being, no matter how low and down and out, has a chance for redemption."

Faith's eyes opened wide. "You know, Jeremy, I never really understood what you meant by that, until I came to the Foundation and saw what you've done here."

"It's not easy. It's a struggle. And we take it a day at a time."

"I'm proud of what you do here, and thank you for letting me be a part of it."

AFTER FOUR WEEKS, and only four Wednesdays, of volunteering, Faith was happy. She felt like she was in heaven until the call came from Bill Ludwig.

15

"Hi, Faith, how's my favorite hotel executive?"

"Well, the good news first. I wanted to do something worthwhile with my life, and have been volunteering at Jeremy's Mothers and Kids Foundation. It's the most rewarding activity I've ever participated in. Now please don't ruin that good time feelin' with some bad news."

"I'll try not to. Late this afternoon I heard from Luciano Garibaldi, Doug's attorney. Nothing hard and fast yet. He called to try to soften us up, says the whole matter can be resolved quickly and easily with two names and addresses."

"And you told him what to do with that offer?"

"No, the time for tough language comes later. I told him I would relay the offer to my client, but thought there was little to no chance you would accept his solution."

"You're right. I can tell you that now and don't need to consult the family. Does this mean he will file a petition with Family Court?"

"He says that's what Doug wants him to do."

"Okay, bottom line. What do we need to do?"

"Be sure to let Scott, and Jeremy and Jonathan, and their wives know so that we're all on the same page. Miriam and I will start preparing an opening statement and put together a character analysis of Doug. Please check with Jeremy and Jonathan to see what they have prepared for a deposition—a statement of why they don't want to meet Doug."

"Okay, I'll do that. By the way, we're always talking business. How's your health?"

"Much better, thank you. Well, thanks to my doctor, who made me exercise and lose a few pounds. And thanks to my wife, who controls my diet."

"Taking time off to volunteer has done wonders for me. I hope you find a way to lighten your schedule and enjoy some leisure activity."

"Have you been talking to my doctor and my wife?"

"Seriously, Bill, give it some thought."

WHEN SCOTT CAME HOME, he read the worry on Faith's face.

"Problems at the Foundation?"

"No, Doug's lawyer called Bill with a throwaway offer to settle everything quickly just by handing over Jeremy and Jonathan."

"That's a load of BS we don't even have to consider."

"No. Bill and Miriam will start preparing opening statements for court, and Bill wants Jeremy and Jonathan to work on their depositions."

Scott enfolded Faith in a bear-hug. "Hey, Babe, we beat Doug before, and we'll do it again. The last time was worse because the health of the twins was at stake."

"Uh, yeah, but the welfare of the family is up for grabs in this go-round."

"Don't worry, Miriam and Bill won't let Doug crash the family picnic."

"Just when I got involved in the Foundation and discovered something heartwarming, Doug barges in and tries to ruin it."

"No! You can't let him do that. If you do, he wins. You've got to keep going to Jeremy's place because since you started volunteering, I can see how your mood has been more upbeat."

"You're right. I'll keep on volunteering unless a court date conflicts with my Wednesdays."

Scott joked, "Well, I guess you'll be going to the South Side soon, right?"

"Yes, my father confessor can't change the situation, but he's a good listener, helps me sort out my thoughts, and I feel better, more sure of myself after talking to him."

Faith called Church of the Redeemer for an appointment, and several days later went to see Father Whitmore. She had a longer than usual conversation with Mary and Harriet, thanking them for help in counseling the residents at the Foundation.

Father Whitmore teased her. "Must be something heavy today because your two favorite saints had a long consultation."

"Yes. I want to tell you, too, that one day a week for the last month I've been volunteering at Jeremy's Mothers and Kids Foundation, and it's been a marvelous experience. I'll tell you more about that some time. For the moment, the bad news is that Doug will probably take us to Family Court to request Jeremy's and Jonathan's identities and addresses."

"Are you ready for the next legal tussle?"

"As ready as I'll ever be."

"You all agree not to allow any contact with the twins?"

"Uh ... yes."

"Hmm, did I notice some hesitation there?"

"Some slippage and uncertainty. This past month I've been interviewing and counseling the young women who live at the Foundation. Something Jeremy said made me rethink my view of human beings. Jeremy said that no matter how bad off a person is, whatever they've done, even attempted suicide, there's always a glimmer of hope. Oh, he didn't put it in those exact words, but he got me to thinking. I used to consider Doug as the devil, one hundred percent, not a bit of good in him. Now I realize I may have been too radical."

"How does that change your position in the legal proceedings?"

"Not a bit. As I told you before, I'm not concerned for the twins so much, but want to protect the grandkids."

"So how have things changed?"

"Well, I thought about pity and compassion, and I looked up the word 'compassion' in a concordance to the Bible, and found a passage in Mark where Jesus says he was moved to compassion because the people were like sheep without a shepherd."

"Yes, I think that's where Jesus fed a large number of people with five loaves of bread and two fish."

"Father, frankly, I'm confused. I'm dead-set against letting Doug into the family, but he does seem to be like a lost sheep without a shepherd to guide him. So I'm stuck with a twinge of compassion that seems to have no means of expression or path of action."

After they kicked around this dilemma for a while, Father Whitmore finally concluded, "I know you'll do the right thing at the right time."

"But you don't know when or what that is."

"My child, we never know."

He ended the session with a plea to Our Heavenly Father to bless all of his sheep and lead them to salvation.

16

W hen Scott came home that evening, he teased Faith. "Well, did you get your priest-fix today?

"Yes, like you've said about your dad counseling parishioners, Father Whitmore was very effective, some of the time just listening and letting me sort things out, and then showing me the path forward."

"I'm glad you saw him. We'll need all the resources we can muster to get through Family Court."

"Scott, I want to change the subject. You know how meaningful it's been for me to volunteer at the Foundation."

"Oh-oh, here comes a biggie."

"No, not a biggie, but an important change. Instead of just Wednesday, one day a week, I'd like to see about Tuesday and Thursday, two days a week. Horton Hotels should allow me to shift some of my workload to the Manager and Assistant Manager."

"Babe, whatever suits you, fine. I've heard lots of people say it's better to move into retirement gradually, rather than abruptly leaving forty hours a week for zero hours."

"Well, if it's fine with you, I'm going to run it by corporate head-quarters."

.   .   .

FAITH HAD no trouble receiving approval for her three-two work week, and Jeremy welcomed her offer for more volunteering.

"Mom, if you're coming Tuesday-Thursday next week, can we set aside next Thursday for brainstorming on the funding for a new facility?"

"Sure. I've been thinking about it a lot, and have some ideas I'd like to share with you."

"I can't wait to hear what you have to say."

THE FOLLOWING TUESDAY, Faith showed up for breakfast at the Foundation. The kids peppered her with questions about what she would do for playtime, but she just said they'd have to wait.

When it was play time, she asked kids to raise their hands if they liked television. Everyone raised their hands. Then she asked how many had been on TV. Several of the children raised their hands, but Leonard objected loudly, "You ain't been on television."

Faith announced, "All of you can be on television today. I'm going to ask each one of you what you want to be when you grow up. And why that's what you want to be, and what you're going to do to make sure you can be what you want to be. I have a video camera in my bag and will record what you say, and then we'll play it back on the television. Who wants to be first?"

Leonard said, "I know what I want to be."

Faith had her camera out, pointed it at him, and said, "What would you like to be?"

"I want to be a fireman. Because they help people and have a good time running around in the red firetruck, and, uh, I'm gonna grow up and be strong, so I can be a fireman."

Faith spent about twenty minutes interviewing the kids, then used a link from her camera to the television in the lounge to play back the kids' statements. They cheered so loud that Jeremy came out of his office to see what was going on. The mothers applauded. Jeremy walked over to Faith.

"Mother, where do you come up with these tricks?"

"I have a good role model in Scott."

LATER IN THE DAY, after two interviews with residents, Faith asked Jeremy for a few minutes. "Jeremy, I'm glad to give you suggestions on fund-raising, but warn you, just like when I did the consult for One Way, my advice may be tough. With the kids and play time, I'm the fun-loving joker. Talking to the mothers, I'm a warm and fuzzy friend. Giving institutional advice, I'm the hard-hitting, no-nonsense business executive."

"Wouldn't want it any other way."

"I found a Jewish delicatessen not too far from the Foundation, and want to take you out to a business lunch Thursday. We'll get more done if you aren't interrupted by phone calls and settling squabbles in the lounge."

THURSDAY MORNING, when Faith got to the Foundation, Amelia and Robby were waiting for her and asked to eat with her.

Waiting in line, Amelia pulled a few papers out of her purse. "My first writing assignment in my online course. Got a B+ on it. We had to read a book and write a report. Mine was on *The Red Badge of Courage*. It's about a civil war soldier, and I didn't look forward to reading it, but it turned out to be very interesting. It's a story of being a coward and then finding courage. You won't believe it, but it helped me think about my situation. Like the soldier in the story, I ran away from responsibilities, and need to have the courage to face difficulties."

"Amelia, I remember reading that book, years ago. And I'm glad you liked it. But more important, congratulations on beginning your course work and getting a good grade."

Faith just picked up a coffee and went to a table with Amelia. Faith held Robby while Amelia ate.

After two morning interviews with residents, Faith went to see Jeremy. Kids surrounded her, expecting her to lead play time, but she said it was someone else's turn to have fun with them.

Faith took Jeremy to a Jewish deli, where they ordered food, and then she said, "This is a business meeting, so I'm going to launch into an overview of how I see your present situation, and plans for the future."

"I'm all ears."

"First, congratulations on establishing an excellent program. You have a good facility with everything necessary to take care of twenty mothers and their little children. And you've set up an efficient, caring plan to lead these residents back into mainstream society.

"This success is the best rationale for expanding your mission. I am guessing here that Melanie, who kept a file of testimonies for One Way, also has a collection of letters from your transitioned women praising your outfit."

Jeremy smiled. "You guess right. The letters are heart-warming."

Faith nodded. "And those letters will open purses and corporation treasuries. Well, look with me into my crystal ball. I see a facility like what you have here, including a large meeting area, dining room, kitchen, and thirty to forty individual rooms. Frankly, I have only one upgrade consideration. Your inner city setting has no lawn or playground. I looked out the back door, and the only extra space is a place where smoking is allowed. For a future facility, I highly recommend a building with enough outdoor space, maybe a lawn, where you could let the kids play, and have a small playground with swings. Is that a reasonable snapshot of your future Foundation?"

"Mom, you're right on target."

"Okay, next on the agenda is how you acquire such a property. Have you started looking around?"

"I watch the real estate listings in the newspaper, but haven't seen anything that matches our specifications."

"Your next priority should be engaging a commercial real estate agent. They work on commission so that it won't cost a cent upfront. They'll tell you not only what is available, but give you details and sales figures of what has been sold in the past five years or so. That will provide you with a realistic notion of how much money you need. A good agent will be on the lookout, may find a property before it comes on the market.

The next item on the agenda is a little more sticky. I think you mentioned Jim Anderson, your financial officer, who is a holdover from One Way."

"That's right; he did such a good job that we brought him with us."

"And that's one reason I said he should not be replaced. He can continue to do what he does best, keeping the books in order. But to be upfront, I think you need a professional fundraiser. Good ones don't come cheap, maybe $25,000 to $50,000 for a six-month campaign. If they bring in millions, that's a sound investment.

"A good realtor will give you an idea of how much you'd need for outright purchase or a mortgage. That will provide a target for the Fundraiser. On the financial side, I propose a bold two-pronged approach. One prong is substantial lump sum donations. The other prong is what I would call 'sustaining contributions,' agreements from corporations to pay a certain amount each month for five years or so. This kind of support would be essential if you had a mortgage. We'll have to look at your books and figure out how to balance initial outlay—say the actual purchase of a property—and operating expenses, including a mortgage if you have one."

Jeremy had almost finished his meal; Faith had only picked at hers.

"Mother, I can't believe that you figured all this out, and could explain it in less than a half hour without a single note."

"This is my executive business mode, not my kid-fun, or resident-counselor mode. If you like my ideas, I'll do my part and look for the best possible realtor and fundraiser."

"You have an excellent plan; go for it!"

They went back to the Foundation. Jeremy insisted that she had put in more than a full day's work, and should make an early start for home, beating the afternoon rush. Faith was tired, so she just dropped Jeremy off, and headed for the condo.

When she opened the door, the phone was ringing.

17

"Hello, Faith. Bill Ludwig here."

"Hello, Bill. Before we get into business, how are you?"

"Much better, thanks. My cardiologist says I've recovered remarkably well."

"That's good to hear. I wouldn't want our troubles to affect your health. Now tell me what's up."

"Well, part of the waiting is over, and now we enter a new period of waiting. Doug's lawyer, Garibaldi, called to try once more to persuade us to set up a meeting with the twins and avoid court. I told him we couldn't in good conscience bring Doug together with your boys. He tried to pry information out of me, asking why the objection to Doug. I said we'd become acquainted with him through complicated negotiations, and didn't want to travel that road again."

"So he's proceeding with a petition to the court?"

"That's what he says, and I think he knows how weak a position he's in, but Doug insists on it."

"What happens now?"

"He files the papers with the court, you know, the petition, and the court notifies me. I respond on your behalf, saying we do not accept the petition. Then comes the waiting period, when we appear before the judge. That will take a month or two."

"So in the meanwhile, the guys have to write their depositions?"

"Yes, that's what I was going to mention to you. Miriam and I would like a look-see at them, to make sure our formal statement to the judge dovetails with their depositions."

"I'll pass the word along to them."

She waited until Scott came home to give him the news.

"Well, this is what we expected."

"Uh-huh. I think I'll send an email to Jeremy and Jon because there's nothing new in what Bill told me."

THAT WEEKEND the family had a get-together at Jonathan and Rachel's house. While Scott entertained the grandchildren, Faith had a brief talk with the twins and their wives.

"Write whatever you think is best. The only suggestion I have is that you don't draft a joint statement. It will be stronger if each of you writes independently. Then Miriam and Bill can comment on whether you might add or delete something."

Jeremy and Jon nodded. Jon said, "Whatever you think is best."

FAITH KEPT busy with the day-to-day routine at the hotel, resolving minor problems. She loved the satisfaction of helping out at the Foundation. Using her connections at Horton Hotels, she had connected Jeremy with a first-rate commercial realtor, who met with him and provided a list of a half dozen properties in the Chicago area that matched his specifications and had been sold in the past five years. The sale prices of ten to fifteen million gave him a financial target. That prompted Faith to pass on the name of a leading fundraiser in metropolitan Chicago. Jeremy insisted Faith be at the meeting with the fundraiser.

Faith told Jeremy, "I'm glad to see the future Foundation project moving forward, but I'm more satisfied with the volunteering with residents. You know, Amelia is finishing her first online course and is signing up for another. I've talked with Julia Kaminski, and we think Amelia's getting close to transitioning out of here."

"You were the spark that lit her fire."

"I've become attached to her and Robby."

"That's a hard part of our work, befriending women and kids, and then seeing them leave."

AT HOME, Scott and Faith talked about the upcoming court appearance. "Faith, the fact that you can juggle the hotel, major negotiations for a new Foundation property, and your twice a week volunteering convinces me that you'll handle the court situation well."

"It's great to have your support, Scott."

JEREMY AND JONATHAN prepared their depositions separately, then met with Miriam and Bill. Faith said she thought it was better for her not to be present at that meeting because the depositions should come straight from each twin, and not appear as if she was telling them what to say. If asked by the judge, the twins could honestly say they had written the statements themselves, without any input from her. Miriam and Bill liked the depositions, making only a few minor suggestions.

THE NIGHT before the court appearance, Faith was a little tense. She and Scott went to bed about eleven. She waited until after midnight when he was snoring, and got up, taking her journal out of her dresser drawer. Opening it to a new page, she wrote:

Trouble.
Trouble with Doug.

I am prepared.
Jeremy and Jonathan are ready.
Miriam and Bill will handle this well.
In all this mess, volunteering at the Foundation helps me, because
it shows me what is more important than legal wrangling.

She felt better just writing out her thoughts. Closing the journal, she replaced it in its dresser home and went back to bed, snuggling next to Scott.

She finally fell asleep having strange dreams about appearing in court.

18

Faith carefully selected one of her power suits for the court appearance and then met Bill and Miriam in their office. Miriam told Faith, "We drew Amanda Hernandez as judge. I've appeared in her court before. She's tough but fair, and she will call you to testify. Just answer her as briefly as you can. She doesn't like witnesses to beat around the bush."

THE THREE TAXIED to the courthouse, and they went up the elevator to the courtroom, waiting for their case to be called. When the clerk asked them to come forward, Miriam and Bill had her take the seat between them. She had seen Doug, who at least had cleaned up his appearance, and had a white shirt and tie on. She avoided looking directly at him.

Judge Amanda Hernandez entered, and everyone rose. Faith thought the name Hernandez was Hispanic, but the judge did not look Hispanic. She wondered if Hernandez was her married name.

The judge walked quickly into the chambers and assumed her seat behind the bench. Faith figured she must be in her late forties or early fifties. With slightly graying hair, worn short with a slight curl, her black robe and horn-rimmed glasses lent her an air of authority and dignity.

After the formalities, Judge Amanda Hernandez asked Luciano Garibaldi to make his opening statement for the plaintiff.

"Your honor, I am glad to present the case of Douglas G. Parinello in his petition to have access to his twin sons. I have tried repeatedly, through the attorneys of the mother of the twins, to resolve this case out of court, but have not received a favorable response. I regret that we have to take up the valuable time of the court to consider what is a rather modest and straightforward request.

"Mr. Parinello and Ms. Faith Armstrong are the parents of twin sons, born some thirty years ago. Mr. Parinello was not notified by Ms. Armstrong of the pregnancy, nor the birth of the twins. Only in this past year, in a separate court case, was Mr. Parinello made aware that he is the father of the twins. We do have a DNA confirmation of his paternity and can provide the documentation.

"Our petition is based on the fact of Mr. Parinello's documented paternity, and the laws concerning parental rights. We ask that the court require Ms. Armstrong to provide Mr. Parinello with the legal names and current addresses of his sons. He has asked her several times for this information, and she has refused. As Mr. Parinello's attorney, I have asked Ms. Armstrong's attorney for this information, which he has told me she would not divulge.

"Your honor, Mr. Parinello has gone more than thirty years without knowledge of, or contact with his sons, and would like to reunite with his sons. It is his fervent wish, and it is his legal right. This we petition the court to honor."

The judge listened closely to Garibaldi.

Faith stared at the judge, unable to see through her stony-faced façade.

The judge announced, "I will speak to you, Mr. Garibaldi, and also to co-counsels Dugan and Ludwig. This is an unusual case because usually such litigation and adjudication involves children, both younger and older, but still minors. In the present situation, the sons of Mr. Parinello and Ms. Armstrong are adults, and we will expect to hear from them. But it is customary to ask counsel for a character assessment of the parent involved in a visitation request. Are you prepared to provide such an assessment now?"

"Yes, your honor. Mr. Parinello is a law-abiding citizen of Peoria. He is a graduate of Western Illinois University, and for decades has managed the construction company he inherited from his family. He is a respected member of the Peoria business community. Recently he has sold his business and is financially well off. He seeks no money in this petition. One reason for his sale of the family business is his earnest desire to develop a strong and warm relationship with his sons, a relationship he has been deprived of for too long.

"Mr. Parinello would like to be a parent in fact and deed, not just in name and legal standing. On behalf of Mr. Parinello, I ask that you honor his petition."

The judge removed her glasses and peered closely at papers.

"Alright, now let's hear the opening statement from Ms. Dugan for the defendant."

"Judge Hernandez, I'm glad to appear before you again, this time not representing a minor, but adults. We understand and support Ms. Armstrong's refusal to provide the names and addresses of her twin sons to the plaintiff. Mr. Garibaldi stated that his client Mr. Parinello has been deprived of access to his sons. Co-counsel and I acknowledge the paternity of Mr. Parinello. Our firm provided Mr. Parinello's attorney at the time of another court case with this information. We will come back to this point when we talk about character. For the moment, we contest that Mr. Parinello has been deprived of access to these sons. He did not contact Ms. Armstrong after their one-time liaison, to see if this liaison resulted in pregnancy and a child or children. So, in effect, he acted, and failed to act, to deprive himself of access to the twins born to Ms. Armstrong.

"Mr. Parinello finished college and married, had children. So he has had, still has, his experience as a parent.

"Counsel for the plaintiff claims that his client would like to step forward and become a parent to his twin sons with Ms. Armstrong. The defendant might have welcomed such a concern three decades ago when her pregnancy during her last year in high school was a cause of embarrassment and interruption of her academic work. The defendant would have appreciated some financial support so that she could raise her boys. With no financial support, as a minor, her parents required her to give up her firstborn for adoption.

"Ms. Armstrong tried, unsuccessfully, to make contact with her adopted sons, but could not. Only in the past few years, was she able to reconnect with them, and has renewed her familial bond. She values this bond very highly, and for this reason, does not welcome the intrusion of Mr. Parinello into this warm and loving relationship.

"For these reasons, we respectfully ask the court to deny the petition of Mr. Parinello."

Faith watched the judge listen intently to Miriam's statement. Faith thought the judge nodded her head, ever so slightly, to each point Miriam made.

The judge briefly looked over her papers, then asked Miriam, "Counsel for the defendant, do you have a character statement?"

"Yes, your honor, I have a double statement, first for Ms. Armstrong, and then for Mr. Parinello."

The judge looked straight at Miriam. "The character statement for Mr. Parinello has already been made by his attorney."

"Yes, your honor, but to understand Ms. Armstrong's position, and why she will not hand over the names and addresses of her sons, we need to understand the context of the relationship and lack of relationship between plaintiff and defendant."

"Alright, I'll allow it, but be brief."

"Your honor, Ms. Armstrong is an upright, law-abiding citizen of Chicago. Raised in Canton, Illinois, after a teenage pregnancy, she graduated from an alternative high school. From these humble beginnings, Ms. Armstrong worked hard at Horton Hotels and became a manager and executive vice president with this firm. She has been in demand as a speaker, for both academic and business conferences.

"As we mentioned in the opening statement, in the past few years Ms. Armstrong has been reunited with her sons and wants to preserve and protect this relationship.

"Ms. Armstrong's one-night liaison with Mr. Parinello, her first sexual experience, came when she was still sixteen, a minor and inexperienced. Mr. Parinello at this time was twenty-one, an adult and a college student. Let me be clear here; we are not raising the issue of statutory rape, nor are we pursuing any financial claim against Mr. Parinello or his business interests. Our point here is the age difference and the contrast of a minor high school girl—just sixteen—and a twenty-one-year-old man—an adult.

"Mr. Garibaldi in his opening statement, in effect blames the defendant for not contacting plaintiff about her pregnancy and birth. We counter that Mr. Parinello did not use a contraceptive to prevent pregnancy, nor did he follow up to see if there was a resulting pregnancy. Ms. Armstrong waited for him to show up, but he did not. He deprived himself of knowledge of the pregnancy and birth.

"Ms. Armstrong suffered from the humiliation of teenage pregnancy and had to graduate from an alternative high school. She had no partner to support her financially or emotionally. In spite of these disadvantages, she has become quite successful.

"Several years ago, she was thrilled to be brought together with her sons. This joy was threatened when one twin developed kidney problems, and the doctors needed family records to see if there was a genetic predisposition to kidney failure, which might affect both twins.

"Ms. Armstrong was able to track down Mr. Parinello and asked for his family medical history regarding kidney disease. Mr. Parinello denied he had ever had a liaison with Ms. Armstrong and insisted he was not the father of her twins. Through the work of detectives and DNA analysis, Mr. Parinello's paternity of the twins was documented and forwarded to Mr. Parinello's attorney.

"At the time, Ms. Armstrong and her twins were desperate to receive the medical records of Mr. Parinello, because one twin was risking kidney failure, and the other twin was facing kidney issues. Even after Mr. Parinello and his lawyer were presented with paternity papers for Mr. Parinello and the twins, Mr. Parinello chose to fight a legal battle that might take six months to a year.

"Your honor, we place this evidence before you, to argue that Mr. Parinello did not assume the responsibility of a parent thirty years ago. Nor did he express the concern of a parent and act for the best interests of his child more recently. Our client sees Mr. Parinello as a parent in name and by biological accident, but not in fact and action.

"We mention one other incident that throws light on the relationship between plaintiff and defendant. When Mr. Parinello first contacted Ms. Armstrong, requesting an introduction to his sons and threatening to petition Family Court if she did not comply, she told him to stop communicating with her and to deal directly with our law firm. He persisted in phoning her, and even posed as a flower delivery man, trying to force his way into her condo. She filed a police report, and our firm obtained a restraining order restricting Parinello from contacting her or approaching her at home or work.

"For these reasons, your honor, we ask you to deny plaintiff's petition."

The judge glanced at Doug and Faith, then announced a fifteen-minute recess and brought her gavel down.

19

During the recess, Miriam went with Faith for a trip to the ladies' room; Bill went to the men's room.

Miriam whispered to Faith, "We may meet Doug or his lawyer in the hall, but just keep moving. Don't make eye contact, say anything, or respond to them."

When they rejoined Bill in the hall, Faith asked, "How are we doing?"

Miriam laughed. "All's well so far. But that was just the warmup. Doug will be sitting in the hot seat next, and that's when the fireworks may go off."

Bill said, "You follow Doug as a witness, and remember what we told you: answer her questions as briefly and as truthfully as you can. By that I mean, if you forgot something, say so. And by the way, when she's grilling Doug, try to show no emotion. No grinning; no frowns."

They saw Doug and his attorney coming out of the restroom, so Bill ushered the ladies into the courtroom.

Following the recess, the judge called Doug to testify, and the bailiff swore him in.

The judge took her time as Doug sat down, fidgeting and looking from the judge to his attorney.

"Mr. Parinello, you have heard two presentations from your attorney, an opening statement, and a character statement. To the best of your knowledge, are these presentations accurate?"

"Yes, your honor."

"Now, for the benefit of the record, would you state why you have authorized this petition, and what you wish to gain from it."

"Your honor, I want to get back together with my sons. I didn't know about them for thirty years, and—well, I'm getting older now, and want to develop a good relationship with them before any more time slips by."

"Mr. Parinello, your formal petition claims parental rights as the legal basis for making this request, is that right?"

"Yes, I'm not a lawyer, but my attorney says a father has the right to see his children. And we submitted the paternity paper, so that should give me the right—he says I have the right—to see my twin sons."

"This proceeding is, as you point out, centered on parental rights, and you are the parent here." She paused, waiting for a reply.

"Uh, yeah ... I mean, yes ma'am, I am the parent of twin sons with Faith Armstrong."

"These twins are not your only children."

"No."

"You are the parent of other children."

"Yes.

"For the record, tell the court about your other children."

"Well, I have two children with my first wife, and two children with my second wife."

"Is that all?"

"Four children with my two wives."

"Is that all?"

"No, your honor, I had another child with a woman I was living with."

"So you have had five children other than the twins mentioned in your petition?"

"Yes."

"And this includes all of your other children?"

"Two by each wife, and one by my live-in."

"I asked if this includes all of your other children."

Doug made eye contact with his lawyer, who jumped to his feet. "Your honor, my client's sexual history is not germane to a petition for visitation."

The judge glared at Garibaldi. "The court is not interested in his *sexual* history, just his *parental* history. He has initiated a petition for parental rights, so the court needs to know his parental record."

Garibaldi sat down.

The judge continued. "I ask you again, Mr. Parinello, and remind you that you are under oath. Are these five offspring all of your children?"

"Well, one other, with a woman in southern Illinois, but that was a long time ago before I got married."

"Did you live with her?"

"No."

"This long time ago southern Illinois child—was this before or after your brief liaison with Ms. Armstrong?"

"After."

"I see. And you didn't live with this woman."

"No."

"Well, now that we have a count of all your children, I want to return to the main focus of your petition, your role as a parent. Let's start chronologically. When was the last time you saw the child you had with the southern Illinois woman?"

Doug squirmed in his chair, pulling at his necktie. "Well, we never lived together, so she took the child and did not let me see it."

"It?"

"Him."

"Did you file a petition for visitation?"

"No."

"What you're telling me is that you have not seen this son for more than three decades, is that right?"

"Yes."

"Let's move on to the children by your first wife. How often do you see them?"

"Not very often."

"How often?"

"Your honor, my first wife remarried, and they turned the kids against me."

"Did you file a petition for visitation rights?"

"No."

"I'm beginning to see a pattern here. What about the children from your second marriage?"

"Your honor, my second wife remarried, and moved."

"So you don't see them?"

"No, not really."

"And you didn't file a petition for visitation?"

"No."

"And you also had a child with a woman you lived with?"

"Yes."

"Do you have regular contact with this child?"

"No, my live-in moved and I lost contact with her."

"Mr. Parinello, with your many children it takes a long time to get your parenting history in the record. Let me cut to the chase, and ask you what it means to be a parent."

"I don't know; what do you mean?"

"I ask the questions. You are claiming a right as a parent. As a parent, you should know what it means to be a parent."

"Uh, well, I care for them."

"Let me help you out. In each divorce, you were required to pay alimony?"

"Yes, alimony, and also I lost a house with each divorce."

"So being a parent means providing financial support for children and assistance for your ex-wife. Uh, ex-wives."

"Yes."

"What about the child with your live-in?"

"She moved away, and I lost track of her."

"Hmm, hard to keep track of all these children. Did you pay support for the child with the woman in southern Illinois?"

"No."

"She did not ask for support?"

"We made a lump sum payment to her, out of court."

"Out of court—what kind of court case?"

"A paternity case, but we settled out of court, so I never formally admitted to paternity."

"You made a lump sum payment to avoid the court suit?"

"I was busy with my construction business, just wanted to settle it and get on with my business."

"Well, I can understand that with a construction business you have many responsibilities."

"Yes, your honor, hiring people and managing them, bidding on projects, and overseeing them."

"I won't waste time with business responsibilities but will focus on parental responsibilities. You come before the court emphasizing parental rights. Rights always come with responsibilities. A driver's license gives you the right to drive a car. But it also requires you to follow the laws and drive responsibly."

"Yes, I understand."

"You are claiming parental rights. What are parental responsibilities?"

"Uh, like I said, I paid alimony and made sure my wives' kids had a roof over their heads."

"But not for your live-in?"

"She moved away."

"The bottom line is that you see parental responsibility mainly as financial support?"

"Well, that's all my wives would allow. Like I said, both wives—and their new husbands—turned the kids away from me."

"Hmm, did the new husbands adopt your children?"

"Yeah. I didn't like it, but had to go along with it."

"Mr. Parinello, according to your testimony, parental responsibility for you is mainly financial support. But now your twin sons are adults and don't need any support. And the defendant says, through her lawyer, that she seeks no money. So that leaves the court and me asking why you want to exercise your parental right for visitation. If we would grant your petition, what would you expect to do with them."

"Get to know them, be friends with them. Maybe go to a ball game with them."

"Let's finish your testimony with some specific questions about the twins you have not seen for thirty years."

"Well, I saw them just once, in the lawyers' offices, a year ago."

"Let's go back thirty years where this all started. You and Ms. Armstrong had sexual relations, just once, and that resulted in her pregnancy, right?"

"Yes."

"After that one time when you had sexual relations, did you meet her again?"

"No, not until last year."

"Let's concentrate on thirty years ago. Did you call her?"

"I went to the pizza place where she worked and tried to get her phone number, but they wouldn't give it to me."

"So did you try to contact her?"

"I didn't know how to contact her."

"You didn't write her a letter."

"I didn't have her address."

"When you met her at the pizza place, did you ask her how old she was?"

"Uh, she looked older, and I didn't ask."

"You knew she was a high school student."

"Yeah ... I mean, yes ma'am."

"Mr. Parinello, did you take a biology class in high school or college?"

"In high school."

"So you knew about human reproduction, and how pregnancy takes place."

"Yes."

"But you had unprotected sex with a high school girl?"

"It just happened. I didn't mean for her to get pregnant."

"And you didn't mean for the girl from southern Illinois to get pregnant?"

"Uh, no, your honor."

"Now let's come back closer to the present, and the defendant's request for medical records for your son. You remember that?"

"Yes."

"Is it correct that initially, you denied paternity of the defendant's son?"

"It was a long time ago, and I wasn't sure who she was, what she wanted."

"Mr. Parinello, let me remind you that your case revolves around events of three decades ago. Did you deny paternity?"

"At first, but not later."

"DNA and fingerprints made you change your mind?"

"Well, yeah."

"Is it correct that you refused to give your family's medical records?"

"At first, but then later I did hand them over."

"Did you delay handing over the medical records for months while the treatment of your son's medical condition depended on those records?"

"I wasn't sure if they were honest with me."

"Did they ask you for child support, any money for medical expenses, or any other payment?"

"No."

The judge thanked him for his testimony and excused him. Beads of sweat trickled down his forehead, and his armpits were dark with sweat.

The judge said court would reconvene at 1:30.

20

Miriam and Bill stayed seated, waiting until Doug and Garibaldi left the courtroom, then stood up. Bill said, "Let's get some lunch."

Faith shook her head. "I'm not hungry."

Bill said, "Honey, you don't want to face the judge on an empty stomach. Let's go out and get you some ice cream. Vanilla ice cream will settle your tummy."

They went to a nearby restaurant, where Bill and Miriam ordered sandwiches, and Faith slowly spooned some ice cream. She said, "Go over it again; what will the judge ask?"

Miriam answered. "Same routine as for Doug. Put in your own words why you oppose the petition, why you don't want Doug to meet the twins."

"Okay, that won't be too hard."

Miriam said, "No, but she's a tough judge, and she just came down pretty hard on Doug. She made him look like the un-parent of the year. So to be fair, or to at least give the appearance of being fair, she'll have to be tough on you, throw some hard questions to you."

"About?"

"About why you don't just go along with Doug and introduce him to the twins."

"I guess I'm as ready for that as I ever will be."

They finished lunch and returned to the courtroom a little before 1:30.

JUDGE HERNANDEZ HURRIED in at 1:35 and called Faith to testify. Faith was sworn in and walked slowly to the witness box. Looking out at the courtroom, she did glance at Doug and Garibaldi but followed Bill's advice to focus on him if she had to, then when answering questions from the judge, look straight at the judge.

Faith felt butterflies in her stomach. She closed her eyes and prayed.

Mary and Harriet, be with me and help me.

The judge squinted at Faith. "Ms. Armstrong, are you okay?"

"Yes, I'm fine."

"Good. You have heard two presentations by your legal counsel today, one the formal opposition to the petition before the court, the other a statement of your character. To the best of your knowledge, are these presentations accurate?"

"Yes, your honor."

"Now, for the record, tell us why you oppose the petition before the court."

"Well, just about everything I can tell you has been said."

"Just put it in your own words."

"Let me say two things first. One, I am opposed to the petition. Two, I am for holding my family together, and that is the main reason for being against the petition. Judge, the only way I can think about this is to go back thirty years and start there."

The judge nodded. "Go ahead."

"Thirty years ago I made a mistake, and have paid for it ever since. I was an innocent, foolish high school girl working at a pizza place, and was flattered by a college man who paid attention to me. I was inexperienced with dating, and the first time alone with a man—I got pregnant. It was foolish, and I regretted it. When I got home that night, I prayed to God that I would never do such a stupid thing again.

"Well, I found out I was pregnant, and finally told my parents. They were as disappointed with me as I was disappointed with myself. When they learned that I hardly knew the father, they realized he had no intentions of marrying me, and insisted I give the babies—we learned it would be twins—up for adoption. I begged them to let me keep them, but they would not agree to that. I knew about abortion but didn't consider that option. I became so depressed I thought of suicide, but ending my life would end the lives of my babies.

"So I carried them for nine months, delivered them, and got to hold them just for ... a few minutes." Faith put her hands in front of her face, sobbing.

Miriam stood up, holding out a handkerchief, nodding to the judge, who motioned her forward. Miriam gave Faith the handkerchief, then hurried back to her chair.

Faith turned to the judge. "I'm sorry, judge, talking about this is very difficult."

"Can you continue, or do you need a few minutes?"

"I'll be okay now." She blew her nose and cleared her throat. "After graduating from high school, I came to Chicago and buried myself in work. Time and again I tried to get in contact with my twins, but that was strictly against the adoption agency's policies.

"A few years ago, my twins were able to locate me, and we have had a great reunion, trying to make up for a thirty-year gap. A little more than a year ago, we learned one twin had a severe kidney problem, and because they are identical twins, the doctors needed medical records for both parents. We were able to locate Mr. Parinello and asked him for his parents' medical records.

"He was uncooperative, did not admit paternity, and would not release family records. Through detective work, we linked his fingerprints and DNA, proving his paternity. So the paternity documents Mr. Parinello provided the court are the ones we gave him.

Well, we needed the medical records right away, for diagnosis of the kidney condition of both twins. However, even after we proved paternity, Mr. Parinello held on to the medical records and insisted on a personal meeting with us. That is when Mr. Parinello had the first meeting with his twin sons.

"It is difficult to describe the trouble and turmoil Mr. Parinello put us through, a life and death situation, and he was ready to let the matter drag through the courts for six to twelve months."

Faith dabbed at her eyes again. "Well, that's my story. I have to tell you because we know Mr. Parinello's family history, we think— our perception is—that he has not been a good parent in his other families, and we don't want him to interfere in our family harmony. These are the reasons I oppose his petition."

The judge finished taking notes, then looked at Faith. "Thank you for your statement. Now I have some questions for you. These identical twins are your only offspring."

"Yes."

"What is your marital status?"

"Three years ago I married."

"No children?

"None."

"You say that over the years you tried to contact your children?"

"Yes, but the adoption agency has a strict policy not to allow contact with adopted children."

"Hmm, but now you are in touch with them?"

"Yes, I couldn't locate them, but through a series of coincidences, they discovered me."

"And you meet with them frequently?"

"Every chance we can. We have a wonderful extended family, and . . ." Faith glanced at Bill, who put an index finger to his lips.

Faith continued, "a wonderful family, and don't want Mr. Parinello to be a part of it."

"Let me ask you, you know about parental rights, don't you?"

"A little."

"Do you understand that a father or mother has the parental right to visitation?"

"What I understand is that a parent has the right to petition for visitation, but it is up to the courts to decide whether or not to grant it. And I am told that a deciding factor is the best interests of the child or children."

Judge Hernandez laughed for the first time. "Ms. Armstrong, you don't need to lecture me on the law."

"Oh, I apologize if I came off that way. I was trying to answer your question about how I understood parental rights."

"No offense taken. Now let's shift back to that time thirty years ago when you got pregnant. Technically, you were under the age of consent, and Mr. Parinello could have been under consideration for statutory rape, but your legal representation is not making that consideration in this case. Are you in agreement?"

"Yes."

"I had some other specific questions about your actions thirty years ago. You said your liaison with Mr. Parinello was your first sexual experience, and you did not meet with him again for thirty years, is that correct?"

"Yes."

"Mr. Parinello says he tried to get your phone number, but couldn't. Were you aware of that?"

"The girls at work said he wanted my phone number, but I didn't let them give it to him."

"Why?"

"I had promised God I would not have another ... 'liaison' with him, and I thought he just wanted to have his way with me again. I didn't want to encourage him, let him think he could call me up and then have sex. This was before I knew I was pregnant."

"I see. Did you think he would marry you?"

"When I learned I was pregnant, at first I fantasized that he would show up and marry me, but when he didn't contact me, I realized that was never going to happen."

"If he had asked you to marry him, what would you have done?"

"I was desperate to keep the twins, so after I found out I was pregnant, I would have married him, love or not."

"For years afterward, you tried to get in touch with your sons, but not Mr. Parinello. Why?"

"I was bonded with my sons, my flesh and blood. But Mr. Parinello and I just had a brief, momentary fling and neither of us was in love with the other."

"Thank you, Ms. Armstrong. The court will take a fifteen-minute recess."

BILL GOT them three bottles of water, so they didn't have to leave their table.

Bill patted Faith on the back. "Honey, you did us all proud."

"That was exhausting. I can't even remember everything I said."

Miriam spoke up. "You made an emotional, convincing, powerful appeal."

WHEN THE JUDGE reentered and convened the court, she announced, "We all know this is a highly unusual case, a petition for visitation of children who are adults. Therefore, 'in the best interests of the children' becomes 'in the best interests of the adults.' So we don't rely on social workers to determine the best interests, we go to the adults. I have asked for a deposition from each of the twins. I ask counselors for the defendant if you have the depositions ready."

Miriam stood up. "Yes, your honor, we have the depositions here and can hand them over now if you wish."

"No, it's getting too late in the day for new evidence. That can wait until tomorrow."

Doug and Garibaldi were huddling, whispering to each other. Garibaldi stood. "Your honor, I request that each deposition be read aloud to the court by the person who wrote it."

Judge Hernandez smiled. "Yes, Mr. Garibaldi, you and your

client might like that, which is the goal of your petition, to bring your client and the twins together. But that would make an end run around the *decision* of the court, which will come after the depositions are submitted and evaluated. Request denied. Court will reconvene at 9:30 tomorrow morning. At that time depositions will be provided. Ms. Dugan, please be good enough to bring three copies, one for the court, one for the plaintiffs, and the original."

Bill said, "Go home, Faith, and get some rest. Miriam and I are used to the adrenalin rush of courtroom drama. Pour yourself a drink, or draw a hot bath. Whatever relaxes you. Tomorrow I'll read one deposition, Miriam the other. You won't be on the hot seat tomorrow, but be prepared for the judge to call on you to confirm that you agree with the depositions."

21

As soon as Faith entered the condo, she headed to the bathroom and turned on the hot water. As soon as she stripped her clothes off, she dipped into the steaming water, letting its heat dissolve the weeks and days of tension that had culminated in the dynamics of the courtroom.

She had soaked for a half hour before Scott burst into the bathroom, eager for a debriefing.

"Give me ten minutes to dry and slip on PJs and a robe, and meet me at the loungers with a glass of white wine."

"You got it, babe."

AT THE LOUNGERS, she kissed him. Scott said, "Well?"

"Yes, Scott, very well. Everything went smoothly. Judge Hernandez runs a tight courtroom. Straightforward presentations, only a few minor objections, and requests, all fielded expertly by Hernandez. Her questions to Doug skewered him like chicken nuggets on a kebob. As Miriam put it, she made mincemeat out of him with queries like, 'What does it mean to be a parent?' and 'You

claim parental rights, but what about parental responsibilities?'
She made him poster boy for the *un*-parent of the year."

"Sounds like the Miriam-Bill tag team came through."

"Yes, Scott. Great preparation. Tomorrow Bill and Miriam will
play tag-team lawyers, Miriam reading Jeremy's deposition, Bill
reading Jon's. Doug's lawyer tried to pull a fast one, requested that
each twin read their deposition. That brought a grin from the judge
when she denied the request. So tomorrow we should have all the
evidence in. Bill and Miriam said it's customary to wait at least a
day or two to 'weigh the evidence,' but the three of us think she's
already made up her mind in our favor."

THE FIRST COURT day fell on a Wednesday and would continue at
least for the next day. That evening she called Jeremy to tell him
she wouldn't be at the Foundation Thursday.

"Take as much time as you want, Mom, you've already earned
the Volunteer of the Year Award."

Faith wished she could spend Thursday at the Foundation,
instead of returning to court.

THURSDAY MORNING before he left for work, Scott kissed Faith. "Eat
'em alive, tiger!"

Later she taxied to the law office so that she could make her
appearance in court as part of the troika. They went to the courtroom and sat on the defendant side, noting that the plaintiff table
was vacant.

Judge Hernandez breezed in at 9:25 and waited until 9:30 to
convene court. "Bailiff, has there been any phone message from
Counselor Garibaldi?"

"No, your honor."

The judge frowned. "We'll wait five more minutes before we
start." At 9:35 she convened the court and told the court reporter,

"Make a note that plaintiff Parinello and his attorney Garibaldi are not present. Ms. Dugan and Mr. Ludwig, do you have the depositions?"

Miriam replied, "Yes, your honor, our original, a copy for you, and a copy for the plaintiff." She handed the two copies to the bailiff.

The judge picked up and slammed some papers down on the bench in front of her. "We have a full docket today. We will proceed without the plaintiff and counsel. Read the depositions."

Miriam stood up. "I will read the deposition from twin number one, the first twin born."

Just as Miriam began to read, Doug and Garibaldi rushed in. Garibaldi shouted out, "Sorry, your honor, traffic problems. We apologize."

Judge Hernandez glared at the two. "You'd be late for your funeral."

Garibaldi's attire was impeccable. Doug showed up without a tie, unshaven, and seemed distracted, maybe suffering from a hangover.

Judge Hernandez announced, "Counselor Dugan is about to read a deposition, a copy of which is on your table."

Miriam waited until Garibaldi positioned the copy between him and Doug so they could read it as she started to speak.

Garibaldi stood up. "Your honor, the reading of depositions by counselors does not give us the tone and emphasis of the authors of the documents. I request once more that the depositions be read to the court by the writers, and that the proceedings be delayed until—"

The judge leaned forward in her chair, raising her voice. "You made that request yesterday if you forgot, and it was denied. Denied again today. Objection noted. Now, Counselor Dugan, give us the deposition."

Miriam began again.

"This deposition is written at the request of my mother Faith

Armstrong's lawyers, William Ludwig, and Miriam Dugan, in response to a petition from Douglas Parinello and his lawyer Luciano Garibaldi to Family Court. The gist of the petition is that my biological father, Mr. Parinello, wishes the court to require my mother to connect my twin and me to him. I join my mother and her lawyers in opposing this petition. This deposition sets forth the rationale for my opposition.

"In this deposition, I am designated as twin one, the first of identical twins born to my mother. My birthdate is December 31, 1979. Shortly after this birth, my mother's parents required her to give her twins up for adoption. I had a great childhood with my adoptive parents and never knew my biological mother and father.

"My twin brother was adopted into a different family from mine, so we did not know of each other until, as adults, accidents of history brought us together. This prompted us to search for our biological parents. Several years ago we discovered that Faith Armstrong is our birth mother. The reunion with her has been an enjoyable experience, making up for decades of separation.

"The joy of this reunification was interrupted by a medical problem. I suffered from potential kidney failure, and the doctors needed medical histories from both parents. My mother was able to locate Mr. Parinello and asked him for his parents' medical records. I think you know this story and will summarize it here. Parinello at first denied paternity. Then when he was shown proof of paternity, he preferred lengthy litigation over prompt delivery of the family medical history.

"I first met Mr. Parinello about a year ago, when he pulled a power play, and would only hand over the complete medical records if he got a meeting with us twins.

"I will make this brief. Mr. Parinello may be my biological parent, but he has not acted as a concerned parent. I understand he has an extensive family and several children. I respectfully suggest that he direct his parental urges to the rest of his family and children.

"My brother will speak for himself, but my perspective is that we have bonded with our mother, and think that Mr. Parinello's presence would detract from, rather than enhance this bond.

"For all of these reasons, I ask the court to deny Mr. Parinello's petition."

FAITH HAD NOT WANTED to read the depositions beforehand, preferring not to influence the guys. Hearing it cold, she marveled at the clarity and cogency of the argument. When she glanced at the plaintiff's table, she saw Garibaldi drumming his fingertips on the table. Doug slumped back in his chair, eyes half closed, frowning.

The judge finished penning notes. "Is counsel for the defense ready with the second deposition?"

Bill Ludwig used his low baritone voice to signal, "Ready, your honor."

"Let's hear it."

Bill Ludwig read Jonathan's deposition.

"FOR THE COURT RECORDS, I will be known as twin two, the second twin born to Faith Armstrong. My birthdate is January 1, 1980, only a few minutes after my older brother's birth, but that puts my birth in a different day and even a different year.

"I write this deposition at the request of my mother, Faith Armstrong, and her lawyers, in response to a petition to the Family Court by Douglas Parinello, my biological father. I'm not very good at writing but will do my best to draft a brief and simple statement of why I, like my twin brother, and mother, stand in opposition to this petition.

"As a newborn baby, I was adopted, so while young I never knew my birth parents. For thirty years I did not even know about my twin. Then a newspaper reporter surprised my brother and me with the fact that we were twins. This led the two of us to search and find our birth mother. We located her, and have had a wonderful time, socializing whenever we can.

"My brother developed serious kidney problems, so we had to get family histories, and that meant we had to find my father. We did locate him, but he was unhelpful, even denied that he was our father! We had to use an investigator to get his DNA and prove he was our father. Nevertheless, he refused to hand over family medical records and was going to involve us in a lengthy court battle at a time when my brother was struggling with a potentially fatal illness. I think you know this story. I retell it to make my point, that this is not the kind of 'father' I would welcome into our family."

Faith heard a noise from the direction of the plaintiff's table and turned to see Doug resting his head on his arms on the table, sobbing.

Bill continued reading from Jonathan's statement.

"I know Mr. Parinello is my biological father, but that doesn't make him a caring and loving parent.

"This deposition is my viewpoint, but I have discussed this matter with my brother and mother, and agree with them that we would not welcome Mr. Parinello into our family.

"Let me conclude this statement by repeating that I am opposed to Mr. Parinello's petition, and respectfully ask the court to deny his request."

As Bill finished reading and sat down, all eyes turned toward Doug, who was crying.

The judge, too, looked at Doug but tried to ignore him. She said, "This concludes the reading of two depositions. I would like to recall Ms. Armstrong to the witness stand."

Faith was sworn in and seated herself in the witness box.

The judge said, "Ms. Armstrong, you have heard both depositions—maybe you read them beforehand."

"No, your honor, I wanted the twins to write their statements without any influence from me, and have heard them now for the first time."

"Do you agree with these two statements?"

"Yes, your honor, I am in complete agreement with their conclusion, asking that the court not accept the plaintiff's request."

At this point, Doug raised his head from the witness table and leaned over to his attorney in an animated conversation.

Judge Hernandez could not ignore this huddle. "Mr. Galibardi, do you have a problem?"

"Please give me a minute." He talked with Doug briefly, then stood up. "Your honor, I have just conferred with my client, and he asks me to speak for him, offering a sincere apology to Ms. Armstrong for his past behavior. He has tried to become a better person, and asks that he be given a second chance."

Judge Hernandez took off her glasses. "Counselor, this is highly unusual. I am asking Ms. Armstrong if she wishes to respond."

Faith looked to Miriam and Bill, then asked, "Can I discuss this with my lawyers?"

"By all means."

Faith hurried to the defendants' table, and asked, "What do you think?"

Miriam said, "This is your call."

Bill added, "If you want to be nice and let him down easy, fine, but don't give the store away."

Faith returned to the witness box.

Judge Hernandez said, "You are still under oath."

Faith looked at Doug and Garibaldi, speaking slowly and deliberately. "My sons and I have talked about how we should respond to Mr. Parinello. Here are my thoughts, which may also reflect their thinking. If Mr. Parinello is trying to become a better person, we are glad to hear that and wish him well. But we think he should go back to his own family—families—to make a new start, not to disturb the bond that we have formed."

Doug had been staring intently at Faith. He jumped to his feet, shouting, "No! Give me a chance! I can be a better person."

Judge Hernandez banged her gavel down. "Mr. Garibaldi, control your client!"

Garibaldi put his arm around Doug, pushing him down in his seat.

The judge looked sideways at the bailiff, who quickly walked over to the plaintiff's table.

The judge said, "Mr. Garibaldi if you don't restrain your client, I will have to ask the bailiff to escort him out of the courtroom."

"No, your honor, that won't be necessary."

The judge turned to Faith. "Ms. Armstrong, you may step down."

Faith took her seat between Miriam and Bill.

The judge sighed. "Good. Well, the plaintiff has had a chance to respond to the depositions. Do the attorneys for the defendant have any additional comment?"

Bill stood up. "Yes, your honor, a comment on a related issue. As has been mentioned several times, it has been necessary to file a police report and a restraining order against Mr. Parinello. We remind the court, the plaintiff, and his attorney that the restraining order is still in effect, and no matter how the court rules, we expect Mr. Parinello to respect the restrictions of that restraining order."

Judge Hernandez said, "Counsel for the defendant's comment is included in the record."

Doug, eyes bulging, scraped his chair on the floor, turned toward Bill, and shook a fist at him.

The judge yelled, "Bailiff," at the same time as this court employee strode over to Doug, grabbed one arm, and raised him onto his feet. Then he pushed and pulled him toward the exit, as Doug screamed, "You lousy bitches and sonsabitches, I hope you rot in hell!"

The judge waited until the bailiff and Doug had made their exit, then said calmly, "This case has taken up a lot of the court's time. In spite of this outburst, and the absence of the plaintiff, I hope that we can wrap this up today. Mr. Garibaldi, are you prepared for a *brief* closing statement?"

"Yes, your honor. On behalf of the plaintiff, I ask the court to accept his request, based on the time-honored principle of parental rights, to require the defendant to provide the legal names and current addresses of their twin sons. I apologize for the flareup of my client, who has been under extreme stress and worry about his sons and did not get a good night's sleep. I hope the court will give him the opportunity he needs to show that he can be a responsible, reliable parent."

Judge Hernandez showed no emotion, raising her eyebrows ever so slightly. "Ms. Dugan and Mr. Ludwig, are you ready for a closing statement?"

Bill whispered something to Miriam, then stood up and said, "Yes, your honor. We prepared a rather lengthy closing statement but will follow the bench's request for brevity. We have submitted an abundance of evidence showing that Mr. Parinello has been found wanting in parenting skills and responsibilities, both for his twins and for a half dozen other children. The eruption of profanity a few minutes ago highlights his unpredictable and unreliable character. The testimony of Ms. Armstrong is supported by the depositions of her twin sons, asking for rejection of plaintiff's petition. We ask the court to reject the petition."

Judge Hernandez nodded. "I will take all the evidence and statements into consideration, and will hand down my ruling within one week. Because the plaintiff and his attorney are from Peoria, rather than scheduling a court appearance, I will notify the attorneys at their legal mailing addresses."

As Garibaldi picked up his briefcase and left the courtroom, Judge Hernandez motioned Bill to the bench. "I don't like the bad behavior of Parinello. You three come with me, through my chambers, and you can use a service elevator. That way, you can exit the building in an alleyway, and avoid any confrontation with him."

Faith, trembling from the turmoil, gladly took the hand of Miriam as they passed through the judge's chambers and made their way to the service elevator.

In the elevator, Bill told Faith, "Give a picture of Doug to your doorman and order him never to let the guy in. You should hand pictures to Jeremy and Jonathan, because who knows, the creep may hire some sharp detectives and find out who and where they are. I didn't like the parting salvos of Doug when the bailiff marched him out of the courtroom. You never know what desperate people will do."

22

When Faith returned to the condo, she did a repeat performance of the previous day, drawing a hot bath and soaking.

A little later Scott popped his head in the bathroom. "Is this the Turkish baths?"

"A good cure for jangled nerves."

"Hurry up and make it to the loungers. I'll have the wine ready."

SCOTT HELD his glass up to Faith's. "A toast to the family negotiator."

"Thanks. I'm still a little frazzled, but it all went in our favor. Later you'll read the two depositions, very well written, making a strong case for killing Doug's petition."

"Any fireworks?"

"Only at the end. Doug overheated, made an outburst, was warned by the judge and bailiff, then when he shook his fist at Bill, the bailiff escorted him out of the courtroom."

"Wow."

"Uh-huh. It's ninety-nine percent in our favor. Ruling within a week."

"I guess that wraps it up."

"I hope so."

"You don't sound so sure."

"As Ludwig summed up Doug, he's unpredictable and impulsive."

"And irrational."

"That too."

Scott took Faith to Berghof's to celebrate the end of the court appearances.

FRIDAY MORNING, Faith called in sick to Horton Hotels. She thought, *Well, I am sick. Sick of worry, tension, court, conflict.*

She drove to the Foundation and entered the front door, seeing Amelia and Robby in their favorite corner. Robby welcomed her with a wide smile. Faith cradled him in her arms, sitting next to Amelia, and burst out crying.

Amelia blurted, "What's the matter?"

"Nothing. I'm happy! Happy to be back where I belong, at the Foundation. I just escaped from a jungle of courtroom misery, and am glad to be back with all of you."

Faith went with Amelia and Robby through the cafeteria line.

Maria joked, "You must be very hungry to come here on Friday."

Faith enjoyed her scrambled eggs with Amelia and several others, then chatted with some residents until Jeremy arrived.

"Mother, what are you doing here?"

"Aren't you glad to see me?"

"Sure, but I thought yesterday you had the crunch court session."

"That's right, I did. And the first thing I want to tell you is that your deposition was excellent. It helped us make our case."

"Nothing is settled, though?"

"It'll work out in our favor. Not only the judge but also Bill and

Miriam destroyed Doug, made him look like a fool. A babbling, crying, idiot. I'll tell you and the family all about it, but if you have time, let's go into your office and talk about plans for the future of the Foundation."

SEATED AT HIS DESK, Jeremy said, "I met with Adam Knox, the realtor you recommended. He seems top notch, gave me some good tips, not only on properties but on how to negotiate. If we buy from a religious organization or a charitable organization, we can probably work a favorable payment plan, guaranteeing them a steady income."

"I knew he was great. How about the fundraiser?"

"That's more complicated but promising. You gave me the name of Samuel Witherspoon, with the leading firm in Illinois. He's cautious, asked for a lot of background information. You know, how we came by the startup money, where we could go back for repeat donations. He'll set up a plan of what he and his people would do in six months for $25,000 to $50,000."

"That's good to hear. Well, today if you need me for playtime, I'd be glad to play with the kids. For me, this is therapy."

She left his office and set up the puppet theatre. Each kid had a chance to act out what he would do when he or she grew up. The kids loved it.

Faith ate lunch with Jeremy, then went back to his office to talk a while before getting an early start for home.

"Mom, I know you don't want to replay the whole court scene, but let me ask you just one thing—how did Doug handle being made the fool?"

"Not well. He pouted, cried, and pleaded, and then ended up in a screaming fit and the bailiff had to remove him from the courtroom while he shouted out obscenities."

"So we're not through with Doug?"

"No, in fact, Bill told me to have you show pictures of Doug to your staff—and Jon will need to alert his security—to keep him away from your premises. Doug is a wounded animal, unpredictable, and there's no telling what he might do."

"What are you going to do?"

"We still have a restraining order for Doug not to contact me or approach me."

"Will that protect you?"

"Uh, it should keep me safe, but I don't know, I realize how devious Doug can be, and I think he'll still try to find his way into the family."

"So how will you handle him?"

"I don't know. Like I told you, he's a wounded animal, and you don't want to kick him while he's down, but you also can't let your guard down."

Jeremy rubbed his chin. "I guess there's no way we can help him."

"I've thought about that, too. I made a gesture of help to him in my parting words. He had his lawyer beg me for a second chance in his attempt to be a better person. I told him to go back and try to reconnect with his own families, not disrupt our family."

"Think he will do that?"

"I doubt it. Doug is his own worst enemy."

"Mom, you look tired. Why don't you get an early start for home."

"I'm more than tired, totally exhausted, and it will take me a while to recover. I'll plan to be back next Tuesday and Thursday."

"The kids adore you. They haven't paid much attention to the days of the week, but now they ask, "Is today a Tuesday or Thursday? That's a Faith day, a fun day."

ON THE DRIVE HOME, Faith felt good. Still tired, but energized by the interaction with Amelia and Robby, and the enthusiasm in playtime with the puppet theater.

Arriving home in mid-afternoon, she didn't want to take another hot bath. She went into the bedroom and took out her journal, walking with it to her lounger. She opened the slim booklet to a new page.

Bad times.

Court is never easy, and the high-powered tension took all the sap out of me.

Good times.

Bill and Miriam proved to be excellent lawyers, and the twins' depositions proved to be marvelous. Hard to judge my own performance, but I made no big goofs and helped make the argument for the court to reject Doug's petition.

Ambiguous times.

Doug's outburst and forced departure from the courtroom left me troubled. Once talking to Father Whitmore, I mentioned the biblical passage about compassion—a sheep without a shepherd. Today I told Jeremy I didn't know what we could do to help Doug. That is IF we should even try.

Yes, that's something I'll have to talk over with the good priest.

SHE PUT the journal back in its drawer, and called Church of the Redeemer, making an appointment for early Wednesday morning. She and Scott needed R & R over the weekend, she'd go to work Monday, to the Foundation on Tuesday, and Wednesday get her father fix.

Monday she was glad hotel matters kept her mind busy, shutting out Doug and the court. Tuesday the Foundation residents and the kids at playtime recharged her batteries.

Driving to Church of the Redeemer on Wednesday morning, Faith made a mental agenda. First stop would be Mary and Harriet. Then bring Father Whitmore up to date on the legal situation. And —what she wanted to discuss—those ambiguous feelings she had toward Doug.

Arriving at church, she skipped up the outside steps and hurried past the priest's office into the sanctuary. She felt better standing in front of the Madonna stained glass window, hands together in prayer.

God, I give thanks to you for bountiful blessings, especially our wonderful family. And I give thanks for your two saints, Mary and Harriet, who have channeled your love and support to me in these difficult times.

Mary and Harriet, I give special thanks to you for being with me in the courtroom. Without your presence, I would not have been able to testify. Not just in the courtroom, I know you are with me every day, everywhere. When I am at the Foundation and hold little Robby, I think of you, and Mary holding baby Jesus.

No matter what problems we face in the future, I know you will be with us. For this we are thankful.

In Jesus' name, Amen.

SHE STOOD before the window for a few minutes in silent meditation, then left the sanctuary for Father Whitmore's office.

"Well, Faith, that was a long session with your two favorite saints. I think I've been demoted to second fiddle in your spiritual orchestra."

"Not at all. It's just that without the help of Mary and Harriet, I don't think I'd have made it through the pressure cooker of court."

"Tough, huh?"

Faith gave him a quick summary of the court proceedings.

The priest shrugged. "Well, at least that marks the end of the matter, right?"

"I'm not sure."

"Why not?"

"I have a strange feeling as if everything's not right."

"What could be wrong?"

"It's strange. We went into court wanting to win, and we won big. Maybe too big. We didn't just beat Doug; we demolished him. I'm not a sports buff, but let me try a boxing analogy. If you're a boxer, you want to win a fight with your opponent. But what if you outbox him, bloody his nose, knock him out, and almost kill him, leaving him with a brain injury."

"Ow, that's painful just to imagine."

"Maybe that's too graphic, but what I'm trying to tell you is that I feel uneasy at how thoroughly we destroyed Doug. And how helpless we left him. The last time I talked with you, I mentioned compassion, and the phrase in the Bible about compassion, when Jesus talked about a sheep without a shepherd. I guess Doug's like that sheep, a lost soul."

"And you feel sorry for him?"

"I can't figure out my feelings. There's a struggle between my head and my heart. I'm sure our family made the right decision not to allow Doug to join us. But I don't feel one hundred percent good about leaving him without a shepherd. Is that sin, guilt, conscience, or just softheartedness?"

"Faith, my dear, compassion exacts a heavy toll. It makes you sensitive to the hurts and feelings of others. Most people, I fear, are deaf, dumb, blind, and oblivious to the pain of others, concerned mainly with self. This is something you'll have to live with."

"Yes, but what will I *do*?"

"No one can give you a road map for the future. But I'm confident that your faith in God, and help from Mary and Harriet, will enable you to do what you need to do, what is right."

23

Thursday morning as Faith drove to the Foundation, she had two things on her mind. She pondered the advice of Father Whitmore, that she would know what she needed to do, and carry through with it when the time came.

Crowding out those thoughts was the prospect of meeting Amelia and seeing Robby's outstretched arms.

Walking into the lounge, she beamed at the broad smile of Robby, scooping him up and cuddling him. Looking at Amelia, she noticed a few wrinkles on her teenage-smooth forehead.

"Troubles?"

"Maybe."

"Want to talk about it?"

"My mother is coming by this afternoon."

"For?"

"She said, 'For a talk.'"

"Clue me in. Is that good or bad?"

"Could be either."

"Do you talk with her often?"

"Every week or two, she checks in with me, how I'm doing, do I need any money."

"Hey, did you tell her about your online class? She should be happy about that."

"Yeah, she's always been proud of how well I did in school, and she was pleased that I got A's on the rest of my papers in the course, and am signing up for another class."

"Hmm, I smell something."

"Your nose is better than mine."

"Amelia, I think she might be wanting to encourage you in school. All parents like to see their children do well."

"Yeah, my folks hated it when I got pregnant and didn't go to a fancy four-year college. Junior college may be a consolation prize, but better than dropping out."

"Be positive. Maybe something good will come of your meeting."

"Faith, will you be with me when I meet her?"

"Would she be okay with that?"

"Oh, I think so. I've told her about you, and how good you are with the kids at playtime, and she said she'd like to meet you."

"In that case, sure, I'll be there. What time?"

"She's shooting for two."

"I'll be here in the lounge about two. If Robby needs a nap, I'll hold him while you talk."

FAITH HAD AN EXCITING PLAYTIME, lining up chairs as she had done for the choo-choo train, but this time having the children stick their arms out for wings on an airplane. Then they made the varoom sound of jet engines, and each kid took off to some other country, telling what he or she wanted to see and do there.

Faith had a brief chat with Jeremy at lunch, mentioning Amelia's mother coming.

"Faith, I never told you about Amelia's background. She comes from big money but left home when her parents wanted her to give up her baby for adoption, and they fought constantly. I'm glad you'll be there to help defuse the tension."

"I care for Amelia and Robby."

FAITH CAUGHT up on paperwork for her interviews with residents, then went to the lounge a little before two. Robby was fussy.

"Amelia, he's tired, needs a nap."

At first, Robby wouldn't leave his mother. Faith sat next to Amelia and Robby, softly singing a lullaby. Robby looked at Faith, and when she held out her arms, he came to her, looking up into her eyes. In a few minutes, he was asleep, but Faith kept singing.

At that moment Amelia's mother entered. Faith made an instant appraisal of her appearance, noticing the designer dress and jacket and fashionable scarf, as well as a diamond pendant. Faith judged her to be in her mid-forties. Her brunette hair flecked with gray, bangs in front and cut short in back, complemented her stylish clothes.

Amelia said, "Faith, this is my mother, Felicia Weatherby. Mother, Faith Armstrong."

Felicia joked, "Well, I've heard of the singing nun, are you the singing nanny?"

Faith laughed. "I've had practice at this with my grandkids, but now they're a little too old to be held for a nap."

"Amelia told me you're very good with kids, and you did a good job putting Robby to sleep."

"You have a lovely grandson. I come here Tuesdays and Thursdays. He and the other kids energize me for the rest of the week."

"You work, but can get off two days a week?"

"My husband says I'm slowly segueing into retirement."

"Where do you work?"

"Horton Hotels."

"What do you do there?"

"My title is executive vice president, but I do a little of everything. Maybe I'm not the jack-of-all-trades, but the jill-of-all-trades."

Amelia and Felicia opened their eyes wide, Amelia gushing, "You never told me you were a *vice president.*"

Faith chuckled. "You never asked."

Felicia wrinkled her brow. "How does a hotel executive find her way to volunteer in a home for mothers and young kids?"

Faith paused. "Well, long story short, I was a teenage mom."

"So you were in a home like this?"

Faith's smile sagged. "No, my folks insisted my babies—twins—be adopted, so I never got to raise them. A few years ago my boys found me, and they have children, so I skipped a generation, and am mothering my grandchildren. My connection to the Foundation is that one of my sons is the head here."

"Jeremy?"

"Yes."

"You should be proud of him; he's doing good work here. Uh, but I'm curious, how you moved into hotel work—college first?"

Faith shook her head. "After I graduated from high school, I was on the outs with my parents because they made me give up my babies. So I came to Chicago and buried myself in work, started with an entry-level job, took some night classes, and eventually climbed the corporate ladder. Hey, did Amelia tell you she is taking a class and getting good grades?"

"Yes. Her father and I were disappointed that her college plans got dropped when she had Robby. We thought she had given up on education, so it's good she's taking classes. She said you and Jeremy encouraged her."

"She's bright, and should get an education while she's young."

Felicia glanced back and forth between Amelia and Faith. "Yes, Faith, my husband and I want to thank you for helping Amelia get back into school. And—that's the main reason I came today—to see Robby, but also to talk about a long-range plan for college."

Amelia looked at her mother.

Felicia stumbled. "Amelia, let me come out with it. How would you like to come home, and not just take online courses, but enroll in a nearby school, maybe a community college, and get your associates degree?"

"What does Dad say?"

"He's a thousand percent for that. He wanted me to talk it over with you because I'd be the one taking care of Robby while you went to classes."

Amelia turned to Faith.

Faith said, "This is a great opportunity for you, Amelia, while you're excited about your classes. You probably know that many colleges accept an associates degree as the first two years of a four-year college degree."

Felicia took a handkerchief out of her purse and wiped her eyes. "Amelia, I know we had some bad times, but when you got pregnant, all the dreams Dad and I had for you seemed to disappear. Now we want to see if we can't make it work."

Robby woke, fussed a little, and looked to his mother.

Faith handed him to Amelia, who said, "He probably needs changing. I didn't bring diapers from my room."

Faith got up. "Amelia, why don't you two go to your room so you can talk. It was nice to meet you, Felicia."

"Yes, same here. And let me thank you and Jeremy for all you've done for Amelia."

FAITH WENT to Jeremy's office. He wasn't busy, so they discussed the realtor and fund-raising projects.

"Jeremy, here's some big news. Amelia's mother asked her to come back home and take classes full-time. Don't tell Amelia I let you in on this. Let her break the news to you."

"That's great news, Faith. Great for several reasons. Not just for Amelia to get on to school, but to repair the family ties, giving Amelia and Robby some stability."

Faith sighed. "I'll miss those two."

Jeremy chuckled. "That's what we're here for, providing a lifeboat for shipwrecked young mothers and their children. But this is not permanent, just a means of ferrying them from a dangerous situation to a safe haven."

"Yes, Jeremy, you know what you need to do, and carry through with it."

Faith suggested, "Why don't we get the family together this weekend. I think it would be okay with Scott to gather at the condo."

"No, Mother, if you don't realize it, you've been frazzled and running on adrenalin for a week. I'll check with Melanie and get back to you about a Sunday meal at our place."

As Faith was leaving, Amelia came running up to her, holding Robby. "Thanks so much for helping me face Mom. I think things are going to work out. At least we'll give it a try."

Faith hugged her. "I'm happy for you. Maybe from time to time, you can come back to the Foundation to visit."

24

Faith felt good when she went to the hotel Friday morning. She still reveled in the meeting with Amelia's mother and the terrific news that the two would have a go at reconciling.

Faith looked back only a few years ago, when she proposed Mothers and Kids to Jonathan and Jeremy, never realizing it would bear fruit like the experiences with Amelia and Robby.

Mid-morning, Faith's secretary buzzed her. "A call from Bill Ludwig. He says you asked him to contact you."

She grabbed the phone. "Bill—court news?"

"Yes, and all good. The judge rejected Doug's petition. I have a client waiting, and know you're busy, so here's the bottom line. Judge Hernandez followed most of the facts and reasoning we provided. Well, also nuggets from her probing questions. The rationale for the rejection is rock-solid. I'll fax a copy to you."

"Thanks, Bill, and give our thanks to Miriam, too."

She hung up and called Scott with the news, leaving a message on his answering machine. Then she waited impatiently for the chatter of the fax machine to end and spit out the court document. After the legal mumbo jumbo came the judge's decision.

After careful consideration of all the evidence in this case, including presentations by the attorney for the plaintiff and attorneys for the defendant, and testimony by the plaintiff and testimony by the defendant, the court has decided to deny the plaintiff's petition to have the defendant supply to plaintiff the names and addresses of their twin sons.

The rationale for this decision is as follows.

The plaintiff has supplied proof of paternity, not contested by the defendant. The plaintiff claims the parental right to seek visitation for his sons. The court and the defendant do not dispute the plaintiff's right to seek visitation.

As in all cases of petition for visitation, the character of the plaintiff is a primary concern. The character of the plaintiff has been evaluated from allegations by the defendant's attorney and the court's questioning of the plaintiff. The court is concerned with the parental history of the plaintiff, specifically his lack of contact with his six children other than the twins named in the petition. The fact that he has not regularly visited these six children, and has not filed for visitation, argues against his present petition to meet with the twin sons he fathered with Faith Armstrong thirty years ago.

Time is of the essence in this case. The fact that the plaintiff did not actively and persistently inquire about pregnancy from his single liaison with the defendant is a fact for which the court has no remedy. The defendant, also, did not actively and persistently try to locate the father of her twins. Ms. Armstrong at the time was a high school student and minor (below the age of consent), a mitigating factor in her not attempting to contact Mr. Parinello. At the time of the liaison, Mr. Parinello was a college student and at age twenty-one, an adult, which argues against a mitigating factor for the plaintiff. An adult should have acted like an adult; a minor may have had some excuse for not acting like an adult.

Coming to the present, in the past year, the defendant asked the plaintiff to forward family medical records to help diagnose and treat *their sons. Plaintiff initially denied patrimony. Then he refused to hand over the records and preferred a lengthy court proceeding rather than a speedy handover of the records. This indicates he has not been the caring and responsible parent who is eager to meet and reconnect with his sons.*

The most unusual aspect of this case is that the plaintiff is seeking visitation for adult sons more than thirty years old. Because of this unusual situation, rather than seeking professional opinions of social workers and psychologists, the court has requested depositions from the adult sons. Each in his deposition provided convincing statements that at present they have no bond with their biological father, nor do they wish to develop a relationship in the future. They cite his past parental history, and recent behavior in the medical record request, as reasons for not meeting him. This argument, by itself, is a compelling reason to deny the petition.

In the court proceedings a few days ago, plaintiff's emotional outbursts, and threats of physical violence, as well as abusive and obscene language toward the court and its occupants, indicate a person who is impulsive and erratic.

For all of the above reasons, the court sees the plaintiff as one who, although he has the right to petition for visitation, lacks the character to be granted that petition.

The court denies the petition requiring the defendant to notify the plaintiff of the twins' legal names and current addresses.

FAITH FAXED the document to Jeremy and Jonathan. She told herself she should celebrate and be happy but still felt too fatigued from the ordeal to party.

She didn't fax the court paper to Scott, just printed it out and put it in her briefcase to show Scott when he got home.

When she returned to the condo, she laid the judge's ruling at Scott's place on the kitchen table. A little later, Scott burst in, saying, "Let me see it!"

She steered him to the kitchen, and asked, "Tea or wine?"

"I have something better, champagne! I picked up a bottle on the way home."

She got out the champagne flutes and set them on the table.

Scott scanned the judge's ruling. "Honey, this is as good as anything we could hope for." He popped the cork on the champagne and started pouring for Faith.

"Not too much for me. Somehow I'm not in the mood."

"Why not? We won!"

"Maybe it was all the pressure of court; I haven't been able to disentangle myself from all the gut-wrenching turmoil of the legal battle. You know, time and again in those hours, I had to relive my pregnancy, the trauma of being separated from my babies, and also the hassle with Doug over the medical papers."

"It's stress. You'll get over it. It just takes time."

"You're right."

She sipped her bubbly, he gulped his down and poured a second.

"No more for me."

Scott laughed. "I'll celebrate for both of us."

Scott wanted to go out to eat, but Faith begged off.

He said, "Let me fix us some sandwiches, and you put your feet up in the lounger."

They had a quiet evening, watching TV. Faith just wanted to be near Scott, holding his hand as they caught up with news and then switched to an old black and white movie rerun.

They went to bed about eleven. Faith snuggled with Scott until he snored, then she tossed and turned until after midnight. She got up and opened the drawer to her little confidante, then took the journal to her lounger and opened it, writing.

Problem?

What problem?

We won.

Why don't you enjoy the victory lap?

Are we through with this?

How can I move past this?

Just writing down her thoughts helped settle her down. She returned the journal to its hiding place, then went back to bed.

THE NEXT MORNING when Scott got up and showered, she said, "Come back to bed for a few minutes."

"Honey, we don't have time this morning. Let's make a date for later this morning."

"Just hold me for a few minutes."

He returned to bed, held her tight, then finished dressing and rushed out of the condo.

Faith eventually fell back asleep and made up for the loss of shuteye. She remembered Scott had promised a "date," and looked forward to making love to him. She had been too tense during the last week to be romantic.

When Faith didn't know what to do with herself, she cleaned. Even though she had a housekeeper, she still was the downstate girl who prized frugality and cleanliness. In an hour she had satisfied her neatnik conscience, and took a cup of tea to the lounger, enjoying the view of the lake.

When the phone rang, she was sure it was Scott, calling to say he'd be home early. Maybe he'd even remind her of their date.

She picked up the phone, and cooed, "Hi, Hon."

After a short pause, the caller did not speak, but sang slowly, "I don't bring you flowers anymore."

Immediately she recognized two things. The tune was from Neil Diamond and Barbara Streisand's ballad, "You don't bring me flowers anymore," with the lyrics slightly changed.

And the vocalist was Doug.

She turned the phone off and slammed it down on the table. She expected Doug to call again, but after waiting for ten minutes, figured he wouldn't redial.

Faith sighed, looking at the silent phone. She got up and got dressed.

SCOTT WAS LATE COMING HOME, held up by several problem articles in the Sunday paper. Walking to the lounger, he said, "Hey, Honey, I didn't forget our date. Hmm, you're dressed, so I guess you changed your mind about—"

"Doug called."

"What?"

"Yeah, late this morning."

"What did he say?"

"It's not what he *said*; it's what he *sang*: 'I don't bring you flowers anymore.' You remember that Neil Diamond and Barbara Streisand tune?"

"Yeah, and I know he's needling you about his impersonation of the flower deliveryman."

She stood up and hugged him. "He scared me. Hold me."

Scott gave her a bear hug, kissing her cheeks and closed eyes.

"Scott, what are we going to do?"

"Two things. First and foremost, we're not going to let Doug win by intimidating us. So we can't have you going into panic mode, which is what he wants. Second, we'll call the police department and file a report of a harassing call. That should give us cause to extend the restraining order." Scott broke away from her and said, "I'd like to drive to Peoria and smash the twerp in the—"

Faith put her fingers on Scott's lips. "Hey, remember what you just told me. I shouldn't panic, which is what he wants. And you shouldn't get your dander up, which is also what he wants. You help me control panic, and I'll help you control anger."

"Right, babe, let's work to keep our lives on an even keel."

He checked the caller ID. "No name, he probably was clever enough to go to a pay phone so that the call wouldn't be linked to him."

"You know, Scott, strangely enough, Doug's call has helped me. After the court struggle, I was uneasy about our big win. And I wondered if there wouldn't be some backlash. Now that I've seen it, I can deal with it better."

Scott suggested, "I have the perfect medicine for you, a walk on the beach."

They walked an hour north and then retraced their steps. Reentering their building, Faith smiled. "We have a great life together, a wonderful family, and a beautiful lake at our front door. We can't let some perverse idiot ruin it."

"Well said."

Back in the condo, Faith admitted, "I didn't sleep well last night, and the beach walk exhausted me. Come lie down with me."

She snoozed for an hour, waking up alone.

"Scott, I've got an idea. Let's go for Japanese at Happi sushi. Take a taxi there so if we want to have beer or sake—maybe both— we won't have to worry about driving home."

They had a great time at the sushi place, starting with beer and edamame, then proceeding to sushi and sake. When they made it back to the condo, Faith said, "We didn't follow through with that date this morning, but now ...."

They made love and fell asleep in each other's arms.

25

S unday morning Scott was the sleepy head who wanted to stay in bed. Faith got up and went to church. Before entering a pew, she made a spiritual stop at her favorite saints, thanking Mary and Harriet for helping her through the court battle and the aftershock of Doug's singing phone call. On the way out after the church service, she quickly asked Father Whitmore about a Wednesday meeting, which he agreed to.

Faith sped home to pick up Scott for the trip to Oak Park for a family gathering at Jonathan's.

Faith quizzed Scott. "Hey, Mr. Court Jester, you don't have any props with you today."

"Who needs props?"

When they arrived at Jonathan's, the kids went wild. "What we gonna do today?"

Scott put his hand to his chin. "I don't know. Maybe not a newspaper."

Groans.

"Maybe not a puppet show or a television show."

More groans.

"Maybe not even a radio show. Hmm, I know, let's go on a safari.

We don't have time to go to Africa, but we could go to your nearby park, and find out how many bugs, animals, and birds we can locate. I can take pictures with my cell phone, and then put together an album of our safari."

The kids yelled with glee. The parents shook their heads in wonder at Scott's juvenile inventiveness.

First, they ate a picnic lunch, which the children gobbled down so they could go on safari.

Leaving the house, Scott asked Faith, "An hour or hour and a half?"

She nodded.

With the dishes cleared away, Faith asked for a prayer circle. They shared prayers of thanks for bringing them through a difficult time and asking for continued help in the future.

Faith opened the meeting. "Folks, I also want to thank each one of you for helping Scott and me get through this latest court battle. It wasn't easy, and I have to admit, I'm still exhausted by all of the tension. But while it's fresh in my mind, I wanted the family to hear about it, ask questions, and take up any issues you have.

"Fortunately, you've read Jeremy's and Jonathan's depositions, and the judge's ruling, so I don't need to go over that. The judge takes many of her points from the opening statements of Bill and Miriam, and also from her sharp interrogation of Doug. Well, I won't waste your time summing up what you already know. Let's hear your questions—or comments. Hey, how about your response? Are you satisfied with the court's decision?"

Jonathan weighed in first. "Mom, it's exactly what we wanted."

Jeremy agreed. "You did a great time representing our interests."

Melanie volunteered, "Well, I'm puzzled by one thing. As a Mom, I'm protective of my kids, and I wondered why they weren't mentioned. Nothing was said about the right of a grandparent to ask for visitation of grandchildren."

Faith answered, "That was deliberate. We avoided any mention of grandchildren because we didn't want to give Doug any ideas. When we discussed this issue with Bill and Miriam, they looked ahead, and said if our argument for rejecting parental rights for the twins was successful, it should also argue against Doug getting visitation rights for grandkids."

Melanie sat back in her chair. "Glad to hear that."

Jeremy wondered out loud, "I can't quite figure out what Doug said and did that got the judge so mad at him she kicked him out."

"The judge couldn't put it all in. I can tell you that the depositions were upsetting, devastating for Doug. Jeremy's deposition came first, and Doug slumped back in his chair. Then when Jonathan's statement was read, especially the sentence about Doug not being the kind of loving parent he would want, Doug laid his head down on the table and sobbed.

"Judge Hernandez called me back to the witness stand to confirm that I was in agreement with my two sons to reject the petition for visitation. I testified to that effect, and then, through his lawyer, Doug made an impassioned plea for one more chance, to prove that he's trying to be a better person.

"When the judge ruled that the petition was rejected, and Bill reminded the court of the police report and restraining order against Doug, he went out of control, shaking his fist at Bill and Miriam. That's when the bailiff escorted him out of the courtroom. The kids aren't here, so I can repeat what he yelled to everyone as he was hustled out: 'You lousy bitches and sonsabitches, I hope you rot in hell.'"

Melanie and Rachel gasped.

Faith continued. It didn't faze the judge, but it did register with her and is indirectly included in her ruling. That's what she meant by abusive and obscene language."

Jonathan chuckled. "He provided the nails for his coffin. I hope that puts an end to the Doug saga."

Faith mumbled, "Well ...."

Jonathan asked, "There's more? You're holding something back?"

"I wanted to deal with the court case first."

Jeremy chimed in, "What else is there?"

"Doug called yesterday."

The two couples slumped shook their heads and joined in a loud moan.

"Yes, and it wasn't what he *said*; it's what he *sang*. Remember, he showed up at our condo door pretending to be a florist delivery man and hid behind the bouquet so I couldn't see who it was. Well, when he called, he sang, 'I don't bring you flowers anymore.' An awkward takeoff on Neil Diamond's ballad."

Jonathan asked, "So what are you going to do?"

"It threw me for a loop, but Scott has a strategy. Doug wants revenge. He wants to disturb my life. But we won't let that happen. We can't let him win by becoming upset and scared. We need to go on with our lives. We have our precautions. Tomorrow I'll file a police report about a harassing phone call. That will help us when we want to extend the restraining order. I've already mentioned to Jeremy, when I was at the Foundation, that he should show a picture of Doug to his staff, and tell them not to let him on the premises. Jonathan, the same is true for you and your security."

They talked around the issue for a while longer, until Melanie and Rachel rescued Faith. "Hey, guys, Mom just spent a few grueling days in court, so let's not grill her here."

Melanie and Rachel initiated a four-way bear hug of Faith. Melanie and Rachel got drinks, which they were sipping when the safari group returned, excited about all the bugs, animals, and birds they had discovered.

Scott saw that the meeting had tired Faith, so he suggested an earlier than usual departure. The kids objected, but Scott said he needed time to process and organize the still pictures for their safari albums.

On the drive home, Faith thanked Scott for giving them an excuse to leave early. "I'm better now, but still suffering from post-traumatic-court-disorder."

. . .

MONDAY MORNING FAITH was able to get a late afternoon appointment with Bill and Miriam.

Bill joked, "You two are becoming Monday regulars."

Faith told Bill about Doug's singing phone call. Bill said she should make a police report of a harassing call, and he promised to call Garibaldi and warn him about Doug's bad behavior. Bill advised them to continue to be careful. Miriam gave Faith a reassuring hug.

Monday Faith enjoyed work even more than usual, because it was ho-hum, everyday routine that required no adrenalin and emotional investment. She looked forward to the next day of volunteering.

Tuesday morning Faith showed up at the Foundation before 7:30 and opened the cafeteria with some of the early birds. She asked, "Where's Amelia?"

"Didn't you hear? She's transitioning, going back to live with her folks."

Faith had finished her breakfast when Amelia rushed in, holding Robby.

"Faith, would you help Robby with breakfast? Here's a bottle, and he can have some eggs and toast. I'm trying to get packed to be ready for Mother when she comes."

Faith and Robby had left the dining room and were sitting in the lounge when Amelia hurried up to them. "Faith, I'm nervous. Just hope that this return to the nest works out."

"Amelia, you have to make it work."

"Sorry to bother you, but I still have last minute details. Can you keep Robby?"

"My pleasure. Take your time."

A few minutes later Amelia's mother walked in, looked around, and smiled when she spotted Robby in Faith's arms.

"Amelia's in her room doing some packing."

"Faith, I'm amazed at you. A corporate vice president, but comfortable as a nanny."

"The kids energize me."

"Well, while we're waiting for Amelia, let's see if Jeremy is busy. I want to thank him."

They walked to his office and found him reading mail. "Come in, Mrs. Weatherby. You must be here to pick up Amelia and Robby. We're going to miss them, but our mission is to make the Foundation a launching pad for putting young mothers back into the mainstream."

"Jeremy, you're doing a wonderful job here. I want to thank you for what you've done for Amelia, but she's just one of the many women you're helping every day."

"We do our best."

"And the best is very good. I mean, you're not just going through the motions. Look at Robby in Faith's arms. That's not an institutional duty, but downhome love." She took out a handkerchief and touched her eyes.

"Thank you, Mrs. Weatherby."

"You can call me Felicia."

"We're not too formal here."

"No, but highly effective, very efficient. I'm from Winnetka and have served on several civic boards there. I know how much energy and personal skills it takes to run a place like this. And *money*! How do you do it—I mean housing and feeding so many?"

"You're right; we're always stretching a buck to make ends meet. Volunteers help us cut costs. You may not believe it, but right now we're starting a funding campaign for a place that will house an even larger number of residents, because we're always full, and have to turn away young mothers."

Felicia opened her purse. "Well, I didn't come here to blow hot air. Here's a check for $100,000 for however you want to use it, for operating expenses, or a new building."

Jeremy gasped. "I ... don't know what to say."

Felicia continued. "We would have paid more money than that to have our daughter back."

Jeremy stumbled, "Well—Thank you. Thank you very much."

"I have a circle of friends in Winnetka, and I've been telling them of your good work here. They're ready to join me with donations."

"That's very good of you. And—uh, if your friends would like to come for a tour, we'd be glad to have them."

Amelia knocked on the door, took Robby from Faith, and the Weatherbys left for Winnetka after long hugs all the way around.

26

Jeremy and Faith sat for a minute in silence.

He was the first to speak. "Did you see that coming?"

"No, Amelia didn't say anything about a check, just mentioning that her folks wanted to thank the Foundation."

"Mother, we both understand the significance of this donation. Felicia has connections to wealthy people in Winnetka, and because she primed the financial pump with a hundred grand, it's likely that several others will follow suit."

"You're quite right. No advertising or promotional is as effective as word of mouth recommendation to friends and acquaintances."

"Right, and you're the one who befriended Amelia and got her started on the education path, that led to her reunion with her parents."

"I'd give most of the credit to you and the Foundation for making it possible for these mothers to keep their children and enabling them to restart their lives."

"One thing I'll do first thing tomorrow is contact Samuel Witherspoon, our fundraiser. He asked for names of people we might tag for contributions."

Faith laughed. "You're a step ahead of me. I was thinking of the same thing. How about this idea? Ask Felicia and her friends to come for a tour of the Foundation, and have a thumbnail overview of what you could do in a larger facility?"

"I may be a step ahead of you, but you're miles beyond me."

WEDNESDAY MORNING, as Faith drove to the south side, she had two items on her agenda with Father Whitmore. She had to bring him up to date on the situation with Doug because her priest had been good to help her weather the court storm. A more important bit of news was Amelia's transition and her mother's generous donation.

Faith, as usual, bypassed the priest's office to commune with her two favorite saints. Then she backtracked, left the sanctuary and paused at Father Whitmore's door.

"Come on in; you're always welcome. Your face tells me things are going well for you."

"Yes, not perfect, but as well as can be expected."

"Did you hit a speed bump on your personal highway?"

"I told you I was uneasy about the big win over Doug in court, but couldn't figure out why. I knew it would be hard for him to drop the matter, and sure enough, he called."

"Did he threaten you?"

"No, he needled me with a phrase he sang, 'I don't bring you flowers anymore.'"

"Oh, reminding you of his flower delivery?"

"Yes, and Scott and I have decided not to let him bother us, and get his revenge by ruining our family harmony."

"That's a good approach."

"Well, you know I've been honest about holding some feelings of compassion and pity for Doug. Nasty tricks like that make me angry and bitter."

"What are you going to do?"

"We have safeguards, filing a police report about a harassing phone call. We can use that if we want to renew the restraining order."

"I guess that's all you can do."

"One more thing that I can do, and am doing, is spending more time volunteering at Jeremy's Foundation. I became friends with one teenage mother and helped her with continuing her education. The long story cut short is that, especially because she's taking college classes, she and her parents have reconciled, and yesterday she moved back to her parents' house in Winnetka."

"Winnetka? Jeremy takes in the rich as well as the poor."

"Family problems know no financial boundaries."

"They could help support Jeremy's program."

"They did, to the tune of a hundred thousand dollars—oh, I shouldn't have told you that. Please don't repeat it."

"My lips are sealed."

"She said he could use it for operating expenses or his financial campaign for a larger facility."

"What does he have in mind?"

"The old residential hotel he took over only has space for twenty mother-child units, and he's always turning away others, so he'd like to expand to a larger place that would accommodate thirty or forty. We've already contacted a professional fundraiser to raise ten million. And we have a realtor looking for a larger building, a small school or seminary or convent that is closing."

"What do you need in the facility?"

"First, thirty or forty individual rooms, then a dining hall and a kitchen. That's the minimum."

"If it were a school, there'd be classrooms."

"Yes, Father, and I haven't explored this with Jeremy yet, but I think it would be a good idea to have classes for these mothers. A whole range of possibilities would help them transition—that's Jeremy's term for returning to mainstream society. It could be parenting skills, or computer instruction, or writing and speaking skills, even mock job interviews."

"Hmm. I see."

"Alright, father-confessor, I can see you have something on your mind. Hey, I'm an amateur in this project. If you have any advice, let's hear it."

"You told me something about your Winnetka donor that is QT, so here's something not on the public radar yet. Some years ago our diocese started a private high school, a combination commuting and boarding facility. They had good intentions, but more enthusiasm than finances. Their expenses outstripped their income, and high tuition helped drive away students. The diocese is considering closing the school."

"Would they consider selling it?"

"It's not so simple as that. They founded the school with sizeable donations tied to a trust. Originally it was a girls-only school, but with lower enrollments, they switched to a coed program. Even so, the trust is pegged to a commitment to fostering the education, health, and welfare of young women."

"I'm not a lawyer, but I can see the complications of an outright sale."

"The diocese has helped support the institution financially, and doesn't want to lose that investment, but can't afford to keep propping it up every year."

"Father, are you free to tell me the name of this place?"

"It's Canterbury Academy. The formal name was Canterbury Women's Academy before it became coed."

"Never heard of it."

"Few people have. It's located in the northwest suburbs, in a rather secluded wooded area. It has all the amenities you mentioned."

"Would you be willing to discuss the possibility of ... I don't know what the term is ... a merger or continuation of the academy's goal of furthering the education, health, and welfare of young women in cooperation with the Mothers and Kids Foundation?"

"The diocese has wrestled with this knotty problem for several years, and in a few weeks we have a meeting to decide on what to do with the academy."

"Father, you told me this in confidence. Can I talk about this with Jeremy, to see if he would like to consider a continuation or merger?"

"Yes, just between you and him."

"Gee, Father, I've taken up too much of your time. But I didn't know our conversation would shift from heavenly affairs to earthly real estate."

FAITH LEFT Church of the Redeemer with a gleam in her eye, focusing on Canterbury Academy, as she drove to the hotel. Busy the rest of the morning and all afternoon, she stayed in the office after five, calling Scott and telling him she'd be late.

Alone in her office, she looked up Canterbury Academy on the internet. The academy had a glitzy website that presented the school as the ideal place for either live-in or commuting high school students, focusing on both academic excellence and social responsibility. She skipped over the hype, concentrating on the physical facilities. The site touted fifty rooms, which would accommodate one hundred live-in high schoolers, and they had a hundred or more commuting students. The buildings included a dining area, kitchen, all-purpose social room and lounge, and even a small gym and fitness area. The wooded lot and green space surrounding the facility impressed her.

In a few minutes, Faith made an assessment that Canterbury Academy would make an ideal home for Jeremy's Foundation. The only mismatch was an overabundance of classrooms, but Faith had her ideas about how to utilize them for the education of young mothers.

Before leaving the office, Faith made the decision not to tell Scott about Canterbury Academy. She didn't like to keep things from Scott, but she had to keep her promise to Father Whitmore not to tell anyone but Jeremy about this possibility. She quickly sent an email to Jeremy, asking him to set aside time Thursday afternoon for a talk, and not to schedule her for any interviews with residents in the afternoon.

FAITH GOT HOME LATE. Scott had dinner waiting for her. "Lots of business at the hotel?"

"Yes, since I'm on a reduced schedule, from time to time I have to put in extra hours." She wanted to share the news of Canterbury Academy with Scott, but that would have to come later.

THURSDAY MORNING FAITH arrived at the Foundation to eat breakfast with the late risers. She missed Amelia and Robby but made friends with the young mother who took Amelia's old room. After an interview with two residents, she let someone else handle playtime. Faith could hardly wait until lunch and her meeting with Jeremy. She went to the lounge, the favorite hangout place for Amelia. She felt sad about Amelia leaving, but was glad that she had transitioned.

She ate lunch with Jeremy, and then they left the cafeteria for his office.

"Mom, what was so important that you had to make an appointment?"

"I want you to look at something. Google 'Canterbury Academy,' and take a look at its facilities."

"Okay."

In a minute he had the academy on his screen. "Looks like a nice place, a lot nicer than what we have here. It's an Episcopalian boarding school. Well, boarding and commuting. Did Father Whitmore mention it? Don't tell me you're about to start volunteering there?"

"Alright, I'll come out with it. In my talk with Father Whitmore, I told him about Amelia's good news, and let it slip—sorry—about the hundred thousand donation to the Foundation. One thing led to another, and when I described the kind of larger place you were looking for, he told me—confidentially—that this academy is in financial trouble, and the diocese may have to close it. I asked him if I could tell you about it, and he said I could tell you but no one else. I didn't even tell Scott."

"This is a blockbuster. Do you think we could swing it to move the Foundation there?"

"If you read the whole site, their rationale, originally, was to foster the education and citizenship of young women. With declining enrollment, they became coed, but the numbers still slid, and they got caught in the squeeze between high tuition and fewer students. It's a long shot and would require some delicate negotiation, but you might be able to arrange a merger of the Foundation with the academy."

"How would that work?"

"I honestly don't know; we'll have to leave that up to lawyers. But the first step was to get your expression of interest. I can take that back to Father Whitmore. He'll have to approach the academy board, and then it would be up to you to have the foundation board agree to explore a merger."

"It's almost too much to hope for, but let's go ahead and see what comes of it."

"Okay, I'll phone Father Whitmore and ask him to see if there's interest from the academy board."

"Mother, I don't know what to think of you. Here you are, a high-level business executive who is also a master family counselor and a low-level baby sitter. On the side, you come up with a real estate deal that even the realtors don't know about."

FAITH LEFT EARLY for the condo so that she could still phone Father Whitmore before he left his office. She told him Jeremy was excited about the possibility of linking the Foundation to the academy, and he would ask his board to okay an exploration of this idea.

"And Father Whitmore, if you don't mind, I'll tell Scott about this. I hate to keep secrets from him."

The good priest laughed. "Okay, but I don't want to read about this in the *Trib*."

THAT EVENING when Scott came home, she brought him up to date on Canterbury Academy.

Scott agreed with her assessment of the academy. "That's great news. Jeremy's Foundation has made quite a name for itself, and he deserves a windfall like this. He can do a lot of good with a larger building."

FAITH WELCOMED Friday with less enthusiasm than the TGIF greetings of coworkers because she dreaded Saturday morning and waiting for a call from the Peoria perp.

Sure enough, mid-morning Saturday, a phone call came in from Peoria. Caller ID didn't give a name or firm, and most likely it was from a pay phone at a bus terminal or train station. She waited to listen to the message.

It was a repeat of the sung phrase, "I don't bring you flowers anymore," followed by the voiced warning, "You can run, but you can't hide."

The call did not make Faith panic, but it did annoy her. Doug knew how to spoil the beginning of a weekend.

A little later the front desk called. "Flowers for you, Miss A. I told the delivery guy I'd bring them up."

"Come by yourself so that I can see you through the peephole."

George came up, knocked, and she checked to make sure he was alone.

She closed the door and took the long box to the kitchen. It held a single long stem rose, with the card, "From your distant admirer."

Scott came home a little later and was furious. He called the local florist, who gave him the number of the Peoria florist who forwarded the order. The clerk in Peoria said a young man came in and ordered the flowers, paid for in cash.

Scott said, "He's slippery and slimy, that bastard. But this is too much. Monday I'll contact Bill, and we'll warn Doug's lawyer that the restraining order is still in effect."

27

F aith sorted her daily life into three categories: what she had to do, at the hotel; what she wanted to do, at the Foundation; and what she dreaded doing, dealing with Doug.

A week went by after the flower delivery, and she spent a quiet Saturday without a call or another surprise package from Doug. Scott and Faith figured that Doug's lawyer had leaned on him not to cause any problems.

The next week, Jeremy fielded a call from Amelia's mother, Felicia Weatherby. She asked if she could bring a half dozen of her Winnetka friends to tour the Foundation. Jeremy wanted Faith to be there, so he scheduled the tour for Thursday.

On Thursday morning, Faith had a slight case of nerves getting ready. She didn't want to dress too casual and offend these ladies, but she would be out of place in the Foundation if she put on one of her hotel power suits. She compromised with a pair of gray slacks and a white blouse.

After a busy morning, she and Jeremy had lunch and then waited for the bevy of socialites. When they arrived, Felicia made introductions, lavishing praise on Jeremy and Faith and the Foundation work. Then she told Jeremy to lead the tour for the other women because she had already seen the place. That left Felicia and Faith in Jeremy's office.

Felicia spoke up. "I know that behind your low-key nanny façade, you're a high-powered executive. I like that. I'm a take-charge person, too. So I don't have to beat around the bush. I understand that you and Jeremy are interested in joining the Mothers and Kids Foundation with the Canterbury Academy."

"Uh, we haven't gotten beyond initial exploration, and were asked not to discuss it."

Felicia laughed. "Don't worry about that. I have connections with the diocese, and they asked me to weigh in on this possibility. I gave the Foundation a glowing recommendation. The diocese values my input because I was honest with them about the academy. They wanted me to be on the academy board, but I turned them down, told them it was underfunded and overly ambitious. Now they see I was right, and they're trying to salvage the situation, to save money and save face."

"You think it's possible?"

"Not only possible, but it's also a win-win. Jeremy would get a much nicer facility in a much nicer setting, enabling him to help twice as many young mothers. The diocese would get rid of a financial albatross while holding true to the academy's original purpose of fostering the education, health, and welfare of young women."

"I think you're right, but how could it work?"

"While Jeremy is finishing the tour, let me give you a quick and dirty. The academy has at least ten million in endowment, and income from the endowment would help with operating expenses, but couldn't be touched for anything else. Let me ask if you two could come up with ten million. I know this is spur of the moment, but am sure you're used to making quick assessments and smart decisions."

"I'll level with you. To begin the Foundation, we raised about fifteen million. We have already contacted a professional fundraiser, and hope to bring in ten million. My idea is to ask ten to twenty corporations and charities for more modest 'sustaining contributions' of about fifty thousand a year for five years. We haven't run the numbers yet, but I think this would support the Foundation for the near future. I haven't had a chance to discuss this with Jeremy, but know the increase in residents would call for another social worker, and the grounds and buildings would require at least one maintenance man."

"Faith, wonderful! I knew you were the same kind of no-nonsense straight shooter like me. Well, another reason I come out with guns blazing is that things might move very quickly. The diocese is under pressure to decide with the academy. If we can provide them a reasonable escape hatch, it will be to everyone's benefit. And of course, this way we don't have to go through a commercial real estate agent, so we can save a bundle of money. If you go over this with Jeremy and it's agreeable to him, I'll start greasing the skids with the diocese. Oh, and by the way, I will be glad to help you with your campaign for the Foundation side of the ten million."

Jeremy returned with Felicia's friends, who said now they understood why Amelia and Felicia had been so upbeat about the Foundation. He asked Felicia if she had a good talk with Faith.

"Yes, we had a nice chat. She can tell you about it after us old hens fly the coop."

"Well, tell me how Amelia is doing."

"Great! She's taking two classes this term, is signing up for three classes next term. She wants to finish her associate's degree right away so she can enroll in a four-year college."

"I'm glad to hear that. She's one of our success stories."

"I give credit to you and Faith for giving her a new start in life. Well ... and being responsible for healing our family rift. My husband and I will be forever indebted to you. Oh, my group is ready to go, so I'll talk to you later."

. . .

Jeremy told Faith, "The women liked the facility, held some babies, and schmoozed with mothers and toddlers. We have some solid supporters."

"Well, sit down in your chair, because you won't believe what Felicia told me while you were playing tour guide. She's a bulldozer and steamroller, combined. I can see why she might have overwhelmed Amelia. To wrap it up in one sentence, she gave me the plans for merging the Foundation with Canterbury Academy."

Faith summed up Felicia's behind the scenes maneuvering for the merger.

"Mother, I was only with the women for a half hour, and you handled all those complicated issues?"

"Yes, and maybe I'm like Felicia, always looking ahead. In the event of a union between the Foundation and the academy, the two boards would disappear, and a new board would be needed. She'd make a good board member, even a chair."

Jeremy stood up and motioned for Faith to sit in his chair. "I think you've made me obsolete, taking care of all my plans for the future."

"Don't worry; there'll be plenty of meetings and glad-handing and discussion before this is finalized. The important thing is that we have a plan, and a dynamo to power it."

"To be honest, only one aspect of their facility bothers me—the classrooms. We don't have any way of using them."

"Oh, Jeremy, that's the beauty of the setup. The rationale of the academy is for the education and welfare of young women. And having those rooms would enable you to fulfill the goal of their endowment while providing training for these young women. Rather than watching TV, they could take classes in parenting, computers, job applications. Hey, I like the gym, which can be utilized for fitness. And there's plenty of outdoors for active youngsters."

"Mom, when's the move-in date?"

"Okay, joke about it, but Felicia says things might move very quickly, and it's better to have plans and be prepared."

. . .

FAITH HURRIED home so she could phone Father Whitmore in the privacy of the condo.

"Father, do you know Felicia Weatherby?"

"Sure, she's from Winnetka, a strong supporter of the diocese."

"Well, I've told you about Amelia, who did so well and transitioned. Felicia Weatherby is her mother."

"What a coincidence!"

"Yes, and you probably know she's a go-getter. I didn't tell her anything about the possible merger of the Foundation and Canterbury Academy, but she had an inside track to behind the scenes discussions, and she helped me plan how we could make it work."

"That's either serendipity or a miracle, maybe both."

They laughed and joked about the good news.

WHEN SCOTT CAME HOME, Faith told him about Felicia Weatherby and her plans.

"Hmm, I've seen her name on the social pages in the *Trib*. She's a mover and shaker. You're lucky to have her as a supporter. I knew Winnetka meant money but had no idea Amelia was connected to the Weatherbys."

After Faith had told Scott everything about the potential merger, Scott said, "Let me change the subject. I'm still concerned about Doug and what he might do. Let's file a complaint with the judge who granted us the restraining order. You said he acted like a wounded animal, and he's irrational even when he's not wounded."

"Oh, Scott, is that necessary? I finally got over the stress of the visitation mess, and don't want to go to court again."

"Hell, almost no one wants to go to court, but it may be the best insurance policy we can buy. Uh, of course, it's up to you, because you'd have to be the one to file the formal complaint, you know, take in the recordings of his phone calls."

"Well, he didn't call or send flowers last week, so maybe he's losing interest."

"That's not in his character."

Faith said, "Well ... let's wait a while before we do anything."

"Okay, if that's what you want."

FRIDAY FAITH HAD a busy day at the office and was glad to have a little Saturday morning solitude. George from the front desk called. "Miss A, just wanted you to know. The man who delivered the flowers, and tried to push his way into your unit, I have his picture, and he was hangin' around the lobby. I asked him what he want. He say he just lookin' for a friend. He say his friend Smith. I tell him he can call him, but he can't hang around the lobby, and not to come back unless he with his friend Smith."

"Thanks, George. You didn't get a picture of him, did you?"

"No, Miss A, but maybe it's on the security camera."

"Make sure you retain today's recording. You did the right thing."

Faith called Scott. "It's not an emergency, but George let me know Doug was nosing around the lobby."

"Is Doug there now?"

"No, George told him to leave. I asked George to make sure the security camera footage was not erased."

"I'll be home within an hour. Don't open the door, and don't answer the phone unless you see it's from me."

AN HOUR later Scott burst into the condo. "Are you okay?"

She ran to him and hugged him. "I was okay. With you here, I'm fine."

"Honey, we've got to file a complaint."

"You're right. I hoped Doug had learned a lesson, but he's a slow learner."

. . .

MONDAY MORNING they were in Bill's office.

"You mean he showed up in your building's lobby?"

"Yes, Bill, and I have the security camera footage."

"That, with the phone recording—what did he say? 'You can run, but you can't hide'? That's a threat. And I communicated with his lawyer to stay away. On top of that, it's in the court proceedings for visitation that we had a restraining order on him."

Scott smiled. "So it's an open and shut case?"

"A slam dunk if I ever saw one."

Faith asked, "How will this work?"

"First there's a long form, a verified petition for an order of protection. I'll fill it out, including all the times we've told Doug to contact our firm, not you. Then there's the phone calls, the flower delivery, and also his appearance Saturday. We'll need recordings of phone calls, the security camera footage. And I want the hospital records for your panic attack."

Scott smiled. "That ought to convince the judge."

Faith added, "What happens next?"

"The court will notify him to appear in court. We'll have the phone recordings and security camera footage, which he can't dispute. His lawyer will plead a distraught man did something foolish, but he won't do it again."

Faith frowned. "Punishment?"

"Depends on the judge. Could be a fine or jail time or both."

"We don't have any choice in the matter."

"Oh, no, that's up to the judge's discretion."

Faith asked, "Bill, I hope you have a few more minutes, for something completely different."

"Sure, what's on your mind?"

"Jeremy has done so well with the Mothers and Kids Foundation that he's looking for a place about twice as large. I can't give you the details, but we have the possibility of acquiring a great facility, and need funding for an endowment and also what we're calling a 'sustaining contribution' of fifty thousand a year for five years. I would appreciate it if you'd mention this to your partners and see if they would be able to help us."

"Jeremy is doing wonderful work, and I think that's the kind of contribution our firm would look favorably on."

"Thanks so much."

28

Faith spent the rest of the day taking care of business at the hotel, but her mind was on Tuesday and a session with Samuel Witherspoon, the fundraiser she had recommended to Jeremy.

Tuesday morning Faith made it to the Foundation in time for breakfast, and had one interview with a resident, then went to Jeremy's office to wait for the ten o'clock meeting.

Witherspoon arrived just before ten. He had on charcoal slacks, a navy blazer, and a white shirt with a striped tie. Armed with a leather briefcase, he walked briskly into Jeremy's office, introducing himself and giving firm handshakes.

Jeremy had Faith summarize the meeting with Felicia Weatherby and the prospect of a merger with the Canterbury Academy.

"Wow, sounds like you've done the initial spadework. What did you leave for me?"

Faith answered, "We'd like to hear your strategy for raising at least ten million, and to secure ten sustaining contributions of fifty thousand a year for five years."

"That's a tall order, but we have experience in similar campaigns."

They talked for an hour as Witherspoon pulled glossy brochures from his briefcase, full of pictures and graphs of his firm's previous successes.

At the end of the hour, Faith raised her eyebrows, asking Jeremy, "Have you heard enough this morning?"

"Yes, I guess so."

Witherspoon assured them, "Let me know what you'd like, and I'll be glad to come back any time with a detailed plan."

After the fundraiser left, Jeremy said, "I don't think you were too impressed."

"Long on hype, short on substance. The trip through his promotional material left me uninspired."

"What do you think we should do?"

"If we're serious about hiring him, he'd have to come back with a solid proposal tailored to the Foundation and the academy."

"Hmm, you said 'if.'"

"Yes, if. And I have another idea that I'd like to float. We have a valuable ally in Felicia, and she has tons of experience raising money for charities and the church. I want to ask her about who she would recommend."

"Go ahead, and I'll hold off on contacting Witherspoon."

FAITH CALLED FELICIA, who recommended Thomas Stinson, a top fundraiser for charities and religious organizations in the Chicago area.

Faith and Jeremy arranged a meeting with Thomas Stinson, who had been briefed by Felicia. Stinson's attire was as neat and proper as Witherspoon's, but his presentation proved to be far superior. He had a plan to parlay the Foundation's proven record of transitioning young mothers, with the academy's lofty ideal of cultivating and enhancing the education and maturity of young women. He admitted it would be difficult to pull off the two-pronged approach of landing one-time endowment donations and securing sustaining contributions.

"My strategy would be to ask for endowment lump sums from heavy hitters, and I think some social agencies who don't have large bank accounts might be able to promise fifty thousand a year for five years."

Stinson's ideas and enthusiasm won over Jeremy and Faith. It only took them a few minutes to agree to hire him.

Jeremy and Faith congratulated each other on a job well done. With the help of Father Whitmore and Felicia Weatherby, they had found a good site for the Foundation, without having to hire a realtor. And with Stinson aboard, they could look forward to a successful financial campaign.

THE NEXT DAY Faith's secretary buzzed her for a call from Bill Ludwig.

"I'll take it."

"Hello, Faith, are you having a good day?"

"I'd like to tell you good news about Jeremy's Foundation, but I imagine you have bad news from the realm of Doug."

"I'm afraid so. Not all bad, but court appearances are never pleasant. We have a date for Doug's hearing on violating the restraining order, and the judge will have to hear from you. Why you authorized the original order, and how it upset you to learn he was snooping around in your building."

"Although I don't look forward to it, I realize that's the price we have to pay. You understand, of course, I'm not thinking just of myself, but the twins and the grandchildren."

"Naturally."

"How do you want to play it?"

"This time I'd be the lead lawyer, and Miriam will be co-counsel. If need be, she can recite the character profile she gave so effectively in the visitation case."

"Sounds good to me."

"We need to have a conference with you and Scott before the hearing, to prepare you for your testimony at the hearing."

.   .   .

FAITH GAVE the news to Scott over dinner that evening.

"The perp deserves what's coming to him. Sorry, I can't be with you, but he would recognize me from our beer-soaked talk at Shorty's in Peoria."

"No need for you to be there."

FAITH MADE a trip to the south side, thanking Mary and Harriet for help in the past, and praying for assistance in the hearing. Father Whitmore first had to hear about the fantastic progress with the merger talks for the Foundation and the Academy. Then he gave his prayerful guidance for the hearing.

THE WEEK before they went to court, Scott went with Faith to Bill's law offices. Miriam and Bill asked probing questions of how Faith had been scared by Doug, especially when he tried to barge into her condo.

Scott added, "She was hyperventilating, and her heart was racing. She had to go to the ER and stay overnight."

Miriam said, "Be sure to bring the hospital record."

Faith gave a "tell-it-in-your-own-words" version of how she was afraid of Doug.

Bill and Miriam said she had a straightforward story that would be effective in court.

29

W hen the day of the hearing rolled around, Faith dressed in one of her gray power suits that matched her graying hair.

She arrived at court with Bill and Miriam and saw Doug across the courtroom. He looked thinner and pale, not in good health.

Miriam told Faith, "We drew Walter Montgomery as judge, a fair-minded and no-nonsense man."

Judge Montgomery entered, and court convened. He settled a few other cases and simple motions before the bailiff called their case.

The judge wasted no time. "Violation of a restraining order is a serious complaint. Attorney for the defendant, do you contest the complaint? The plaintiff has offered considerable evidence to support her complaint."

Luciano Garibaldi stood. "Your honor, my client has been under considerable stress because he has not been able to reunite with his sons. If he is guilty of anything, it is his earnest desire to be rejoined with his flesh and blood. He has shown evidence of paternity for his twin sons and asks the plaintiff to provide him with the exact names and current addresses of his twin sons. He has been overzealous in pursuing his parental rights."

"Mr. Garibaldi, we are more interested in Mr. Parinello's actions, rather than his intentions, and whether in fact, his actions violated the provisions of a restraining order. Let's hear from him."

He was sworn in and entered the witness box.

"Mr. Parinello, you received a certified letter from the law firm of Mr. Ludwig, asking you not to contact Ms. Armstrong, but to communicate directly to Mr. Ludwig."

"Uh, yes, I did."

"Did you make telephone calls to the home of Ms. Armstrong?"

"I wanted her to help me contact my sons."

"So you did call her?"

"Yes."

"That is a violation of the restraining order."

"In a phone call, did you say, 'You can run, but you can't hide'?"

"Well, I was joking."

"The court considers that a threat, not a joke. That also is a violation of the restraining order."

"Did you impersonate a florist delivery man, and deliver flowers to Ms. Armstrong's condo?"

"I was just trying to be nice with flowers since she wouldn't take my calls."

"That is a violation of the restraining order."

"Did you try to force your way into her condo?"

"I was trying to get her to talk to me."

"I have a sworn statement from Ms. Armstrong's neighbors that you tried to push the door open, and Ms. Armstrong told them to call the police. I remind you, Mr. Parinello, you are under oath. Did you try to force your way in?"

"I put my foot inside so she couldn't close the door."

"The restraining order stated you could not approach her at home or her office. Stepping inside her condo is a serious violation of the restraining order."

"We have security camera video footage of you in the lobby of Ms. Armstrong's building. Do you deny you were there?"

"No, I was there, hoping to run into her."

"Which would have been another violation of the restraining order. You can step down."

He then called Faith to the stand. After being sworn in, she stepped briskly into the witness box.

"Ms. Armstrong, your attorneys have submitted considerable evidence of Mr. Parinello violating the terms of a restraining order. Did you provide this evidence to them, and are you in agreement with the complaint presented to the court?"

"Yes, your honor."

"I don't need you to ask you about each item, but would like to hear how you understood Mr. Parinello's phrase, 'You can run, but you can't hide.'"

"He scared me. I understood that no matter what, he would come to get me."

"After one of his many phone calls you were so frightened and upset that you had to be hospitalized, is that correct?"

"Yes, the doctors said the fright led to hyperventilation, rapid pulse, and high blood pressure. I had to go to the hospital and stay overnight."

"Are you still frightened of Mr. Parinello?"

"Yes, in a recent court appearance for a visitation petition, he threatened everyone in the court, used obscene language, and had to be marched out of court by the bailiff. So, yes, I am still frightened by Mr. Parinello."

"You may step down."

As she took her seat, Faith glanced at Doug, who glared at her.

Judge Montgomery shuffled the petition papers, then asked, "Mr. Garibaldi, do you have any statement?"

"Your honor, I repeat that my client only had good intentions. His only mistake was he got carried away trying to make contact with his twins. I ask you to consider this."

"It is in the court records. Mr. Ludwig, do you have a statement?"

"Yes, your honor. My intention and the intention of my client is to preserve her safety and peace of mind. Mr. Parinello has terrified my client, given her cause to worry by persistently contacting her on the phone, and even using a ruse to try to gain entrance to her condo. He has repeatedly violated the terms of the restraining order. We ask that you decide in our favor, determine the appropriate punishment, and extend the restraining order indefinitely."

Judge Montgomery looked through his papers, jotted down his notes, and looked over the courtroom. "Plaintiff has presented overwhelming evidence of a violation of a restraining order. The defense has shown no facts to contradict this evidence, and the defendant has admitted to repeated violations of the restraining order.

"The court finds Mr. Parinello guilty of willful violation of the restraining order. Punishment, in this case, is a way of deterring Mr. Parinello from again violating the restraining order. The court imposes a fine of $1000. It also imposes a jail sentence of one day. Mr. Parinello caused Ms. Armstrong to spend one night in the hospital. In turn, he should spend at least one overnight in jail. I add that if Mr. Parinello is brought before this court for another instance of violation of the restraining order, the fine will be much greater and the jail time will be thirty days. The restraining order remains in effect."

Garibaldi rose to his feet to object.

"Mr. Garibaldi, you may appeal if you so wish."

"Your honor, my client only had good intentions, and—"

"Mr. Garibaldi, I should not have to remind you of the cliché that the road to hell is paved with good intentions. The court has no way of knowing Mr. Parinello's intentions but has clear evidence of his actions. And actions have results, disturbing the peace of mind of the plaintiff, even causing her to be hospitalized. In the future, your client should be more concerned, like the court is, with actions rather than intentions. Sentencing is delayed for one month to give the defendant time to appeal."

As the judge rendered his verdict, Faith glanced at Doug, who glared at the judge, and then twisted in his chair to stare directly at her and Bill.

Faith turned toward Bill, whispering, "I'm still afraid of him."

"Don't worry; we have your back."

Bill stood and asked, "Your honor, may I approach the bench?"

The judge motioned him forward, where the two had a brief talk.

Bill returned to his chair. "I told the judge that in his last court appearance, Parinello got out of control, and had to be escorted out by a bailiff, and the judge let us out through his chambers to a service elevator. The judge said this courtroom doesn't have easy access to a service elevator, so he'll have the bailiff tell a policeman in the hall to see us safely to the ground floor and a taxi."

Doug stayed seated in his chair, stiff as a statue. Garibaldi stood behind Doug, trying to get him to stand up and leave. The two exchanged sharp words that Faith couldn't hear clearly.

Bill said, "We'll just wait here until the bailiff brings a policeman, who will escort us to a taxi."

Garibaldi grabbed Doug by the arm, managing to get him on his feet, and Doug shuffled out, turning sideways, scowling at Faith.

A few minutes later a policeman approached the plaintiff's table. "I was told to take you to a taxi at street level."

They followed him to the elevator and went down to the lobby. As they exited the building, Faith noticed Doug standing on the sidewalk. He had his arms at his side, but she saw that each hand was doubled up, with a middle finger extended. Garibaldi quickly stepped in front of Doug and turned him around.

Faith asked the policeman, "Did you see that?"

He shrugged. "A double middle finger salute. Well, here's a taxi. I've got to get back to my post by the door of the court. Have a good day."

. . .

IN THE TAXI, Bill told Faith, "You could come back to the office with us, but I'd prefer to drop you off right at your condo. You should be okay there, but we've whipped Doug twice, and a cornered animal is unpredictable. So be careful."

Faith welcomed the safety and security of the condo. She called Scott. "Well, one more court appearance, and one more for the home team."

"The court could hardly ignore all the evidence. How did Doug take it?"

"Not well. If eyes could kill, I'd be dead."

"He didn't do anything, did he?"

"Well, the judge had a policeman walk with us to a taxi, and on the sidewalk outside the building, Doug was waiting. As the policeman put it, Doug gave us a double middle-finger salute."

"Yeah, that's Doug, he never gives up. But I hope we're done with him."

"I'm afraid not."

"What do you mean?"

"He seems so bitter, so full of anger, that I wouldn't put anything past him."

"I'll talk with your building security, and you should probably do the same with hotel security."

"Oh, Scott, I'm so tired of court and Doug, and looking over my shoulder."

"I think you need to make a trip to the south side."

"Yes, I'll call Father Whitmore now."

30

A few days later, Faith traveled the familiar road to Church of the Redeemer and quickly stepped past the priest's office. Proceeding to the familiar stained glass window, she gave her heartfelt prayer of thanks to Mary and Harriet.

Then she sat in a pew and had a good cry, releasing the tension of the past months. She was drying her eyes when Father Whitmore touched her on the shoulder.

"Faith, are you alright?"

"Much better now, thanks. I shared my trials and tribulations with these two saints. They're good listeners, and helped comfort me."

"Whenever you're ready, come to my office."

They walked to his office.

"Father, the court hearing is over, but it seems like it's never over."

"What is never over?"

"Doug has to pay a large fine and spend a night in jail. He'll never forgive me for that, and will find a way to make me pay for it."

"The court, and if necessary, the police will protect you."

"And I'm fortunate to have Scott, who will look after me."

"What else do you need?"

"I have to protect me from myself. After the judge ruled against him, Doug was so beaten down he looked pathetic. Before, when I talked to you, I said Doug was like a sheep without a shepherd. He's all of that, the lost sheep, but at the same time, he's like a wolf. Scott would say he's a wolf in sheep's clothing. So I'm back to the inner battle between softhearted and hardhearted me."

"It says something about you that you're having this dialogue. Many people don't listen to their conscience—if they have one."

"Well, Father, I don't need to harangue you with my troubles. Let me share some good news. You gave me a very valuable tip on Canterbury Academy, and thanks to Felicia Weatherby, we seem to be on the initial steps of the negotiation for a merger."

"I'm glad to hear that. Not only for you and Jeremy and the Mothers and Kids Foundation, but also the Academy and the diocese. It's good when you have a business deal or real estate negotiation that's a win-win."

"Felicia is a smart cookie. She's aware of the complexities behind such a negotiation and has a good plan to handle the difficulties. She even offered to help the Foundation come up with the millions needed to swing the deal."

"She's known throughout the diocese for being generous with money, but tough with finances and negotiations."

"I'm glad she's on our side."

Faith and the good priest ended their session with his prayer, concluding with, "And we give thanks for the support in helping mothers and kids."

Faith called Jon, asking him to set aside a half hour of his time. They agreed on early Tuesday afternoon after she had lunch with Jeremy at the Foundation.

In Jon's office, she joked with him. "I want you to know I'm not playing favorites volunteering at the Foundation and spending more time with Jeremy than with you. But I can do so much good there, and it's so satisfying. I don't have anything to offer Jontronics."

"Mom, we're still benefiting from the business consult you gave us."

"Well, I'll come right to the point. Jeremy is doing a terrific job at the Foundation in a made-over residential hotel that can accommodate about twenty mothers and their children. But he's always turning away others and would like to expand. I won't give you the long version of the story, but he has the possibility of taking over the facilities for a boarding school that's closing. It's a nice place in a nice setting and would house fifty mothers and their kids. It's an Episcopalian academy with a sizeable endowment, and we need to match that endowment to bring off a merger. We're looking at ten million. I've talked to my financial advisor, and since I don't have to worry about leaving money to you and Jeremy, he says I can donate a million and still be quite comfortable. If you or Jontronics could come up with a million, that would be good seed money to persuade others to donate. That's the pitch, and I don't expect you to give me an answer today. Think it over and let me know if you can help."

"I'm always interested in helping Jeremy, who is donating more than any of the rest of us because he's giving more than money, he's giving his life. Hmm, you said this is an Episcopalian place. I smell Father Whitmore in the background."

"You have a good nose. I see him quite a lot, and when I told him Jeremy was looking for a place, the good father said their diocese was going to close their academy. Originally it was a girls school and had as its mission the education and welfare of young women. So a merger with the Foundation is a good fit."

"Tell you what I'll do. I'll discuss a corporate donation with my board, and talk to Rachel about a personal donation from the two of us. Rachel is very impressed with Jeremy's project."

Faith ended the meeting with a hug. "I don't want to take up any more of your time. Let me hear from you."

. . .

IT WAS STILL EARLY ENOUGH for Faith to beat the afternoon rush, so she drove straight to the condo. She was sure Jon would come through with a significant donation.

Entering the condo, she heard the beep of the answering machine, and her heart skipped a beat when she saw it was from Bill Ludwig. She immediately called his office, and the secretary said he'd get back to her soon.

She got a soda from the fridge and waited fifteen minutes until the phone rang.

"Hi, Bill, I hope we don't have more doo-doo from Doug."

"Why Faith, do you think I always call with bad news?"

"I'm still suffering from court stress."

"I won't bother you with that mess. I have good news — double happiness. You asked for a donation for Jeremy's Foundation. Our firm will donate a hundred thousand. Also, I understand that you're not going through a realtor, you're making a direct offer to the academy. You'll need a good lawyer to handle all the complications of an endowment, a new board, and the like. I don't handle real estate, but the firm is willing to have one of our real estate specialists represent you, pro bono."

"That's super news, Bill. You just made my day!"

"Always glad to make a client happy."

FAITH AND SCOTT had a lot to talk over that evening.

Scott shook his head. "I think you should update your resume by another page, including fundraiser and babysitter, as well as legal adviser."

"It's good to keep busy, prevents me from thinking about the guy you call the Peoria perp."

"Have a good time. Enjoy your time at the Foundation. In the future, people won't remember you as a Horton Hotel VP, but as the founder of Mothers and Kids Foundation."

"If we can just make the merger between the Foundation and the Academy work, I'll be on cloud nine."

At that moment, a call came in from Felicia.

"Faith, sorry to bother you at home, almost at dinner time, but can you talk for a few minutes?"

"Sure, we haven't started dinner."

"We have a snag in the negotiations with Canterbury Academy. One of the academy board members, Agnes Stuart, has dug her heels in, and won't go along with a merger. She claims trying to blend the Foundation and the academy would violate the provisions of the endowment."

"Has she lawyered up?"

"Not yet, but threatens to."

"Here's some good news from our side. Bill Ludwig, who handles all my legal work, has sweetened a hundred thousand dollar donation with the offer of pro bono lawyer's services for the transaction."

"We may need him eventually, but I'd like to avoid a lawyers' cat fight. I prefer what I call soft diplomacy, working behind the scenes. Could you and Jeremy come to my home in Winnetka next Tuesday at two for a tea? Agnes will be there, along with some of my friends who've heard about the Foundation and would like to learn more."

On Tuesday Faith skipped the morning trip to the Foundation, waiting for Jeremy to come to the condo ahead of the meeting with Felicia. He picked her up at the curb and drove while Faith talked.

"Agnes Stuart is the holdout on the academy board, blocking a merger. Felicia and I didn't talk strategy. She's just relying on us to describe what we do at the Foundation. By the way, I emailed Melanie for copies of some glowing testimonials from residents who transitioned—you have them?"

"In the manila folder in the back seat."

"Good. Jeremy, you and I have worked together so closely these past months, we're like a tag team. We can just be ourselves, not talk too long, and let the women ask questions."

Arriving at the large lakefront house in Winnetka and parking in the semicircular drive, Jeremy jested, "My Toyota doesn't fit in with all the luxury vehicles. Hope I don't get towed."

Felicia greeted them at the door, ushering them into a large living room of chattering women. "Ladies, these are the heroes of Mothers and Kids Foundation, Faith Armstrong and Jeremy Goodman."

At that moment, Amelia entered the room with Robby, who was fussing. When Robby saw Faith, he held out his arms.

Faith scooped him up and cradled him. "I think someone needs a nap. Amelia, take me to your rocker." As Amelia led her to another room, Faith hummed a lullaby, and Robby quieted down.

Amelia said, "She's the only one at the Foundation who could hold him like that. I wish I could have her here every afternoon."

Felicia introduced the ladies, one by one, to Jeremy.

Five minutes later, Faith reentered, still humming, with Robby sound asleep. Amelia took him from her.

Felicia did a round of introductions again for Faith. She didn't have to be told who Agnes Stuart was, sitting stiffly upright, nose in the air.

Agnes said, "You seem to have a way with children."

"Yes, I had good training with my grandchildren."

"Not with your own children?"

"No. Several of the women here came for a tour of the Foundation, so they know my story, but here's a recap. Like many of our Foundation residents, I was a teenage mom."

Agnes interrupted, "And you went to a place like the Foundation?"

"No, my parents insisted on adopting out my twins, so I didn't see them for three decades."

"What did you do?"

"Buried myself in hotel work, became an executive vice president, and made a lot of money, but was unhappy. Then my twins found me, and I've gone from the dark ages of my life to the golden age. Well, I had saved a lot of money, so I decided to invest it in a fund for young mothers who wanted to keep their children. Because Jeremy had started his career in a youth ministry, it was an easy move for him to head up the Foundation.

Oops, forgot I'm not a hotel vice president holding a board meeting, and shouldn't dominate the conversation. Jeremy and I will be glad to answer questions, but he should have a chance to speak."

"I'm not as accomplished a speaker as my mother, but here's an overview of what we do at the Foundation. We started with a modest budget and helped young mothers with money for housing and food. When we had a chance to rent a former residential hotel on the west side, we saw a real opportunity to house and nurture young women with preschool children. Our goal is to help these women move back into the mainstream. We call that transitioning. Ideally, we like to see a woman get on her feet and move on after three months or so.

"Our problem, if you want to call it that, is we're too successful. Various agencies are always referring women with small children to us. Now our limit is twenty units. So we've been looking for a facility to at least double that number."

Amelia had put Robby to bed and took a seat with the women. "I can tell you; the Foundation is a wonderful place. Being a teenager is difficult enough, but being a teenager and pregnant is a double whammy that few girls—and that's what we were—girls, can handle. The Foundation for me was a safe haven where I could start life anew. Faith and Jeremy believed in me, persuaded me to start taking classes, and now that I'm back on track, nothing will stop me from completing a degree."

Jeremy said, "Amelia is a good example of our success stories. We have thank you notes from others who have transitioned, and I'd like to pass them around and share them with you."

Agnes spoke up rather sharply, "Faith, are you against adoption?"

"No, that's an individual decision every woman should make. We want her to have the option of keeping her child. We are not *against* anything; we are *for* mothers and children being together if at all possible."

Felicia announced, "We have some high tea fixings in the

dining room, even cucumber sandwiches. Come out and spoil your appetite for the evening meal."

During refreshments, people switched seats. Agnes brought her plate and sat down next to Faith. "From what you and Jeremy said —he's one of the twins you were separated from for thirty years?"

"That's right."

"It's wonderful that you got back together."

"We cherish our time together."

"I guess Felicia told you that I'm not for joining together your foundation and our academy. We worked very hard to set it up, and I'd hate to see it disappear."

"What would you like to see for the academy?"

"We emphasize the education and welfare—you know, responsible citizenship—for women. And I wouldn't want to see the academy become a daycare center."

"That's understandable. From my perspective, the classrooms at the academy present a bright opportunity for the foundation. In our present building, we can't provide education. But if we were at the academy, education would be a major focus. We have some women who didn't graduate from high school, so they could work on their GED. Those with a high school degree could take online classes. That's what Amelia did. And to help the women become self-sufficient, we could have training sessions in computers, reading and writing skills, and sessions on interviews and job applications."

"I didn't realize you had plans like that."

"For the moment we're focusing on fundraising, with a target of ten million. If we reach that goal and have a larger facility, I'm convinced we could staff an in-house instruction faculty with volunteers."

"You certainly seem to have this well thought out."

Robby's crying interrupted them. Amelia ran to get him. When he saw Faith, he readily came to her. She hummed a lullaby, and he stopped crying, relaxed, and fell back asleep. Amelia smiled and took Robby back to bed.

The questions to Faith and Jeremy petered out, and a few women began to leave. Faith and Jeremy took that as their cue to go.

Some women brought up the thank you notes Jeremy had passed around. "Oh, no, you can keep them, share them with friends."

Felicia saw them off at the door. She said, "Thanks for coming," and winked at Faith.

31

On the drive back into the city, Faith and Jeremy compared notes on their high tea.

"Mother, let me share something with you. The very first time Jonathan and I met you was at the high-powered executives' seminar, where you presented your half dozen business 'secrets.' Both of us were impressed with your entrepreneurial savvy, and especially your speaking abilities. But today you showed another talent, a downhome storytelling style. I guess the French would say you were a raconteur, spinning a tale that wove your personal experiences into the dynamics of the Foundation. Wow! And Amelia came in, right on cue, with Robby. The way you soothed him and lullabied him to sleep made points with the women."

"Well, Jeremy, you did a great job quickly summing up the history and work with Mothers and Kids."

"After Felicia broke for refreshments, one lady buttonholed you —was that Agnes?"

"Yes, she's the holdout to preserve the academy, and she grilled me about what we would do with it in a merger. She made a rather snide remark that she didn't want to see the academy turned into a daycare facility. I tried out the same educational ideas on her that I mentioned to you. In other words, we would use the classrooms for educating and training."

"Did she buy it?"

"She seemed interested, at least surprised, that we had learning objectives in mind. Hey, fill me in on what you talked about with the rest of the women."

"They liked what you and I said when we introduced the Foundation. They commented that Amelia was, as one of them put it, 'the proof of the pudding.' They knew the background of Amelia and Felicia, the heartbreak of the family separation, and the joy of their reconciliation. And they were impressed with the thank you notes from former residents."

"So they were in favor of the merger of the Foundation and the academy?"

"They didn't come out and say it in so many words, but all of their comments were positive. One woman remarked, 'Look at the way Faith comforted Robby. That's not institutional care; it's down-home love.'"

Jeremy dropped Faith off at the condo. They agreed to talk more about the meeting on Thursday when Faith volunteered.

THAT EVENING when Scott came home, he pranced across the room with dainty steps, holding an imaginary cup with forefinger and thumb, his pinky finger extended, and said in a falsetto voice, "May I have high tea with thee?"

Faith laughed. "Have your fun, but it was a good conference. The lone holdout on the academy board and I had a long one-on-one chat."

"But you didn't settle anything?"

"No, it was a social gathering, so we didn't talk formalities."

They had supper and were watching television when at eight o'clock the phone rang. Faith saw from caller ID it was Felicia.

"Oh, Felicia, thank you so much for the high tea. It was a

pleasant diversion from my hurried coffee breaks. And it was nice to meet more of your friends."

"You're welcome. But I'll get right to the point. You know I wouldn't call mid-evening unless I had something to say. Agnes was bowled over by you. Partly it was what you—and Jeremy—said, and she couldn't believe that a hotel vice president was so good with Robby. She had resisted making the academy a babysitting operation, but she liked your plans for educating and training young mothers."

"I take it she's still getting used to the idea of a merger, but hasn't yet agreed to it."

"Well, you know, I said I preferred soft diplomacy rather than hard lawyering. Let's compare this tea to dating. It was like a blind date. Feeling each other out, a getting to know you dance. Today we went as far as the handholding stage, not the first kiss."

Faith laughed. "What's the next step?"

"I told Agnes she should come to the Foundation. The women who'd already visited your place agreed she would be pleased with what she saw."

"Jeremy and I would welcome her anytime. Just let us know so that we'd both be there. I volunteer on Tuesdays and Thursdays."

"I'll let you know when Agnes and I can come."

When she hung up, Faith told Scott, "Felicia is as smooth and efficient and perceptive as any executive I've met."

THURSDAY AS FAITH drove to the Foundation, she reviewed the high tea and the followup phone call with Felicia.

Pulling into the parking lot, she saw Maisie Bedford's new Buick, so she knew Maisie would be cooking and the scrambled eggs would be perfect. In the cafeteria line, she told Maisie, "I've never eaten better scrambled eggs than what you cook."

"Don't praise me; give the hens all the credit." She let loose a cackle that even the egg layers would have been proud of.

"Tuesday I had high tea and tasty cucumber sandwiches, but I'd prefer your breakfast any day."

"Where in the world did you get cucumber sandwiches?"

"Winnetka. You remember Amelia, don't you?"

"Sure, lovely lady and cute baby."

"I had tea with Amelia's mother."

"Who is ...?"

"Felicia Weatherby."

"I know her; in fact, I used to be in that high society crowd, but got more satisfaction out of volunteering here."

Faith said, "I guess it's a small world, after all."

She ate breakfast with some residents, then waited for Jeremy to show up.

"Hi, Mom, come into my office. We didn't have enough time on the drive from Winnetka to your condo to talk over the high tea."

"Jeremy, there's more. Tuesday night, Felicia called and said that Agnes is quite impressed with the foundation and us. She likes the idea that we would use the academy for educating our young women."

"That's great."

"It's not a done deal, but I think we should move ahead with fundraising. I'll donate a million, and I asked Jon for another million. Bill Ludwig's firm will contribute a hundred thousand, and has pledged pro bono lawyer services for handling the merger."

"That's terrific."

"My idea is that if we have two or three million in the bank, it will grease the skids for Thomas Stinson to ask for large donations."

"I follow you. It'll take time to make it to ten million, but it's going to be a while before the formalities of a merger can be worked out."

"My guess is the diocese will announce soon that this is the last academic year for the academy. At that point, we want to be well on the way toward our ten million dollar goal."

Jeremy leaned back in his swivel chair, hands behind his head and feet up on the desk. "Mom, when we first opened that shoe-string operation for Mothers and Kids Foundation—remember that decrepit Montgomery Ward store where we were running both One Way revivals and the new Foundation—did you ever dream we'd be where we are today, ready to move into a nice facility?"

"No, I never imagined we'd come this far. So far and so soon."

"It's taken years."

"Good years."

"Any regrets?"

"Sure. I don't like to talk about it, but the decades separated from my twins are what I call my dark ages."

"You mentioned that at Felicia's, and how you've moved into your golden age."

"Yes, and if we're cleaning out the Armstrong attic, I can tell you that being a part of Mothers and Kids is the most satisfying thing I've ever done. Fancy titles at the hotel, money in the bank, lectures at conferences, and honors at universities—they pale before the contentment of seeing these young women raising their children. Something I was not able to do."

"So the regrets of your dark ages are outweighed by the satisfaction of your golden age?"

"I try not to think about it, just bask in the wonderful harmony of our family."

"You do a remarkable job of staying focused on the family and the Foundation, with all the legal problems you've had to handle."

"You're right; my dark ages still throw shadows on the present. And in the shadows, you know who is lurking."

"Do you think about him?"

"As little as possible. Busy work at the hotel and volunteering here shuts Doug out of my mind, but he's always in the background. Meeting him was part of my destiny, as was having you two guys. I didn't choose this life, but have dealt with it as best I could."

"How do you see Doug now?"

"Maybe we'll get together Sunday and talk about it. I go back and forth on him. Father Whitmore is my priest confessor. I told him Doug is like a poor lost sheep, but at the same time he's a dangerous wolf in sheep's clothing."

"Do you feel sorry for him?"

"I guess so. I pity him; he's so pathetic. I don't want him in the family, yet I see him as a bitter, lonely old man. I'll tell you more about this on Sunday. It's difficult to talk about."

"I know what you mean. I feel sorry for him, and pray for him, but am not sure what we could do for him."

"Hmm, you're not my father-confessor, but I know you well enough to realize that you have an idea about Doug. Maybe you don't want to share it. If you don't, we can drop it."

"I didn't plan to mention this today, but here's something I've been thinking about. You know I've never given up on Doug completely. Partly because he's my father, but also because he's a human being, and my faith tells me that no person is beyond redemption. So I've searched for a way that he can redeem himself—"

"You don't mean to bring him into the family?"

No, that's out of the question. But I surveyed Doug's weaknesses and strengths. He was a Casanova, and better at producing children than being a family man. You tell us he's alienated from all of his female partners and offspring. That's his downside. What are his strengths? He spent his life in construction, so he knows blueprints, materials, designs—how to build. I checked with some of my minister friends, and they told me about a program called Redeemed Souls and Reborn Homes. They take their inspiration from Jesus, who was a carpenter. They help people build, repair, and remodel homes. It's almost entirely a volunteer organization. The pay is the satisfaction of helping others. My friends tell me they have plenty of men who can handle a wheel borrow and swing a hammer, or use an electric saw. But they're short on people with construction know-how. So that's where Doug comes in. He says he's born again and wants a second chance at life. This might well be his opportunity."

"You've thought this out, haven't you?"

"Well, yeah. What do you think about it?"

"Your idea has real possibilities. I mean, when there's a national or international disaster, the politicians mouth 'Our thoughts and prayers are with you.' But you go beyond thinking and praying to what people can *do*. And do it themselves."

"Uh-huh. The only catch is how to clue him into this program."

"Jeremy, are you looking in my direction?"

"I don't know how else—who else—could make such a suggestion."

"You know that Doug and I are not on good terms, in fact in this last court appearance he glared at me like he wanted to kill me."

"Mom, today we started out talking about the merger of the academy with the Foundation, and somehow we wandered down memory lane. I apologize, I didn't mean to spring this on you so suddenly. Let me ask you to think about this."

"That's not too much to ask. But frankly, I feel this should be between the two of us. You haven't discussed this with Melanie, have you?"

"No. She won't have anything to do with Doug."

"Good. For the moment I won't talk to Scott about it. He's like Melanie, sees Doug as a total zero."

They parted with a hug, and she left early that day.

32

The clan met at Jon and Rachel's house Sunday. Scott had a trick up his sleeve to get the kids out of the house.

As soon as Faith and Scott arrived, the kids besieged him, wanting to know what they were going to do.

"Well, not a newspaper, not a television show, not a radio show. Not the zoo or a safari."

The kids wanted to know what it was.

"All I'm going to tell you is that it will be sky high."

The cheers rang out.

"But first we have to eat lunch, and then everyone makes a stop at the bathroom."

The kids gobbled lunch and got ready to go with Scott to a nearby park.

Faith asked, "Sky high?"

He whispered to her, "Kites."

"Clever."

After lunch, with the kids out of the house, Faith convened the family circle, starting with a prayer asking for divine guidance.

Then she cleared her throat, and announced, "I think you know most of what I can tell you, but let me sum it up quickly, and after that, you can ask questions.

"The early part of the hearing went as expected, an opening statement by Doug's attorney asking for rejection of our complaint, claiming a violation of the restraining order. He said Doug had been 'overzealous' in trying to contact his sons. Then his lawyer gave a rather thin defense of Doug's sterling character.

"The judge had Doug take the stand, and peppered him with sharp questions. He forced Doug to admit that he had called me and tried to force his way into the condo, both of which acts were violations of the restraining order. When the judge asked Doug what he had meant by 'You can run, but you can't hide,' Doug said he was joking. The judge cut him short, saying the court saw it not as a joke, but a threat.

"The judge excused Doug and called me to the stand and asked me if I agreed with the formal complaint and all of Doug's actions that we considered as instances of harassment. I told him I agreed with the claim. Then he asked me specifically about how I under-stood Doug's phone message, 'You can run, but you can't hide.' I told him I was terrified by Doug's call and had such a severe panic attack that I was hospitalized. So that was my reason for asking for the complaint to be accepted.

"Next Garibaldi, Doug's lawyer, was given a chance for a final statement. He said Doug only had good intentions, and he mentioned again Doug meant no harm, he just got carried away because he was so eager to meet his sons. The judge rejected the argument of good intentions, saying the court was only interested in actions, and actions have results, like forcing me to go to the hospital.

"Bill Ludwig spoke next, saying our side's intentions were my safety and peace of mind. He quickly summed up the instances of Doug violating the restraining order, asked the judge to find him in violation, punish him appropriately, and to continue the restraining order indefinitely.

"The judge decided in our favor and sentenced Doug to a thousand dollar fine and one day in jail—because I had been forced to be overnight in a hospital. The restraining order was extended, and if he violates it, he will be fined more, and spend thirty days in jail. Garibaldi tried to object, but the judge said he could appeal, and he delayed sentencing to give time for an appeal.

"The judge had a policeman escort us from court to a taxi. Sure enough, Doug was waiting on the sidewalk outside the court building and made obscene gestures, but his lawyer hustled him away."

Faith stopped and caught her breath. "Sorry that took so long. I imagine you have questions."

Melanie spoke up first. "I'm always concerned for the children, but they weren't even mentioned."

"Yes, and deliberately so, on lawyers' advice. Don't give him any information he can use."

Melanie continued, "But you don't think he can ask for visitation rights to grandchildren?"

"He can ask, but Bill and Miriam will use the same flawed character argument against him that she presented in the visitation case, and a reasonable judge should deny any such petition."

Jonathan bit his lip. "I hope that means we're through with this creep. Mother, you've gone through holy hades dealing with him. Well, that's the end, isn't it?"

"I honestly don't know. He was so depressed and angry after the judge ruled in our favor, that he might do something irrational, irresponsible. So we should all be careful. That's not just my opinion; it's what Bill strongly advised."

Rachel asked, "Mom, is there anything you or we should do?"

"No, legally, the matter is settled. He's forbidden—restrained— from contacting me, and we don't have to contact him."

Jeremy said, "But nothing would prevent us from contacting him."

All eyes turned toward Jeremy.

Jonathan blurted out, "But why would we want to get in contact with him?"

Jeremy replied, "I was just asking for clarity."

Faith said, "Well, if we ever have any need to contact Doug, the best route is through Bill, our attorney."

Faith and Jeremy exchanged glances but said nothing.

Melanie and Rachel stood up, signaling the end of the session, and initiated a four-way hug of Faith. Her daughters-in-law cried softly, thanking Faith for protecting them and the children.

BEFORE LONG, the children burst into the house, excited about how high their kites had flown. Faith breathed a sigh of relief.

After some refreshments, Scott said, "Grandma's had a hard few weeks and needs some rest, so we're going to get an early start for home.

In the car, Faith said, "Thanks for rescuing me. Just retelling that scene makes me relive it. I don't ever want to go through that again."

She went to bed early and slept well, relieved that the family get-together went smoothly.

MONDAY MORNING FAITH went in early to the hotel and looked up the website for Redeemed Souls and Reborn Homes. It turned out to be a barebones site asking committed Christians to volunteer to work on homes for needy people or to donate money. "If you can't swing a hammer, open your wallet." They were listed as a non-profit organization, making donations tax-deductible. People in need of housing or repairs were advised to write to a committee stating what they would like the volunteers to do for them. The site encouraged volunteers to indicate such skills as carpentry and painting.

Faith waited until after nine to call Church of the Redeemer and set up a Tuesday meeting with Father Whitmore. Next, she phoned the Foundation and left a message that she would come in Tuesday about noon and hoped to have lunch with Jeremy.

Tuesday morning Faith arrived just before her ten o'clock appointment with Father Whitmore, stepped into the sanctuary for a brief prayer to Mary and Harriet, then hurried to the office.

Father Whitmore motioned her in. "That was quick. I've heard of speed reading, but you must have developed speed praying."

Faith laughed. "Yes, I have a busy day planned."

"Well, fire away. What's at the top of the agenda?"

"Good news first. The initial planning for the merger of the Foundation and the academy is going well. Jeremy and I went to a tea at Felicia Weatherby's home, and had a good talk with Agnes Stuart, who had been opposed to the merger, but seems to be coming around to the idea."

"I'm glad to hear that. You're helping out the diocese. In the next month or two, we'll probably be announcing the closure of the academy."

"We've gone ahead with fundraising, and should have at least two or three million in our coffers by the time of the announcement."

"If that's the good news, what else is on your agenda?"

"I saved the heavy lifting for last. And here I need your help, not just lifting, but—some snooping. Detective work."

"Sounds interesting."

"You know, Jeremy and I have been carrying a load of guilt for not helping Doug, and he came up with an idea. He said if Doug is reborn and wants to make a fresh start on life, why doesn't he volunteer to help repair and remodel homes, because he's good at construction. Jeremy found a non-profit called Redeemed Souls and Reborn Homes. They have people donate money and labor, and help out low-income families with essential home improvements."

"Sounds interesting. Where does the snooping and detective work come in?"

"When I leave today, you can do an internet search for this organization and their Peoria unit. I've looked at it, and it's minimal information. I'd appreciate it if you could use your connections, maybe contact the Episcopal church in Peoria, and the ministerial alliance, to see if this group is on the up and up. If it's a viable endeavor, it might be a good way for Doug to help others and in the process rehabilitate his life. Well, what do you think?"

"Let me say first that you and Jeremy should be commended for listening to your conscience, and letting your conscience lead you to a meaningful solution to a knotty problem. That's what I meant in one of our earlier sessions when I said you would know what to do and then do the right thing."

"So you'd be willing to serve as a sanctified snoop?"

"I should be able to do that."

Faith said, "Call me as soon as you find something out." After a quick goodbye, she left for the Foundation.

FAITH PULLED into the Foundation lot next to Maisie's shiny Buick. She knew that meant Maisie and Maria would have a good meal ready. She joined Jeremy in line for the cafeteria. He said, "You're just in time for Maisie's tasty meatloaf and mashed potatoes, and corn."

As other volunteers served them, Faith asked Maisie, "How do you do it, always preparing good meals?"

Maisie's laugh shook her ample midriff. "You don't know the balancing act. I have to be economical, and the state requires me to have a nourishing meal—you know, with vegetables—and find something that people will eat. I don't like to see my food thrown in the garbage. It's almost as difficult as a juggling performance."

"You're doing great."

Faith and Jeremy finished their meal, then went to his office.

She looked down at the floor, then raised her gaze to meet his eyes. "I might as well tell you, I looked up Redeemed Souls and Reborn Homes Peoria on the internet, and read their website. Not much information on it, mostly about volunteering and donating, and the possibility of getting your house fixed up by them. I just came from my father confessor, and asked him to nose around, see what he can find out about this organization."

"Yeah, Mom, I looked at their site, too, and it has potential. You're smart to check into the local situation, because most of these volunteer outfits are shoestring operations, and they seem to vary from place to place."

"I'll see what my priest comes up with. I'm still not sure how this would work, and I'm uncomfortable doing a behind-the-scenes plan with you, not letting the rest of the family in on the idea. Scott and I don't keep things from each other, and I assume it's the same with you and Melanie."

"Yeah, Mom, we don't have secrets."

"Well, if it doesn't work out, then maybe it's better we not upset them. If the Peoria branch looks promising, then we'll have to let the family in."

"You're right."

Jeremy's phone rang. "Jon, good to hear from you. What's on your mind? You want to talk to Mom? How did you know she was here?"

He handed the phone to Faith.

"Jon, do you have me bugged with a GPS?"

"Mother, I know you two are busy, and I am, too. I just wanted to let you know that our corporate people okayed a million dona-tion for the Foundation. Rachel and I talked it over, and we'll match that with another million. That should kick-start your fund for the new facility."

"Jon, that's terrific! Thanks a lot. I know you've got a busy day, so I'll let you go."

She handed the phone back to Jeremy and gave him the good news.

"Well, Mother, with Jon's two million, your million, Felicia's hundred thousand, and Bill's hundred thousand, that puts us at three point two million. I'm going to let Thomas Stinson know so that he can rev up the fundraising."

"That's good. Jon's call reminds me that we can't keep him out of the loop too long. As soon as I hear from Father Whitmore, I'll let you know. Right now my idea is twofold. First, anything we do for Doug has to be discussed at family council. Second, any good deed for Doug should be channeled through Bill. No direct contact from any of us to Doug."

"I was thinking about the same thing. In dealing with Doug, we have to keep our hands clean."

33

Tuesday evening Faith shared with Scott the good news of Jontronic's, and Jon and Rachel's, million dollar donations.

"Hey, babe, I'm thinking of buying the *Trib*. Would you handle the financing?"

"This is a one-shot deal for me. I'd much rather work with warm human beings like Amelia and Robby than with cold cash."

They had a light supper and a nice evening, but Scott asked, "Are you okay? Ever since the court hearing, you've been distracted."

"I've got a lot on my mind."

She went to bed early. At one o'clock she woke up, tiptoed across the bedroom to retrieve her journal, and took it to the lounger to write.

Trouble.
I've never kept things from Scott before.
He knows something is wrong.
I can't keep this up for long.
It's not fair to him.
And it's driving me crazy.

She went back to bed, tossing and turning.

Wednesday, Faith managed to take care of some paperwork and appointments at the hotel, yet couldn't keep Doug and Jeremy from crowding into her mental space.

Mid-afternoon Father Whitmore called. "I don't like to bother you at work, but you said to let you know as soon as I found out something about the Christian building organization."

"Good news?"

"Mostly good. It's an up and up group, with too few volunteers and too little money. Several ministers I talked to said these redeemed souls had helped out low-income parishioners with marginal housing. Fixed leaky roofs, installed insulation, that kind of work. And they need someone like Doug to oversee projects, to get the right materials and plan the remodeling."

"Father, that's good news, indeed."

"Can you take more good news?"

"Dish it out."

"The diocese has an active grapevine, and although it's not public yet, the finance committee of the diocese has made a decision that they can no longer subsidize the academy. Without the church subsidy, the academy can't operate."

"Well, the Foundation now has almost three and a half million in the building fund, so when the academy is formally closed, the Foundation should have enough money to talk seriously about a merger."

"Great. I won't keep you any longer. Congratulations!"

. . .

A FEW MINUTES later Jeremy called. "Mom, Felicia just phoned, said she'd like to bring Agnes Stuart by for a tour Tuesday. I wanted to make sure you'd be here."

"Sure, count me in. What do you have in mind?"

"No special deal. Just give her a tour, and you and I have clear ideas about how we would make use of the academy facilities that would expand the program of Mothers and Kids while continuing the academy's mission of educating and nurturing young women."

"Sounds like a plan."

"Good. Felicia and Agnes will come mid-morning, may eat lunch with us in the cafeteria."

"Let me throw in something here. Father Whitmore called a few minutes ago, and without going into details, he has checked out Redeemed Souls and Reborn Homes and gives us the green light for encouraging Doug to volunteer there. Think about this, because I don't want to keep it from Scott much longer."

"I'm in the same limbo with Melanie, and would like to come clean with her."

"Tuesday morning we'll be busy showing Agnes and Felicia around. Let's set aside some time in the afternoon to talk about Doug and the charity building group."

The next morning in the breakfast line, Faith greeted Maisie. "We have a guest this morning, Agnes Stuart, and she may stay for lunch."

"Should I prepare some cucumber sandwiches?"

They laughed.

Faith had one interview before play time at ten. She got out the cardboard theater box and had each child talk about their favorite cartoon character or another TV star. In the middle of Faith's video-taping of the kids, Felicia and Agnes arrived. They watched the rest of the kids act out their skits and then see themselves on television when Faith used a lap link to play it back.

Felicia and Agnes clapped.

Faith greeted the two ladies. "Welcome to the crazy world of the Mothers and Kids Foundation."

Agnes asked, "Was this a special performance?"

"No, we have play time every day, and always get the kids involved."

Agnes said, "That helps them develop verbal skills."

"We hope so. And it's fun, not an assignment."

Jeremy heard the women talking and came out of his office. "Glad you could come by. This is our general lounge and meeting area."

He led them through the dining room and into the cafeteria. When they entered the kitchen, Maisie shouted, "Agnes, how are you? Can you stay for lunch? By popular demand, we're having tube steaks and baked beans."

"Tube steaks?"

"Yeah, hot dogs. That's one entrée everyone eats, kids and adults."

Agnes hugged Maisie. "So this is where you've been hiding."

"Yeah, since my husband died, I didn't like cooking for one. I get a lot more satisfaction preparing a large meal."

Jeremy and Faith took Agnes and Felicia up the back stairs, and they looked into several of the residents' rooms. One resident had some papers, and a book spread across her bed next to a sleeping little girl. Agnes asked, "Can we come in?"

"Kinda messy, but yeah."

"I'm Agnes."

"My name's Louann."

"What are you reading?"

"A novel, *The Red Badge of Courage*. It's for an online literature course, and requires us to write."

"How did you happen to take an online course?"

"Well, Amelia took this course and recommended it. She read this novel and liked it. I've just started it. I didn't like history in high school, but this book makes history come alive. Have you read it?"

"To be honest, I read it as a sophomore in high school because it was required, and I didn't care for it. Later, in college, when I understood more about war, I read it and liked it."

"I hope to be able to get a college degree."

"If you want it and you're able to work for it, you'll get there."

They went back to the lounge, where Leonard was bouncing a large ball. It ricocheted off his shoe, and the ball rolled to Agnes. She tossed it back to him.

Leonard's eyes sparkled. "Will you play catch with me?"

They threw the ball back and forth a few times before Jeremy rescued her.

He led the women into his office.

Agnes said, "That young woman doing the online course should have a desk."

Jeremy replied, "I agree. Not just a desk, maybe a library or reading room. We could use the classroom space. I think mother told you we'd like to offer mini-courses and training sessions if we can get a larger facility."

Agnes screwed up her face and sighed. "Well, it's not public yet, but the church can't support the academy financially so that it will close at the end of the academic year. Seeing what you've done here with just the bare essentials, I can see how much more you could do with the amenities of the academy. Amelia gave a glowing recommendation of this foundation, and I'm willing to support bringing it together with the academy."

Felicia smiled. "Well, Agnes, we have an invitation for lunch, so let's get in line."

Faith and Jeremy led the way to the front of the line. Maisie served Agnes first, giving her a hot dog on a bun and a dipper of baked beans. Then she reached behind her and grabbed a quarter of a hot dog bun that had two slices of cucumber and mayonnaise on it. "In honor of our guest."

"Maisie, you haven't lost your sense of humor."

"Well, I have a cucumber sandwich for each of the rest of your party."

They enjoyed lunch. Agnes had to go back to the kitchen to find out how Maisie had spiced up the canned baked beans to give them a tangy flavor.

Agnes thanked Faith and Jeremy for the tour. "Hey, it was worth it to see my old friend Maisie. And she's still the same old clown."

Felicia winked at Faith. "We'll be in touch with you."

34

Jeremy and Faith went to his office to relax after the tour with the Winnetka guests.

Faith winked at Jeremy. He asked, "What?"

Faith smiled. "When we left Felicia's house after high tea, she winked at me, signaling that our meeting with Agnes went well. A few minutes ago she gave me another wink, which means Agnes agrees to the merger."

"I must say, Amelia is the girl that keeps on giving. At the tea, she chimed in with a strong recommendation for the loving care at Mothers and Kids. And a little while ago upstairs, Louann gave Amelia credit for persuading her to take an online course. That proves we don't just talk about education; we actively facilitate it."

"You're right, Jeremy, although we've got a lot of hard work ahead of us, today we should be glad that the road is clear for the Foundation to merge with the academy."

"What comes next?"

"The fundraising. Why don't you push Thomas Stinson's buttons, and see if he can get past five million in the next month or two? That would put us halfway to the ten million mark."

"Good idea. I'll call him later this afternoon."

"Jeremy, we have some other unfinished business, something as difficult as it is delicate. I'm open to your idea of recommending the Christian building program to Doug. It makes sense for him to rehabilitate himself while he rehabilitates houses. I like the title of that group, Redeemed Souls and Reborn Homes. And well, I like what you proposed, yet I don't know how and when the message can be passed on to Doug."

"You don't think it's impossible?"

"Let me think out loud, telling you how I see the situation. First and foremost, our extended family has to know about this and agree with it. And we've all spent so much time and energy keeping Doug outside the family; we don't want to do anything that would bring him inside the circle. One way of handling this is to make sure, whatever we do, that everything is channeled through Bill's law firm, and no personal names are mentioned."

"Good thinking, Mom, we don't want to upset our family, and using Bill as a go-between would give us insulation, protection."

"How about this? Why don't we both try to draft a statement between now and Tuesday, and we can look them over next week?"

"I'm not very good at writing. I'll do my best."

FAITH HAD TROUBLE DRIVING HOME, thinking about how to word her draft to Doug.

Friday at work she had difficulty concentrating on business.

That evening Scott asked, "Are you still bent out of shape over the court hassles?"

"Oh, with that, and the planning for the merger of the Foundation, I'm juggling a lot. Sorry I'm such bad company. Tomorrow after you get home from the newspaper, why don't we go to the Art Institute? Seeing the impressionists always lifts my spirits."

Saturday morning Faith got up early when Scott left for the paper. When he went out the door, she booted her computer and forced herself to type out a rough draft of the letter to Doug. She didn't like it, and over the new few hours rewrote it again and again.

Finally, she emailed the file to her account at the hotel and got dressed.

Scott got home in time for a quick sandwich, and they left for the Art Institute. As they viewed more and more of the French artists' masterpieces, Faith's lips curled upward in a smile.

Scott gave her a quick kiss. "That's the girl I love."

They finished the afternoon with a cup of tea in the snack shop and went from there to Boccaccio's for dinner.

SUNDAY MORNING FAITH attended services at Church of the Redeemer. On the way out of church she asked Father Whitmore for a morning appointment Tuesday, which he agreed to.

Faith wished the clan was getting together Sunday, but both the Goodmans and the Rockwells had other plans. She and Scott enjoyed a lazy morning and then a two-hour walk along the lakeshore in the afternoon. She felt recharged after Saturday's session with the impressionists, Sunday morning's church services, and a refreshing stroll Sunday afternoon.

Monday morning she arrived at the hotel early, and took care of all urgent emails, before turning to her letter for Doug. She fine-tuned it and concluded it was ready for showing to Jeremy Tuesday afternoon.

Mid-morning, she took a call from Bill Ludwig.

"Bill, I know this isn't a social call—what's up?"

"This morning I got a strange letter from Parinello's lawyer, together with a letter from Parinello."

"You've read them?"

"Yes. The good news is that Parinello and Garibaldi are smart enough not to appeal the judgment on the restraining order violation."

"And there's bad news?"

"Well, strange. Garibaldi speaks for Parinello, regretting the past 'misunderstandings,' and wanting to avoid any future problems. Then he comes to the point. They know they lost in court, so they make a special appeal to have mercy on an old man and let him meet with his sons."

"What's in Doug's letter?"

"I'll fax it to you so you can see for yourself. As Scott would put it, Doug's still in the 'pity me' phase of denial."

"What do they expect?"

"What they've asked for all along, a meeting with the twins."

"That's not going to happen. Well, do they mention any time-line of when they expect this meeting to take place, or do they have any other legal strategies?"

"They know they've exhausted all the legal angles. In football and law practice, this is called a Hail Mary pass. When all else fails, throw yourself on the mercy of the court or the generosity of your opponent. And no, they didn't mention when they expect an answer."

"Bill, I've already told you what I think. Still, I have to run this by the guys. Fax me both of the letters. Maybe I can pull the family together this weekend, and get back to you next week."

"No hurry."

The fax machine began printing out the letters. Faith told her secretary to hold all but urgent calls. Faith ignored the lawyer's letter, grabbed and read Doug's.

Faith,

I said it before, and I'll say it again. I'm sorry for all the trouble I caused you in the past. And I apologize for bothering you recently. I promise not to trouble you any more with phone calls or flowers or hanging around your place.

I asked my lawyer if there was any way I could contact you, and he said the only thing I could do is have him send this letter on to you. So that's what I'm doing.

You know my situation, my parents are long gone, and I'm separated from all the family I was close to. I'm old and getting older, and all by myself.

A year ago, when I handed over the medical papers and saw that I had twin sons, I was so surprised I didn't know what to say. And they take after me, look like I did at that age. Ever since then, I can't stop thinking about them and wanting to get together with them.

No, the way I've acted, like the judge said, I'm not a model parent. No, I don't deserve another chance. But since I got religion, I learned that it's never too late for forgiveness and starting over. That's what I'm asking for, something I don't deserve, the chance to start over.

If there's any way for me to meet my sons, let my lawyer know what I can do to make that happen.

Thank you,

Doug Parinello

FAITH SAT with her hands over her closed eyes, digesting Doug's letter.

She called up the draft of her letter to Doug on the computer. Then she re-read Doug's letter to her.

She picked up the phone, put it back down, and reread Doug's letter. Once more she picked up the phone and dialed Jeremy.

"Hi, Mom."

"Morning, Jeremy. Do you have a few minutes?"

"Sure. Something important? About your draft?"

"Indirectly. Ludwig got a letter from Garibaldi and a letter from Doug. The bottom line is an apologetic and polite appeal to our mercy, and another request to get back together with his sons."

"What do you think of it?"

"Two immediate reactions. First, our family would never allow him into our circle. Second, this might be an opening for your proposal to have him renew his life while renewing houses."

"I see what you mean. Well, would you fax me the letter?"

"This caught me by surprise, and I had to think about it a few minutes even before calling you. If I send it to you, then I think it also has to go to Jon. Honestly, I don't know whether to use a hot or cold metaphor. We're skating on thin ice or playing with fire. If we don't handle this carefully, it will upset our happy family."

"If you don't want to send the fax to me, okay."

"I think you're right, but I'll send it simultaneously to you and Jon. Maybe that's the fair way to do it. You two guys can let in your wives, and I'll have to tell Scott about it when he comes home tonight."

"That seems to be a good way to update everybody."

"What do you say, Jeremy, can you revise your draft to take into account Doug's appeal?"

"I'll do my best."

All day Faith switched between hotel business and rewriting the draft to Doug.

LATE AFTERNOON, Faith called Scott. "Bring a pizza home with you."

"Oh-oh. Sounds like you have something serious to talk over."

"Bill forwarded letters from Garibaldi and Doug, asking us again to let a lonely old man get together with his sons."

"Almost brings tears to my eyes."

"I didn't want to interrupt your day. You can read the letters when you come home. Not a very good appetizer for pizza."

When Scott arrived at the condo, he let Faith open the pizza box, and quickly read Doug's letter. "The same narcissistic con man."

"Bill called it the Hail Mary pass."

Scott belted out a bitter laugh. "But we don't have to play ball with him."

"I faxed the letters to Jeremy and Jon. This probably calls for yet another family council. This time, though, you have to be present. So after you do your schtick with the kids, maybe they can watch cartoons while the adults talk."

"Sounds like a plan."

.   .   .

TUESDAY MORNING FAITH went to see Father Whitmore and knocked on his door even before visiting her two favorite saints.

"Holy moly. This must be urgent because you detoured around Mary and Harriet."

Faith chuckled. "I'm on a tight schedule this morning, so I gave my two saints a wireless prayer."

"What's on your mind?"

"I should tell you first that, thanks to you and Felicia, and now with the support of Agnes, we seem to be proceeding on a path to the merger of the Foundation and the academy. Agnes came with Felicia to the Foundation and was impressed with what we're doing there."

"Glad to hear that. What other breaking news do you have?"

"Yesterday Bill Ludwig received faxed letters from Doug and his lawyer. Because they've exhausted all legal possibilities, they appeal to our sense of mercy to let a lonely old man see his sons."

"You haven't changed your mind on that, have you?"

"No, but it's still a dicey situation with the family. Jeremy and I agreed to draft a letter to Doug about working out his problems through the Redeemed Souls and Reborn Homes project. You're the only other one who knows about this angle. Yesterday I sent Doug's letter on to Jon and showed it to Scott last night. But only you, Jeremy, and I are privy to the proposal for Doug to volunteer rehabbing houses."

"A tough situation. How are you going to deal with it?"

"When I leave here, I go to the Foundation. Jeremy and I will compare drafts of a reply to Doug's request, and try to fold in the rehab option. Sunday we have a family conference, and want to be ready with a tentative response to Doug."

"I wish you the best."

"Father, I've heard that no good deed goes unpunished. Is it also true that no good conscience goes unpenalized?"

"Believe me, Faith, if you follow what you know is best, in the end, it will come out alright."

She was in such a hurry she said farewells without the usual prayer.

GOING DIRECTLY from Church of Redeemer to the Foundation, she thought over her letter to Doug, wondering what Jeremy had penned, and hoping they could put together a draft that would satisfy the family.

She arrived at the Foundation in time to eat lunch with Jeremy, but only picked at her food. They entered Jeremy's office and exchanged copies of their letters. The two drafts mentioned about the same information, in a slightly different order. As they spliced the two accounts together, Jeremy sat at his computer and composed a hybrid version.

Mr. Parinello,

Your recent letter proposes the same meeting with the twins that was requested in the court filing for visitation. Our response to this proposal remains the same. We have formed a tight family bond, and do not want to make changes in that bond.

It is challenging to move beyond the gap of three decades. We have been able to do that with our family, and, again, urge you to renew the bond with your family units. We have prayed for you in the past and will continue to do so in the future.

You write about your religious change and your desire to become a better person. It is good to hear this, and we offer a suggestion that may help you improve your situation and develop a new friendship group.

We saw on the internet an organization called Redeemed Souls and Reborn Houses. They have a branch in Peoria. These people are Christians dedicated to helping needy people repair and remodel living quarters. With your experience in construction, you could provide valuable assistance. The reward for such volunteer work is not financial, but satisfaction in helping others less fortunate. Faith and charity are beyond payment; they are priceless. We hope this suggestion is helpful.

> *Good luck,*
> *Faith*

JEREMY PRINTED out copies of the letter. "I don't know, Mom, do you think the rest of the family will agree with this?"

"I'm not sure. I talked this over with my father-confessor, and he says if you follow your conscience and do what you think is right, things will turn out okay. We have to move slowly, carefully. Sunday I'll ask the others to respond to Doug's letter. Then I think we have to feel our way through their thoughts and feelings. That would be the point where you could bring up the double rehabilitation of Doug and homes. All we can do is our best and hope for the best."

35

F aith left the Foundation early Tuesday afternoon, too caught up in the letter to Doug to do any interviewing of residents.

That evening she was still distracted, and Scott noticed it. "Hey, dear, are you uptight about the family confab on Sunday?"

"I'm always a little tense, not knowing how things will go."

"After all the hot button issues we've tangled with, this is negotiation-light."

Faith laughed. "I hope you're right."

WEDNESDAY FAITH MADE it to the hotel early so she could read, for the umpteenth time, the letter she and Jeremy had written to Doug. She asked herself how the rest of the family would comment on it.

What had she left out? What would they want to add? How would they want to modify it?

A little after nine Jeremy called.

"How's my favorite Mom?"

"Fine, thanks. I was poring over our letter, but can't see any way of improving it."

"Oh, the letter will be fine. I was calling with kind of a surprise. Maisie talked to me as soon as I arrived, and asked to have a meeting with you and me tomorrow morning after breakfast."

"About what?"

"She said she had several things she wanted to mention, and preferred to discuss it with the two of us."

"That's strange."

"She seemed serious. I hope it doesn't mean she's thinking of quitting on us. She keeps the kitchen humming."

"Well, Jeremy, thanks for letting me know."

"Let's plan to do some brainstorming tomorrow, especially on fundraising. I've been in touch with Thomas Stinson, and it would be good to fine-tune our approach.

THURSDAY MORNING FAITH arrived at the Foundation hungry for breakfast, but even more eager to learn what Maisie wanted to talk about.

As Faith was getting her breakfast, Maisie walked up between two moms who were servers. "Faith, glad you're here. I know how busy you and Jeremy are, but I want to talk to you."

"Sure, Maisie, I'll wait in Jeremy's office."

Faith had her eggs, toast, and coffee, and was leaving the kitchen when Maisie hurried over to her. She whispered, "Sit with Louann; she's in line now."

Faith waited outside the kitchen door for Louann and her little girl. "Could I sit with you, Louann?"

"Sure."

"Your little girl's name is Lorraine?"

"Yes."

"Lorraine, could I eat breakfast with you?"

"Uh-huh."

They sat down and began eating. Faith said, "You were reading *Red Badge of Courage*. Did you like it?"

"Yes. It's the best novel I ever read. Well, I haven't read that many. But now, the problem is writing a report on it. I've never written a report like that before, and don't know how to begin."

"Didn't the instructor have any suggestions?"

"Sure—'Tell the story in your own words.' 'Who is the main character, what problems does this character face, and how does the character resolve the problem.' But I'm still stuck. I was talking to Maisie, and she said maybe you could help me or find someone to help me." Louann stopped eating, took a handkerchief out of her purse and wiped her eyes. "I was excited taking this course, but now I don't know if I can finish it."

"You can. I'm sure you can. I'll talk to Maisie, and we'll see about getting some help for you. I've got to go to a meeting now, but I'll try to get back to you today."

Faith went to Jeremy's office. He showed up a few minutes later.

"Mom, I don't know what Maisie wants; she wouldn't tell me."

"I think part of it is Louann and her online course. Maisie asked me to sit next to Louann at breakfast, and Louann said she's having trouble writing her first book report. I think Maisie has an idea how to get help for her."

Maisie knocked on the door, then walked in. "I know how busy you two are, so I wanted to wait until I could talk to you together, and not waste your time. I haven't told you what I did before retiring. I was a superintendent of a school and swore I would never mess with administrative matters again. I love to cook, and just wanted to retreat into the kitchen.

"But something came up, and I can't let it go. Yesterday I saw Louann crying, and we had a long talk. She feels she's messed up her life, and taking a college course was her first step to straightening herself out. The problem is, she's never written a report before, and she's got writer's block, and is afraid she'll flunk the course. I could help her, but the one who can get her on track is Agnes. She has a degree in English and taught literature in high school. So—excuse me—but I called Agnes to see if she would help Louann. Agnes remembered meeting her and talking about the novel she read. And she'd be tickled to help Louann. I didn't mean to go over your head, but felt it was the right thing to do."

Faith and Jeremy had been listening carefully. Faith nodded to Jeremy, who spoke up. "Maisie, that was what you should have done. I'll give Agnes a call and see when she can come to tutor Louann."

"Well, while I'm sticking my neck out, you can chop it off or tell me to pull it back in my shell. I've talked to Agnes. She told me the backstory of the merger. In the new place, you'll have classrooms, and Agnes says you plan to have volunteers give mini-courses to the residents. I think Agnes would make an excellent recruiter and coordinator of volunteers."

Faith smiled. "Well, I bet you made a good school superintendent, with that kind of foresight."

"I'm glad you didn't tell me to get back in the kitchen and tend to cooking."

Jeremy said, "If that's what you're cooking, bring it on."

Maisie took a deep breath. "Well, one more thing before I go back to KP. Agnes and I discussed your financial strategy, the two-pronged approach. I've had to deal with budgets, and think that's a smart approach. Frankly, the reason Canterbury Academy is going under is that they didn't plan for operating expenses. Last week I talked to my financial adviser, and I have some investments that I don't depend on for living expenses. I've been considering donating that money to various charities and got to thinking about all the good work you do at the Foundation. I decided to commit to your 'sustaining contribution" fund, fifty thousand for five years."

Faith and Jeremy gasped. He said, "That's very generous of you."

Maisie laughed. "One more thing. Maria and I get along well. She does most of the cooking, while I do the meal planning, and take care of the state requirements of a log of the calories and balanced diet. So far the state hasn't complained too much, because you're providing a valuable service they don't have to pay for. And I had some home economics classes in college, which gives me some qualification as a dietitian. But once you move into the academy, and have a fancy setup, probably the state is going to ask for a part-time or full-time nutritionist. I figure my fifty thousand would help pay for a pro. Right now my legs are pretty good, but my trick knee may make me leave the kitchen, and you might have to hire someone, even before you merge with the academy.

"Well, that's the end of my story. Now you see why I wanted to lay all this out to the two of you."

After they gave profuse thanks to Maisie, she excused herself to get back to her cheesy mashed potatoes.

Faith joked, "The Bible talks about manna from heaven, but we receive money from the kitchen."

"We'll take anything we can get. Maisie raised the issue of funding, so here's an update from Thomas Stinson. He hasn't been able to snag any million-dollar donations but did get promises for several commitments in the hundred thousand range. That puts us above three point five million in endowments. He found it easier to get sustaining contributions at fifty thousand a pop. He has five of those lined up, so five more, and we should be comfortable with a half million a year in operating expense funds, in addition to income from the academy's endowment."

Faith nodded. "Yes, the heavy hitters may take a little more time. He can keep making the rounds for big endowment donations while beating the bushes for sustaining contributions. I know you're going to be talking to Agnes, and she'll probably be coming to help Louann. When the time is right, either you or Thomas Stinson might approach her to do some fundraising among her social circle. I understand she helped finance the academy, even though she considered it underfunded and doomed. Agnes seems to think our program deserves support."

Jeremy asked Faith to wait while he called Agnes, who readily agreed to help Louann. Faith went to Louann's room and knocked.

Lorraine said, "Come in."

"Thank you, Lorraine. Can I talk to Mommy?"

"Yeah, I guess so."

"Louann, Agnes would be delighted to help you think through your paper. She'll call, and the two of you can set up a time."

Louann shut her eyes tight, tears starting to trickle down her cheeks, and gave Faith a bear hug.

Lorraine said, "I like hugs, too."

Faith hugged the tyke and was rewarded with a super smile.

36

The rest of Tuesday, Faith kept busy with the day to day activities of the Foundation, while she thought ahead to the weekend family gathering. And she had on her mind Louann, Agnes, and the discussion of fundraising with Jeremy.

When Scott came home that evening, he joked, "Faith, are you here or somewhere else? I'll be glad when we pass through the barrier of Sunday."

"Sorry, I'm just preoccupied."

WEDNESDAY FAITH HAD hotel business to keep her from over-thinking about the letter.

Thursday morning when Faith arrived at the Foundation, she was not too surprised to see Louann and Lorraine waiting for her.

Lorraine asked, "C'n we have breakfas' with you?"

"Of course, Lorraine."

Louann said, "I'm nervous because Agnes is coming in this morning to help me with my writing."

Faith laughed. "She won't bite. As a teacher, she's worked with lots of students. You'll do fine."

They chatted while eating. When they finished, Louann said, "Thanks for eating with us. You helped me get over the jitters."

Faith had an early interview, then came back to the lounge to schmooze with residents.

About ten o'clock Agnes walked in, and Faith greeted her. "We're just getting ready for playtime. I ate with Louann this morning. She's looking forward to having you help her."

"I'm a little rusty, but writing and editing are like riding a bicycle. Once you've done it, you never forget how."

"Agnes, I'll walk with you to Louann's room. Maybe Lorraine will join me for play time. That way you can concentrate on the report."

As they went to Louann's room, they chatted about Maisie and her fantastic career, ending up in the Foundation as a cook.

At Luann's door, Faith knocked. Lorraine opened the door. Faith said, "Lorraine, it's play time. Shall we go down and join the other kids?"

"Is Mommy coming?"

"She needs to talk to Agnes. Do you like to sing?"

"Yeah."

"What's your favorite song?"

"Um ... small world."

"It's a small world, after all?"

"Yeah!"

"Well, let's go down and sing it with the others. Everyone gets to pick a song and sing it."

"C'n I go, Mommy?"

"Sure. I'll come down later."

Faith held Lorraine's hand as they went to the lounge. Faith rounded up the kids and explained the singalong. Leonard tried to push his way to the front of the line, but Faith told him, "Today Lorraine is first."

Faith told the kids, "We'll sing everyone's favorite. If you don't know the words, just hum the tune. You're not hummingbirds, but you can be hummingkids."

She had her video camera and shot footage of each child. The kids knew what to expect. As soon as they finished singing, they sat in front of the television, waiting for the playback. The hoops and hollers were so loud that Jeremy came out to see the excitement.

Amid the excitement, Agnes and Louann entered the lounge. Lorraine ran to her mother. "Mommy, we *sang*! Miss Faith, play it again."

The kids echoed, "Play it again."

Faith started the video again, to the delighted screams of the children.

Agnes told Faith, "I think you're the pied piper of Mothers and Kids."

"It's fun. I never had so much pleasure, even when I was their age. The children recharge my batteries."

"You get a kick out of playing with youngsters. I just had a good time working with Louann."

"It went well?"

"Yes. Louann's very bright, just scared. I didn't tell her, but brought along a mini recorder, and taped what she told me about the novel, the characters, the plot, and how the story ended. I let her borrow the recorder, so she can jot down what she said as the basis for her paper. Hey, I'm an old hand at this, and I never write papers for students. I use the Socratic method, ask the leading questions, and the students speak 'in their own words' what they will write."

"Clever. Louann must be happy."

Louann brought Lorraine over to Agnes and Faith and said, "Agnes got me on the right track. Now I'm sure I can write the paper. She says she can come back next Tuesday, and we'll go over what I write down."

Faith hugged Louann. "Good girl! I knew you could do it."

Lorraine pulled at Faith's dress. "I like hugs, too."

Faith leaned over and hugged Lorraine, as Louann embraced Agnes, saying, "I can't thank you enough."

Jeremy approached the ladies. "What is this, a lovefest?"

Agnes said, "Yes, and the celebration isn't over. I want to get in line for lunch, and see what amazing Maisie has for us."

They filed into the kitchen, where Agnes ran to Maisie. "I'm glad you told me about Louann. She's bright, just needed some direction."

"I told Jeremy and Faith you'd be able to help Louann."

Agnes said, "We're holding up the line. What's for lunch?"

"I deliberately made a double batch of cheesy potatoes Tuesday, and let them set up in the fridge. Today we're having a kind of potato pancake, with hamburger gravy."

Agnes leaned back as if fainting. "I just died and went to heaven. Food like my mother made."

They held out their plates for the servers to fill them and carried them to the dining room.

Agnes said, "With food like this, you could have successful fundraising dinners."

Faith joked, "Even without cucumber sandwiches?"

Agnes laughed. "My cucumber sandwiches are better than her hot dog bun versions."

After lunch, Faith, Jeremy, and Agnes walked to his office.

Agnes said, "I think you heard me say I'm coming back Tuesday to look over Louann's paper. And I'd be glad to continue helping her."

Jeremy nodded. "You can see we're hampered here, urging residents to take online courses, but we need a plan for helping the moms get ahead with their education. We would never try to become a for-credit school, but the gals need help with reading and writing, and other skills that would make them more employable and self-supporting. What would you recommend?"

"Let me say first that you have the most important ingredient for a successful learning program. You have a harmonious setting with a trusting relationship. Given that, and a little motivation from the residents—you know, like Louann—the rest is simple and straightforward. We could recruit some volunteers to give brush-up exercises on writing, speaking, job interviews."

Faith added, "I don't want to interrupt such a great set of ideas, but that's just what we've been looking for, and you're just the kind of dedicated and qualified person who could guide such a program."

"You have a very heady atmosphere here. I'm drunk with enthusiasm, and you can count me in. It's funny; I had a different speech prepared today. What I wanted to tell you is that I'd help with fundraising. It's not nice to brag, but I raised a lot of money for the academy. Frankly, I was an unwilling co-conspirator. The only reason I did it is that a number of my friends had daughters in the academy, and they leaned on me. I kept telling them we were pouring water into a leaky bucket, and we couldn't ever fill the bucket. I'm impressed with your two-pronged approach to fundraising, which will guarantee five years of operating money. At the end of five years, if you're successful, the money will pour in."

She paused to catch her breath. "You know me; I get right to the point. I can tell Thomas Stinson that I'll work on the sustaining contributions, and he can focus on endowment lump sums."

Faith and Jeremy exchanged glances. Jeremy turned to Agnes. "You are a double dipping dynamo, giving us a strategy for an educational component, and providing a crucial boost to our funding drive."

Agnes excused herself to beat the afternoon rush.

Jeremy shooed Faith out of the office so she could get an early start home.

Faith couldn't wait for Scott to get home so she could tell him the good news about Louann's tutoring and the well-thought-out proposals of Agnes.

When Scott entered the condo, he pretended to be a sailor, with his hand shading his eyes and scanning the horizon. He focused his eyes on Faith's face. "Land-ho, safe haven ahead."

"Ha-ha. You said I should never play poker because I can't conceal my feelings. It was a red-letter day, with Agnes and Louann having a successful tutoring session. On top of that, Agnes has a blueprint for an educational program for the academy. The frosting on the cake is that she'll work hard for funding the operational expenses."

She gave him the details of the day with Agnes.

Scott bowed to Faith. "Congratulations on a wonderful day. A glass of wine to celebrate?"

"I don't need alcohol. I'm on an adrenalin rush with all this good news."

"Okay, I don't usually drink alone, but will tipple for two of us. It's good to see you out of the doldrums."

FRIDAY FAITH HAD a ho-hum day at the hotel and a lovely evening with Scott.

Saturday morning, as soon as Scott left for the office, Faith sat at her computer, rereading the letter to Doug. She felt so antsy; she had to keep busy. Faith knew the condo was clean, almost spotless, but she used her nervous energy to re-clean the place, even emptying leftovers and shriveled fruit from the fridge. Then she hit the bathrooms with tile and toilet cleaner.

As soon as Scott opened the condo door, he lifted his head and sniffed. "Has Miss Neatnik been at it again?"

"I had to keep busy."

"I've got a better idea. After lunch, let's take a long walk on the beach. Then it's your choice for dinner. How about Happi sushi?"

"Yes, and let's taxi over, so we don't have to worry about drinking too much and driving."

They had a lovely sushi dinner, came home and shared a love dessert in bed.

37

Sunday morning Faith went to church. In the greeting line after church, Faith said, "Pray for me, Father."

He asked, "Tuesday morning?"

She said, "I'll see how today goes, and email you."

LATER IN THE MORNING, Scott and Faith were driving out to Oak Park. Faith asked, "Scott why in the world did you bring gunny sacks?"

"You'll see."

As usual, their arrival at Jeremy's place marked the eruption of excitement by the kids.

"Grandpa, what are those things?"

"Gunny sacks."

"What's a gunny sack?"

"They're used to hold things like potatoes or coffee beans."

"Why did you bring them?"

"You'll see."

After lunch, Scott took the kids to a nearby park for fun and games.

Faith announced to the two couples, "I know what's on your mind, but let's hold off talking about the letter until Scott returns. I want him to hear what you have to say, and be a part of the discussion. Jeremy, why don't you tell us about the remarkable progress with Mothers and Kids."

Jeremy brought them up to date on success stories like Amelia and Louann, the educational plans Agnes proposed, and the advance of the fundraising.

Faith commented, "Jeremy and I were thinking out loud about the wonderful accomplishments of the Foundation, going from a part-time operation in a decrepit Montgomery Ward store, to a thriving residential program, and the prospect of a move to an upscale facility."

They talked about the Foundation until Scott brought the children home. They were excited about their gunny sack races.

Faith laughed. "So that's what you were up to."

"Give me a couple of gunny sacks, and I can keep kids happy for a long time."

After refreshments, they installed the kids in front of cartoons.

FAITH ASKED the family to form a prayer circle before discussing Doug's letter. Each member asked for divine guidance in doing the right thing.

Faith announced, "We've all seen the two letters sent to Bill Ludwig, so I don't need to summarize them. Let's hear what you all have to say."

After an awkward silence, Jon spoke first. "It's the same bull. . . baloney we've heard all along—poor me, pity me, I made a mess of my life, so feel sorry for me and be nice to me."

Melanie added, "I only have to say what I've said before. My main concern is for my children; we don't want Parinello in the family. So I'm against having the twins meet him because that would open the door to our family. And the children."

Jeremy sighed. "Remember the depositions Jon and I wrote. We said then, and can repeat here, that we don't want a meeting with him.'

Rachel nodded. "Melanie spoke for the children, and I second her view: we want to protect our kids, and that means keeping Parinello away from him. I went along with Jeremy that we can pray for him. We pray for everyone. Excluding him from our family doesn't mean excluding him from our prayers."

Faith looked toward Scott.

"Okay, I'll weigh in, and start by saying that I'm the 'Grandpa' who has a vested interest in the grandchildren. I didn't have children of my own and feel blessed to be included in the family and share the love of these wonderful kids. Even if I have a vested interest, I go along with Melanie and Rachel that it's important to protect these treasures."

Jon said, "I don't know what we're discussing. It's unanimous that no meeting will take place. Is that what we need to tell Doug? I mean, tell Bill to pass on to Doug."

Scott turned to Faith. "Bill didn't say we had to even answer Doug's letter, did he?"

"No, this is not a hearing or a formal court ruling. We aren't required to reply."

"That's our option."

Jon asked, "What does Bill think?"

"He leaves it up to us. The only thing he strongly advises is that any response goes through him, to Doug's lawyer. All communication should be lawyer to lawyer."

Scott rubbed his chin. "I seem to remember, when we discussed the visitation ruling, that Doug was prevented from approaching or contacting any of the family. You know, the extension of the restraining order. On the other hand, Jeremy mentioned that nothing was preventing us from contacting Doug." Scott turned to Jeremy. "Are you for contacting Doug?"

Jeremy squirmed in his seat. "No. I think we've all agreed on two things. One, no meeting of Jon and me with Doug. Two, Bill

Ludwig handles any response. As Mom said, and as Bill recommended, any reply is lawyer to lawyer."

Jon almost jumped out of his chair. "What in the world would you want to say to this perp who caused us so much grief?"

Jeremy agreed. "He certainly is a disaster, self-inflicted, and doesn't deserve any pity. He has sinned against God and sinned against his fellow man. But in my ministry, I have dealt with many sinners, and feel a Christian duty to help every sinner I can. Parinello claims he found religion. We can doubt that sincerity, the authenticity of that religious change. But we can also try to find a way to help him become a better person."

Scott nodded. "Yes, I thought you might have some notion of how to save this lost soul. Listen, I know and recite the Lord's prayer, about asking forgiveness for our sins, as we forgive the sins of others. But I don't want to take responsibility for cleaning up Doug's mess."

Jon chipped in. "I'm less charitable. Isn't it in the Bible that you reap what you sow? He's spent his entire life sowing lies and deception, so let him reap the loneliness of old age."

Jeremy looked down at the floor. "I understand how you feel about him, Jon. As you put it, he is reaping what he sowed. His loneliness is self-imposed. He is his own worst enemy, and he is punishing himself. So there's no need for anyone else to penalize him."

Jon softened his tone. "I didn't mean to be vicious. I didn't mean we should try to punish him. But his personal crisis shouldn't hurt us. It shouldn't hurt the children."

Scott looked to Faith. "I think we've aired our viewpoints. Isn't this where you mention the consensus and the remaining issues?"

Faith closed her eyes for a moment. "Let me try. It's easiest to point out what we all agree on. First, no meeting of the twins with Doug. Second, no direct contact of Doug with the family, especially the children. Third, any response to the letter goes through Bill Ludwig."

She paused. "The remaining issue is whether a reply is given to

Bill Ludwig to forward to Doug's lawyer. And if there is a reply, what that would be."

Scott faced Jeremy. "Let's cut to the chase. From the first time we had to litigate with Doug, you were more for a care-for-the-sinner approach, and you've held out for the possibility of indirectly praying for Doug or helping him. I think you have a pastoral message for Doug, so let's hear it."

All eyes focused on Jeremy.

"You're right, Scott. I've thought and prayed about this for quite a while. Here's what I came up with. I began where all of you began, three main considerations: no meeting with Doug, protect the children, and everything goes through Ludwig. Then I asked myself, how we could help Doug if he has had a religious change. If he has—"

Jon interrupted. "We heard that born again story before when we negotiated for the medical records. And Jeremy, he used your One Way materials to justify his ego trip and manipulated my Digirel program to reinforce his selfish attitudes. So no, I don't buy his religious change claim."

Jeremy nodded. "I can't argue with that. Honestly, I don't know what's in his heart. I leave that to the powers above. But here's what we can do. Well, we already told him if he values family bonds, then he should mend fences and get on good terms with his families."

He paused. "Then there's one new idea I want to try out on you. He sold his business, and he's lonely. What he does well is construction work. I asked around to my minister friends, and they told me about a volunteer organization, Redeemed Souls and Reborn Houses. They help low-income people build, remodel, and update houses. So he could rehabilitate his personal life while giving new life to houses. The plus of this idea is it's something he can do for himself. I checked, and there's a branch of this home restoration organization in Peoria. Well, what do you think of this possibility?"

Jeremy looked around the room.

Faith broke the silence. "What do you think of this idea?"

Jon asked, "Do you mean to give him this suggestion, and let him run with it? We don't have to be involved?"

"That's right. He can follow up or not. But this way, we've given him a good avenue for creating a new friendship circle while acting on his Christian charity."

Rachel shrugged. "I don't see any harm in it. Melanie and I have been Mama-bear protectors, and so long as the children are safe, it's okay. Right, Melanie?"

"Sure, his first three points give us plenty of protection."

Scott had a half-smile, half-smirk on his face, winked at Faith and turned toward Jeremy. "Well, Mr. One Way, I doubt you would make such a proposal if you didn't have a printout of your idea to make the point."

"Yes, Mr. investigative reporter, your news antenna is excellent. I have some one-pagers I can let you read and comment on." He walked across the room and picked up a manila folder, handing a sheet of paper to everyone. "Read through it and see what you think. This is just a rough draft."

After a few minutes, Jon spoke up. "The protections are built in. What I like about this idea is that it's up to Doug, what he has to do for himself. We don't have to do anything for him."

Jeremy nodded. "Yes, we provide him with an opportunity, and he has to make the decision, you know, the commitment, to do something."

Scott said, "This is good for a draft. I have two comments to make. One, I would add at the end that this is a one-time suggestion. This letter does not open a new negotiation but closes an old negotiation. And we do not expect; in fact, we do not want, a response from him. I don't think any of us look forward to regular family circles reading his letters and writing back."

Jon raised his fist. "Good idea, Scott, I'm all for that."

Melanie and Rachel nodded.

Scott turned to Faith. "Miss negotiator-in-chief, what do you say?"

"I sense a consensus. We all agree on three basic principles and think it's good to urge Doug to renew ties to his families. Also, it is good to give him encouragement for self-improvement, letting him know he's on his own, with no continuing input from us. Jeremy can add a few sentences about this being a one-time suggestion with no future correspondence."

People glanced around the room and made eye contact.

Faith said, "Let's close with a prayer circle."

Right on cue, the kids barged in. "Cartoons are over."

Mark said, "Great, a prayer circle!"

Heartfelt petitions and thanks were offered up by everyone, including the children.

38

S cott knew the meeting had tired Faith, so he suggested they leave early. As they pulled out of the driveway, Scott asked, "Are you satisfied?"

"No, not really."

"Why not?"

"I talked about this problem to Father Whitmore, and told him that just as no good deed goes unpunished, no good conscience goes unpenalized."

"How so?"

"I followed my conscience and tried to do what is right for Doug —I don't like Doug. I don't approve of Doug. Doug doesn't deserve any slack from us. But my conscience told me to try to help him."

"Hmm, so why aren't you satisfied?"

"For one thing, because giving Doug a break caused trouble in the family. Fear on the part of Melanie and Rachel. Anger on the part of Jon."

"Don't worry about Jon; he's a good guy; he'll come around."

"And then there's another reason I don't like what we did ... well, how we did it."

"Which is?"

"You know, and if you don't want to say, it, I will. You understood that Jeremy and I put together his response to Doug."

"I knew, this past week, you were carrying a heavy load, but couldn't figure out what it was. Once Jeremy read his statement, I knew the two of you had to work together polishing it."

"Don't be mad at me, please. Jeremy felt he had to do something, and he needed my help. We knew we had to wait for a family circle to introduce his proposal, so we agreed to keep it mum, not mention it even to spouses."

Scott whined, "So you don't trust me."

"Oh, no! Don't think that."

He chuckled. "I knew that would get a rise out of you."

She slapped him on the shoulder. "Well, Mr. Smartypants, I didn't do something like you did, when you walked out of the apartment and drove to Peoria to spy on Doug, leaving me alone for several days and nights."

"I just did what I had to do."

"And that's what I did, following my conscience. In the future, I think we'll look back on this, and all agree it was the right thing to do. But for a while, there may be some tension and hurt feelings."

"Tell me, what drives your conscience?"

"Well, preacher's son, you know the Bible as well as I do, probably better. As I was thinking about doing a good deed for Doug, I was reminded of the story of the shepherd who had a hundred sheep and lost one. So he left the ninety-nine, and looked for the lost sheep, and was happy when he found the lost sheep."

"Yeah, I know that Bible verse, I think it's in Luke. Dad preached on that several times."

"Well, let me put it to you this way; what would your dad say we should do about Doug?"

"Touche! You touched my weak spot. He would say to follow your conscience, do the right thing."

"That's what I thought."

"You know what you are? You're a killjoy. I was having a good time razzing you for keeping me in the dark, and you made me admit that my father would have sided with you. Dad always told us, 'Just do the right thing.'"

When they arrived at the condo, Faith gladly joined Scott in a toast of wine to celebrate a productive family get-together.

MONDAY FAITH ARRIVED at the office early to take care of email and correspondence. At ten o'clock she called Church of the Redeemer and talked to the secretary, setting up a nine thirty appointment with Father Whitmore on Tuesday. All of Monday, the Sunday family circle rolled around in her head as she tried to figure out how to quickly summarize it to her priest.

Tuesday morning Faith climbed the steps to Church of the Redeemer and made a brief stop in front of Mary and Harriet before continuing to Father Whitmore's office. He motioned her in.

"This weekend I wondered about you and your negotiations. Looks like you survived."

"Yes. As expected, some friction between Jon and Jeremy, but we smoothed it out."

She gave a rundown of the meeting.

"So you and Jeremy followed your conscience?"

"Yes, and the penalty was minor differences of opinion, but the letter will go out, suggesting that Doug mend fences with his own families, and work out his rehabilitation while giving new life to rundown houses."

"Congratulations on a job well done."

"I hope that's the end of the story for Douglas Parinello. Now I'd like to focus my attention on the Mothers and Kids Foundation and the merger with the academy. I don't know what you can tell me, but you're an insider. Any tips on how to approach the academy?"

"You seem to be doing everything right, especially the finances. The academy never had a solid funding base. And you've made a valuable connection with Agnes. She can help both with raising money and soothing any negative feedback from alums and their parents. I guess my only suggestion is to go slow and expect some waves, which eventually will subside."

"Thanks for the advice. I want to add that without your support I don't know how I would have made it Sunday."

"That's what I'm here for."

He concluded with a prayer of thanksgiving, and Faith left for the Moms and Kids Foundation.

DRIVING TO THE FOUNDATION, Faith felt energized, with the Sunday meeting and Doug's letter now history. She looked forward to the future and the merger.

She arrived too early for lunch and found Jeremy in his office. He stood up to greet her. She ran into his arms. "You were brave, sacrificed yourself by taking responsibility for our letter. When I saw what you were doing, I thought it would go better if it came from you. Thanks to your thoughtful, diplomatic presentation, the family accepted it. You sent our letter to Ludwig?"

"Yes. I tacked on Scott's two sentences and forwarded the letter to Bill. He said he'd fax it to Doug's lawyer."

"Jeremy, now we need to go full speed ahead with the merger. Well, excuse me, I'm used to being the top executive. I didn't mean to take charge here. But I do think it would be good to have Agnes help us with planning for the best use of the academy's facilities. For example, we could use some or all of their library holdings. And Agnes can help us prepare a basic set of mini-courses. The next step might be recruiting volunteers."

Jeremy laughed. "It's just like being back in your "Faith's Half Dozen Secrets" talk. Your executive mind is sharp as a scalpel. And we need that, to make sure the transition is smooth."

"Any word from Thomas Stinson on fundraising?"

"He has a half dozen prospects for major donations. He doesn't think any of them will put up a million, but he may string together several donations in the hundred to five hundred thousand range."

· · ·

AGNES CONTINUED to tutor Louann in her online literature course, and the example of Amelia and Louann persuaded other residents to sign up for the same class. Several followed their fellow residents in choosing *The Red Badge of Courage* for their reading and writing assignment. Some read other novels. Soon Agnes developed a whole afternoon of tutoring. As more students enrolled in courses, she expanded to a Tuesday and Thursday afternoon tutoring schedule. Because this program started with *The Red Badge of Courage*, Agnes initiated a "Red Badge" award for every resident who was taking a class. She found some red badges at a novelty store and handed out a badge to Amelia, Louann, and other students. Agnes told them, "This badge is a symbol of the courage you show by taking a class."

At the end of the academy's school term, students left, and it was officially closed. Felicia and Agnes took Faith, Jeremy, and Maisie on a tour of the facilities.

The fancy kitchen impressed Maisie. "I always hoped, when I died, to go to heaven. Now I don't have to wait to die, because I'm in heaven right now."

They looked at all the dorm units, the dining room, the all-purpose gym area, and the library, and walked around the grounds.

Faith gushed, "This corner by the back door entrance is an ideal location for a playground."

FAITH AND JEREMY had to sit through several lengthy sessions with Bill Ludwig and his firm's real estate specialist. Faith told Jeremy, "Let them do whatever they have to do. It's a black box to me, especially the convoluted wording about how we will conform to the specifications of the academy endowment."

Jeremy agreed. "So long as we can finalize the merger, that's the only thing that matters."

Fundraising had accumulated about eight million in endowment, and nine sustaining contributions of fifty thousand a year.

The merger went ahead, with the understanding that fundraising would continue until they reached their ten million goal.

The negotiations for uniting the two institutions took all summer. The boards of each organization had to meet separately and then come together for a joint discussion. Felicia and Agnes became board members. By September the formalities concluded with the signing of documents, and it was moving day.

39

The children were the ones most concerned about the move to the academy. Some kids with bad memories of being shuffled from one temporary residence to another had grown comfortable at the Foundation in the company of so many moms and other boys and girls. They tended to stick close to their mothers as they packed and prepared to get on a chartered school bus for the trip to the academy.

"Will all of us be together?"

"Will we still have playtime?"

Once they arrived at the academy property, the youngsters were thrilled with the spacious buildings and grounds. The moms loved the upscale setting.

Faith and Jeremy frequently met with Julia Kaminski, their social worker, reading and evaluating applications for new residents. The new facility would house an additional thirty mom and kid combinations. They hoped to add five or six every week, to let the newcomers blend in with the current residents of the Foundation. Julia Kaminski led Getting to Know You meetings in the all-purpose room, asking everyone to briefly introduce themselves. This approach helped the new residents blend in.

. . .

SEVERAL MONTHS AFTER THE MOVE, the Canterbury Mothers and
Kids Foundation reached its capacity of almost fifty mother-child
pairs. Not only did they have more residents, but the increasing
number of transitioned moms who needed follow-up interviews
presented a heavy workload that Julia couldn't handle by herself.
They followed their plan of hiring a second social worker.

Jeremy and the Foundation suffered from the growing pains
that every renter experiences when becoming an owner. At the old
residential hotel, he had to negotiate with the landlord for repairs
and updates such as painting, and resist rent increases to offset
major renovation. Moving into the academy dumped the responsibility for all upkeep on him. Fortunately, they could keep on the
full-time handyman they inherited from the academy, but he only
had time to keep the place running, fixing leaky faucets and
handling minor repairs. Faith had a maintenance supervisor from
Horton Hotels look over the academy's books, and help them plan a
rainy day fund. They set up a schedule for big-ticket replacement
items, such as roofing. Jeremy followed Faith's suggestion of
contracting with a professional accounting firm to keep track of
expenditures and reserve funds and provide an annual audit. With
all his additional responsibilities, Jeremy hired a full-time secretary
to handle the phone and office details.

The location of the academy in an unincorporated area of the
northwest suburbs meant a longer commute for Faith, and she
couldn't always make it for breakfast. Maisie said, "Just give me a
call if you're gonna be late, and I'll set aside breakfast for you."
Jeremy and Faith gradually settled into a new routine, adjusting to
a more hectic operation.

Jeremy complained, "I feel more like I'm running a business
than heading a social service."

Faith corrected him. "Good service requires good business
savvy. Remember, I included good service as one of my half dozen
secrets."

When they reached a more comfortable fit with the new place, they planned an open house. They sent invitations to a wide circle of donors, social agencies, non-profits, transitioned former residents, and potential new residents. Maisie insisted on preparing refreshments, baking several sheet cakes and fixing many trays of finger food. The paid advertisement in the *Tribune* helped bring in a large crowd.

Even Jon and Rachel came with their kids. Stephie chirped, "This is a fun place, c'n we come here more?"

"Me, too," Jeb said.

Scott persuaded his city editor to let him cover the open house for the *Tribune*, and notified the local TV stations. Scott wrote a glowing account of how Faith and Jeremy had started the Moms and Kids project in a rundown department store, and advanced to a much nicer facility. Scott's connections with the television stations got them good media publicity, including cameo interviews with current residents and praise from transitioned former residents.

The next week Jeremy and Faith basked in the satisfaction of a successful launch of the merger. Letters and checks in the mail confirmed their perception. NPR picked up the story, doing a joint telephone interview of Faith and Jeremy, giving them free national publicity. Several large donations from major philanthropies pushed them over their ten million dollar endowment goal.

In her climb up the executive escalator at Horton Hotels, Faith became accustomed to requests for consults to businesses and speeches at universities and conferences. After the NPR publicity, she now fielded queries from other cities and agencies on how to set up similar operations. She and Jeremy huddled and made more ambitious plans than they had ever envisioned. First, they bought a website, Momsandkids.com, and wrote up a very brief history of their project and an overview of their operation. They didn't want to become a nationwide program but did want to control who could use the "Moms and Kids" name in other cities.

Jeremy joked, "Mother, can we handle success? This is becoming almost a fulltime job for you."

"Funny you would mention that. I've thought it's time for me to hang it up at the hotel and devote more time to the Foundation."

"If you do, we'll have to cook up a special title for you. Already you qualify as the founder."

"Remember, Jeremy; the merger means everything, including titles, has to be run through the new board. I don't need any salary, so whatever the board wants to call me will be fine."

At the next board meeting, they named Faith Armstrong "Founder and Counselor."

Faith's regrets at leaving her longtime career at Horton Hotels was offset by her excitement at her expanded role in the merged Foundation and the prospect of helping start similar programs in other cities.

The Canterbury Moms and Kids Foundation had picked up momentum; she thought nothing could slow them down.

She was at the Foundation when she got a call from Bill.

40

"Hi Bill, I hope this is a social call."

"Well, let me make it social. I want to congratulate you and Jeremy on your wonderful Foundation. I couldn't make it to your open house, but read Scott's piece in the *Trib*, and saw some of the TV footage. Great job!"

"Thanks, Bill. Now ...."

"Yeah, now for the not so good news. Another letter from Mr. Parinello."

"You mean from his lawyer?"

"No, he sent it himself, directly to me."

"He didn't go through his lawyer?"

"He writes that he's done with Garibaldi, who used to represent him."

"What's the point of the letter?"

"It's better that I fax it to you. Another sob story. Doug says he's dying of cancer and is making one last request to you."

"Not to meet the twins?"

"That's about it."

Faith gasped.

"Faith, are you still there?"

"Yes. Fax it to me. We have no way of telling if this is another con."

"No. He does invoke his born again change of heart. And he's authorized his oncologist to confirm his stage four cancer diagnosis, and sends a letter to that effect."

"This is too much to take. I'll look at the fax, and get back to you."

The fax of the doctor's letter and a handwritten letter, along with a hospice information sheet came a few minutes later.

Faith,

This letter is being written for me by a nurse who's taking care of me. A lot has happened since I last wrote to you. The bottom line is that I got prostate cancer, and it spread. Chemo and radiation have made me weak, and I can't travel or do anything. The doctors can't predict how long I will live, but my time is short.

I had my doctor write out a note that I have terminal cancer. I did this because I wouldn't blame you for not trusting me. You can contact his office, and they will confirm this.

Well, let me get right to the point. I am sending you a dying wish. I never got back to my other families, and the only contact I've had with the twins was that half-hour in the lawyer's office. My dying wish is to see the twins one last time.

As I said, I'm too weak to travel. I don't know where the twins are now. If both, or even one of them could come to see me in Peoria, that would make me happy. I include a paper with the name and address of the hospice where I'm staying.

I want to thank you for suggesting Redeemed Souls and Reborn Homes. At first, I thought this was a no-good, do-good make-work bunch. But once I started volunteering, I discovered these guys were sincere, dedicated Christians. They weren't always too good with a hammer or saw, but their hearts were one hundred percent pure. Anyway, I'll say that helping renovate houses with them was more satisfying than all my years in the cutthroat construction business. I wish I had known this kind of Christian friendship and decent companionship when I was young.

I've done a lot of bad things, been a bad guy for most of my life, and can't go back and relive my life. I'm glad that at least I can end my life with a better record of doing some good things.

No, I didn't go to my lawyer Garibaldi to send this. He'd charge me a lot of money and waste a lot of time. So I had my nurse write this out.

I hope you will forward this letter to the twins and that one or both of them will be able to come to see me.

Doug Parinello

FAITH HELD her hands in front of her face as she cried. "It never ends."

Then she wiped her tears away with a handkerchief and called Bill.

"Bill, I don't want to seem coldhearted, but I need to confirm the doctor's letter. Could you call and make sure this is a legitimate letter from his office?"

"I should be able to get the doctor's office to verify that they sent out such a letter. Naturally, their office won't reveal any personal medical information."

"I have to take this to Jeremy and Jon, and I'd prefer to go with sure information, not a hunch."

A half-hour later Bill returned her call. "All the doctor's office will say is that they did give Mr. Parinello a statement of his condition, and if he shares it with others, that is his prerogative."

"Thanks, Bill, that's all I need to know."

FAITH DROVE HOME with the letter, wanting to show it to Scott before she faxed it to the twins.

Late in the afternoon, she phoned Scott. "Bring something home with you."

"Pizza?"

"Anything."

"Sounds bad. Doug?"

"Yeah. I don't want to talk about it on the phone. Just get home as soon as you can."

An hour later Scott walked in with a pizza and laid it on the kitchen table next to Doug's letter, which he quickly read. She opened the box and nibbled on a piece.

Scott frowned. "Sounds bad. Do you believe him?

"I had Bill call his doctor's office, and they admit they gave Doug a statement of his condition."

"So what are you going to do?"

"What I have to do is forward his letter to Jon and Jeremy. Frankly, I don't know what to say to the guys. Any suggestions?"

"That's a tough call. A dying wish, and ...."

"Yeah, I don't know what to propose to the twins, and hate to just leave it up to them."

"Well, here's a reporter's take on it, going back to your last negotiation with Doug. The womenfolk were most concerned with protecting the children, and there seems to be no danger of Scott traveling. I'd guess that Jeremy would be more open to meeting Doug, Jon would be more negative."

"That's a fair assessment."

Faith faxed the letter to Jon and Jeremy, simply adding a note, "Can we talk this over in a family circle next Sunday?"

Then she emailed Father Whitmore, asking for the earliest appointment when he could meet with her.

She and Scott watched television, but her mind was in Peoria.

When they went to bed, she snuggled close to Scott. By twelve-thirty, still awake, she retrieved her journal and went to the lounger. Opening the journal to the first blank page, she wrote:

TROUBLE!
BIG TROUBLE!
The saga of Doug seems never to end.
I hate to admit it, but I'm more concerned for my family than for
Doug. I can't do anything to cure his cancer.
All I can do is hope that this dying wish doesn't harm our family
unity.
Mary and Harriet, help me.

THE PRAYER to her two saints helped her calm down and get back to sleep when she went back to bed.

THE NEXT MORNING at nine an email came in from Father Whitmore, saying he could squeeze her in for an eleven thirty meeting.

On her drive to the South Side, Faith recalled all the other times she had borrowed her priest's ears to listen to her problems. Just talking to him helped her sort out her doubts and fears. She hoped he would be able to set her at ease.

She arrived at eleven-fifteen and had planned to go right into his office when she arrived at Church of the Redeemer, but he was talking to a parishioner, so she detoured into the sanctuary and sat in a pew so that she could view Mary as she prayed. Finishing her petition for divine assistance, she allowed herself a few tears. A few minutes later Father Whitmore put his hand on her shoulder.

"Bad troubles?"

"Yes, a lot of personal conflict and indecision."

"Come on into my office. I've got another appointment at twelve, so we don't have too much time."

They talked as they walked to his office.

"I'll let it all out. Doug is dying of cancer, makes a deathbed wish to see the twins before he dies."

"That's tough."

"Yes, and I said there was personal conflict. It's mostly inside my head and conflict between my head and my heart. You know the story of my heart gauge of warm-cold and soft-hard. The last time we talked, I went along with Jeremy and was more on the warm-soft side. Now, I don't understand it, but I've moved more to the cold-hard side. To be blunt, I'm more against giving Doug his dying wish of seeing the twins. I guess I'm selfish, not wanting Doug to work his way into the family and cause a rift."

"What do Jon and Jeremy say?"

"We have a family circle set for Sunday, so we'll find out then."

"Are you dead set against the twins meeting Doug?"

"I'm not dead set against it, but I feel twinges in my stomach just thinking about it. Doug has terminal cancer, can't travel, so the twins would have to go to Peoria to meet him."

"Well, that means the children would be protected from interacting with him."

"Yes, I know, and that's why I feel ... guilty about denying the guy his dying wish. That must be a sin."

"You think so?"

"Yes, Father, bless me, because I have sinned. Am sinning."

"But you haven't mentioned this to Jon and Jeremy."

"No, I'm still thrashing in my indecision and torment."

"Faith, your family has gone through so much that I know you'll weather this storm. You have God and his two saints on your side, and a solid family bond. Trust them. They'll do the right thing."

Father Whitmore's next appointment arrived, so Faith excused herself.

He called after her, "God be with you."

FAITH STRUGGLED to make it through the few days until Sunday. Busy work at the hotel helped pass the time. Interacting with moms and their offspring at the Foundation refreshed her spirits.

Sunday as they drove to Oak Park for the family circle, Faith asked Scott, "Did you forget to bring your bag of goodies?"

He tapped his head, "It's right in here."

The kids bombarded Scott with questions about what they would do. He just told them, "You know the routine. First lunch, then the bathroom, and after that we're going to do something new."

The children exploded in excitement.

With Scott and the youngsters out of the house, the unannounced family circle began.

Faith heaved a sigh. "Nothing pleases me more than family get-togethers. And nothing disturbs me more than interrupting our social time with yet another negotiation. Well, you've seen Doug's letter and the doctor's note. Just for the record, I did have Bill call the doctor's office, and they told him the doctor's letter is authentic. So, let's hear what you have to say."

Melanie broke the stony silence. "Mom, what do you think?"

"To be honest, I don't know what to make of this situation. I talked this over with Scott, and we can go along with whatever the four of you decide on."

Melanie continued, "Well, my main concern, all along, has been our children, and if Doug can't travel, then there's no problem. I mean, we wouldn't even consider driving the kids to Peoria to see a phantom grandpa."

Rachel nodded. "I agree."

Faith said, "Now we need to hear from the two guys."

Jon blurted out, "Okay, I'll put in the negative vote. Before, I said you reap what you sow, and Doug's loneliness is self-inflicted. Everyone dies, but dying alone is the result of his bad actions. I don't know what to call him—not the prodigal son—may be the prodigal father. We've all agreed we don't want to bring him into the family. And I'm not so sure we should bring the family to him. That's my take on the situation."

Everyone looked to Jeremy, whose lips turned down. "You know, all along, I've looked at Doug as a sinner, someone we should pray for. I'm impressed that he took to heart our suggestion about improving his life as he renovated houses. Now he comes to us with a dying wish. As Melanie and Rachel pointed out, we don't have to worry about him breaking into our family bond. But I am open to seeing him."

Jon shook his head. "Know what this reminds me of? A convicted serial murderer, who just before his execution, calls for a minister, and wants to be saved. If he's honest, then he is a redeemed soul and has undergone a religious change. So nothing any of us could do would make a difference in his salvation or entrance into heaven."

Jeremy nodded. "You're right. His salvation is between him and God. The only thing we can do is to ease his last days. That's why I would be willing to go see him."

Jon tilted his head. "Doug's letter says he'd like both of us to come but would settle for one. Would you go without me?"

"It's up to you if you want to go. If you don't want to go, I'd consider going alone."

Faith frowned. "People, I think we have reached a decision point. I hear Jon saying he will not go to meet Doug, and Jeremy saying he is considering going, even by himself."

The two couples nodded in agreement.

Faith shrugged. "Rachel and Melanie, do you have any objection to Jeremy going solo?"

Melanie looked around at everyone. "Let me put in a condition that I think Scott would mention if he were here. Whoever goes, one or both, I'd like to keep the grandkids out of the meeting. I would hate for Doug to say, 'Now that I've seen my sons, next I want to see my grandchildren.'"

Everyone agreed.

Rachel put water on for tea and coffee.

Faith, glued to her seat, wished Scott could be with her.

Jon broke the tension. "Mother, tell me, how's the fundraising going?"

"The open house led to a lot of local and national publicity, and we pushed over the ten million mark. Thanks again to you and

Rachel for seeding the project. And also for coming to the open house.

Rachel said, "The kids haven't stopped talking about the place. They loved the excitement of all those kids in one place."

Scott and his troupe of admirers returned, full of enthusiasm. The kids bubbled over. "Mom! Dad! We did exercises. Just like grownups."

Scott said, "I looked up several websites, and found a calisthenics and training routine in a nearby park. It's set up after a Swiss model, with various exercises for each station."

He looked around the room, then glanced at Faith, who had a slight frown on her face.

He announced, "Well, I think it's time for Grandma and me to head back to our sky-high condo."

ON THE DRIVE BACK, Scott said, "You could cut the tension in the room with a knife. Not so smooth, huh?"

"You predicted that Jeremy would go for a meeting, Jon wouldn't. So maybe Jeremy will go alone."

"He would do that?"

"He said he was 'open' to it."

"The women agreed?"

"Melanie put in a condition she said you would have insisted on, keeping the kids out of any meeting. She didn't want Doug to say now that I've seen my sons, I want to see my grandchildren."

"Smart girl."

"Scott, I don't like the stress in the family."

"I'm sure it'll work out. What are you going to do?"

"All I can do. Just wait and see."

41

Sunday evening and all day Monday, Faith couldn't get Doug's letter off her mind.

Tuesday morning she made it to the Foundation at the tail end of breakfast. Maisie had saved her something to eat. Then she headed to Jeremy's office, knowing they'd have to talk.

"Good morning, Mother. Those weekend family circles are rough on you."

"Rough on everyone."

"Melanie and I have talked it over. She's not thrilled about me going to Peoria, but she says if I think I should go, then she won't stop me."

"Not exactly a vote of confidence."

"I respect her for wanting to shield the children. Uh, do you think I ought to go?"

"I'm with Melanie. If your conscience tells you to go, then go."

"Without Jon?"

"I understand Jon and don't fault him for not wanting to go. It was a stretch for him to agree to the suggestion for Redeemed Souls and Reborn Homes."

"I'm glad that worked out. It's the only bright spot in this whole mess."

"Jeremy, we did what we thought was right, and it worked. You know I talk to my priest confessor. He encouraged us to set up the rehabilitation program for Doug. And he said the same thing about visiting Doug: each one of us should do what we think is right."

"I've already called the hospice, and their visiting hours are pretty flexible, depending on the condition of the patient."

"Let me know if and when you will go."

"Sure. I may go this next weekend. That way I won't take time away from the Foundation."

JEREMY WENT HOME that afternoon with a heavy heart, thinking of the trip to Peoria. After they had supper and the kids were in bed, he and Melanie sat at the kitchen table sipping iced tea.

Melanie put her hand on his. "You're upset about Doug, aren't you?"

"Yes, can't keep it off my mind."

"Have you decided definitely to go?"

"I think I should go. What do you think?"

"As your mother said, follow your conscience."

"Well, then I guess I'll go."

"Alone?"

"Jon is against going. I mean he's against going himself, but he didn't object to my going."

"You'll let him know?"

"Yes, and I might as well make the call now."

"HELLO, Jon, Jeremy here. Melanie and I were talking, and, well, I've decided to drive to Peoria, probably this Saturday."

"If you think that's what you should do, then I guess you'd better make the trip."

"It's not easy visiting people on their deathbed. As a youth minister, I only had a few of those cases. But I can do it."

"Well, good luck, Jeremy. Let me know how it goes."

"Sure, I'll call or email you."

WHEN JON HUNG UP, Rachel asked him, "Jeremy is going?"

"That's right; looks like Saturday."

"And you're not going with him."

"No, he'll go by himself."

"You don't like Doug, do you?"

"That's putting it mildly. I dislike him. Detest him."

"Nobody likes Doug. Faith and Scott don't like him. Rachel and I don't like him. I suppose even Jeremy doesn't like Doug."

"No, he doesn't *like* Doug, but his Christian faith tells him to *love* Doug."

Melanie chuckled. "You could never *love* Doug, right?"

He shook his head. "Not in a million years."

"Who do you love?"

"Uh, I love you."

"And our kids?"

"Of course."

"And your mother?"

"Yes."

"And?"

"I see where you're going. You're right; I love Jeremy, too."

"And you're not going to visit Doug because you don't love him, you don't even like him. In fact, you dislike him."

"That's right. Uh, you know, Rachel, I think we've had this conversation before when Jeremy was going to meet Doug alone in the lawyer's office."

"You remember that?"

"Yes, and I think this is your cue to ask, 'Am I my brother's keeper?'"

"Do I need to ask it?"

"No, you made your point. Jeremy should visit Doug because of his Christian love for him. And I should go with Jeremy because of my brotherly love for my twin."

"If you think so, Jon."

"Rachel, you devious demon, you, I *love* you."

Jon called Jeremy. "Jeremy, let me know when you're driving down to Peoria, and I'll go with you."

"You changed your mind?"

"Not really. Rachel changed my mind. I'll be perfectly honest with you. I'm going not because of Doug, but because of you. I'm doing it for you. We've been through a lot together, and I want us to be together on this."

"It means a lot to me, Jon."

SATURDAY MORNING JEREMY picked up Jon. "Thanks a lot for coming with me."

"It's for you, Jeremy, not for Doug."

"In the future, years from now, I think you'll be glad you bid farewell to our father."

"I don't want to talk about Doug; it's too upsetting. Let me change the subject, and talk about something we both agree on. You know, in our family conversations, I seem to be Mr. Negative, but I can also be Mr. Positive.

"I went to the open house for the Foundation, and I never really appreciated everything you're doing. You're helping so many mothers and their children. You've created an atmosphere—I guess the French call it ambiance—of love and trust. That in itself is a miracle. You can count on Jontronics, and Rachel and me, to continue to support the Foundation. I told Mom, and I'll repeat to you, that money is crucial to your project. But without tender loving care, the money goes nowhere.

"What I'm getting around to is a suggestion. You know I'm the computer nerd, so if I'm off base, tell me to shut my mouth. But Rachel and I noticed the absence of men at the Foundation. And what I know of children is they need male role models as well as female role models. So, getting around to my suggestion, I'd be glad to volunteer at the Foundation. I'm not as clever as Scott with games, but Rachel and I read to our children, and I figure I could come and read to the kids. We have tons of books, and I have a portable projector so that I could project the pages of a storybook on a blank wall while I read the words. Part of my strategy is for the kids to have contact with a man. Well, that's one thing I wanted to share with you today. Is that a possibility?"

"You're right on target; in fact, you hit the bullseye. Even our social worker is concerned about what she calls the gender gap, kids without a father not having a man to look up to."

"Let me know when you'd like me to come, and if the kids like it, maybe we could have a weekly story time like you have daily playtime."

"That's super!"

"Well, if you can take two surprises, Rachel would like to volunteer, too. At the open house, she talked to Agnes and knows you want to help the moms hone their skills for occupations. Rachel could teach the computer short courses you have in mind, either beginning or intermediate or advanced level. She and Agnes can work out a plan. If you'd take two of us, we could hire a sitter for our kids, and come at the same time. I could do story time; she could do computer time."

"Jon, that's better than a fortune cookie with double happiness."

They talked about the Foundation while driving to Peoria.

ARRIVING AT THE HOSPICE, their cheerful mood changed. Worry lines spread across Jon's forehead. "Brother, you've had more experience with sick calls and deathbed visitations, so you take the lead."

They checked in at the main desk and walked to Doug's room.

An IV was hooked to his arm, and other cords were attached to his chest. Jeremy mumbled, "He's so pale and thin." Doug was sleeping, so they went to the nurse's station and asked about him. The nurse told them he had morphine earlier, and would probably be awake soon; he would have an hour or two of alertness before the next pain medication. They went back to the room and sat down.

Fifteen minutes later he roused and rang for a nurse with his call button. "Mr. Parinello, you have company."

"Company? Who?"

"Take a look."

The nurse came closer to them and whispered, "Because of the medication, it may take him a while to focus."

Doug rolled his head back and forth on the pillow until he looked directly at the twins. After staring for a minute, he closed his eyes, chin trembling, tears dribbling down his cheeks. "Well, I'll be damned! You came — both of you. You ... you don't know how happy this makes me. I thought I'd go to my grave without ever seeing you again. Let's see now; it's been a while." He pointed a bony finger at Jeremy.

"I'm Jeremy."

He moved his trembling finger toward Jon.

"And I'm Jonathan."

"Yes, Jeremy and Jonathan. My sons. My twins. I tried to get in touch with you, you know, the courts and the lawyers, but it didn't work out. That doesn't matter, because now you're here. The only ones who come see me are the Redeemed Souls, the ones I worked with to make over houses. They're terrific people. Good Christians. I wish I had started my life with them. Then my life would have been different.

"I have so much I want to tell you, don't know where to start. Well, if I had been a redeemed soul thirty years ago, I would have married your mother. Then we all would have been happy. Not like now ....

"You two are the spittin' image of what I was like at your age. And women found me handsome. I couldn't help myself. One thing

I want to tell you, don't let your good looks go to your head. Find one woman and stay with her. No monkeyin' around. Later you'll regret it, like me, end up a lonely old man. Won't be many people at my funeral.

"And go to church. Religion will keep you out of trouble. You know the trouble I've been in. Your mother told you all about that."

Jeremy and Jon stood side by side next to his bed, nodding at what Doug said.

"Well, hell's bells, here I am talking my head off, and I want to hear from you two. Where do you live?"

"In the Chicago area," Jeremy replied.

Jon added, "We drove down together."

"If I were healthy, I would've driven clear across the country to see you."

Jeremy said, "Don't worry about that; we only had to drive a few hours to get here."

Doug grimaced, then asked, "What do you two do? I mean, work?"

Jeremy said, "I've been a minister, and now run a social agency for single moms and their kids."

Doug tried to sit up. "A minister! Well, let me tell you who helped me. The One Way people. Have you heard about them?"

Jeremy and Jon exchanged glances. Jeremy said, "Yes, I know them. They do good work."

"I asked one of their ministers to handle my funeral. My time is coming. Uh, and ... Jonathan, what do you do?"

"I work with computers."

"Never really did much with computers. Construction was my thing. I could build anything." They talked for about forty minutes, with Doug dominating the conversation, rambling about his mistakes and bad decisions, running his construction company, and making a mess of his life. "Learn from my mistakes. Go to church, read the Bible, and leave the women alone."

Doug fumbled for his call button and rang for the nurse, who showed up a few minutes later. "Yes, Mr. Parinello, I know it's time for your next pain medication. I'll get it."

"Damned pills and shots. Only last for an hour or two." He shook his head, shutting his eyes and clenching his jaw.

Soon the nurse came in with a hypodermic. "This will give you some relief." She motioned Jeremy and Jon toward the door, and whispered, "The shot will knock him out and stop the pain, and he'll probably sleep for an hour or two. You might as well leave for now; get something to eat or shop."

Jon looked at Jeremy, then turned to the nurse. "We have to head back to Chicago, so we'll probably leave soon."

Jeremy said, "Let's stop for coffee."

Jon countered, "Let's hit a fast food restaurant on the highway. Maybe we can go to a drive through place."

"You want to get home as soon as possible."

"Yes, I'm not used to end of life scenes, and it upset me."

"Want to talk about it?"

"No. Not really. Let me admit you were correct; it was right to come. And it wouldn't be fair to expect you to make the trip and visit by yourself."

They made small talk about the scenery and the weather, stopping to get takeout coffee, and continued to Chicago.

When he dropped off Jon, Jeremy said, "I want to thank you for coming with me. It meant a lot, both to our father and especially to me."

Jon waited until after the kids were in bed to talk to Rachel. "He was extremely sick, on death's door. It threw me for a loop, and I don't want to talk about it."

Jeremy told Melanie, "I respect Jon. He doesn't share my faith, but he went along with me and gave me support. Oh, there's big news.

He wants to volunteer reading stories to the kids, and Rachel will volunteer to help moms with computers."

"How did it go with Doug?"

"He was doped up, had difficulty talking, and hasn't changed, did most of the talking, regrets about how he ruined his life and said for us not to ruin ours. I'm like Jon, not ready to talk about it now. Maybe never."

42

Happily retired from Horton Hotels, Faith was even happier volunteering four days a week at the Foundation. She couldn't decide which she liked better, acting the child during playtime, or becoming a surrogate mother while advising moms.

Faith welcomed Jon for his first crack at story time. He set up a high tech projector in the all-purpose room and brought several children's picture books for the kids to view on a blank wall while he read. When the kids were seated on the floor, he said, "My name is Jon, and I like stories. If you like stories, raise your hands." All hands went up, along with squeals of delight. He had plenty of experience reading to his children, and the Foundation kids ate it up.

After forty minutes, he asked, "Would you like to do this next week?"

A unanimous roar answered him.

"Well, we'll ask Mr. Jeremy and Miss Faith, and see if we can arrange that."

. . .

AFTER JON READ STORIES, Rachel and Agnes were still brain-storming about how to run the computer short courses, so Jon and Faith had some time alone. They went outside the back door, where some playground equipment and one adult-size table had been set up.

"Mom, it's been hard for me to talk about Doug, even to Rachel. All I want to say today is that I was wrong about not wanting to see him. Jeremy was right; if I had not gone, later I would have regretted it.

"That's all I can say now about Doug. You may be interested, though, that this episode made a deep impression on me. And you know nerdy me, always tinkering with Digirel. Even after your Secrets talk the first time we met, I cribbed some of your remarks about Confucius and worked them into Digirel.

"The experience with Doug taught me two lessons. The first lesson is compassion. I learned that compassion goes beyond pity. Pity is just feeling sorry. Compassion involves empathy, feeling for and with another person. I've developed a new segment of Digirel that helps people cultivate compassion. I know you like Mary and baby Jesus, and Mary's compassion for suffering people. There's a deity in Buddhism, Kannon, sometimes known as the deity of compassion. There's even a form of Kannon known as Koyasu Kannon, Koyasu translates something like 'child-rearing.' Women pray to Koyasu Kannon for ease in childbirth, and for divine help raising children. Mary—you know, the Madonna—and Koyasu Kannon will be two visual aids helping people nurture compassion."

Faith raised her eyebrows. "The mother-child relationship is a lot of things, not just biological, but emotional and also sacred. I'll be interested to see how you handle this bond."

Jon continued. "The second lesson is about repentance. Doug regretted very much all the trouble he caused people and didn't get rid of that heavy load. In Christianity, the Lord's Prayer is one way of asking for forgiveness of sins and forgiving others of sin. Other religions, too, have prayers for relieving people of their shortcomings. I'm putting in Digirel a segment on repentance, helping people unload their guilt and regrets for shortcomings and mistakes.

"Well, end of story. I still find it difficult to talk about Doug. My way of working out these things is to incorporate it into Digirel."

"Jon, only a virtuoso like you could turn a sick call into a creative moment."

Rachel came out the back door. "So here you are. How did storytelling go?"

Faith answered. "It was grandiloquent. The kids loved it, and expect a repeat performance next week."

Rachel smiled. "Agnes and I are still working out the details in the levels of computer sessions."

The threesome joined Jeremy in his office for a recap of storytelling and computer classes.

Jeremy joked, "The Foundation is rapidly becoming a family business."

43

J eremy's comment about the Foundation becoming a family business delighted Faith. That phrase tickled her brain and warmed her heart. She went home in a mood of celebration.

Always honest with herself, she realized one reason for the celebration was that Doug's imminent death meant no more tension-filled family circles figuring out how to deal with him. But the main reason for her festive mood was the extraordinary achievements of Moms and Kids, and the involvement of the whole clan in this do-good, feel-good, be-good endeavor.

She couldn't wait for Scott to come home. When he entered the door, he joked, "Turn the lights down; that's a thousand-watt smile on your face."

"Yes. Things went so well today at the Foundation, with Jon and Rachel both volunteering, and Jeremy made my day by saying the Moms and Kids venture had become a family business. So I'm in a party mood. Let's go out to Boccaccio's, and return to the place where we first met. I'm a little romantic and nostalgic tonight."

"Well, if you want to travel down memory lane, I'll have to grow a two-day stubble and stay awake all night, and then show up with rumpled clothes and a lousy attitude. It's a wonder you wanted to see me a second time after that dismal debut."

As they taxied to Boccaccio's, they joked about their first meeting and the followup "dinner dates." Faith remembered the table where they sat that initial time together at Boccaccio's and asked the maître 'd to seat them there. She motioned to the head waiter. "Open a bottle of your house Cabernet Sauvignon and let it breathe while we order."

Scott teased her, "You'd make a good reporter with that memory."

She bantered, "May I suggest the lasagna, with salad and the house dressing?"

"Perfect recall."

She ordered for both of them and asked the waiter to bring the wine. She okayed the wine and had both glasses filled.

She raised her glass in a toast. "To us, and to Moms and Kids, a family business."

They clinked glasses and savored the wine.

Faith and Scott enjoyed the meal, reminiscing over that get-to-know-each-other event.

Returning to the condo, Faith said, "Remember when you first came here, and oohed and aahed over my books?"

"Yes, you impressed me as a self-educated hotelier. Tell me, what prompts you to time travel back to earlier times?"

They sat in their loungers watching night's darkness descend into the lake.

Faith held her chin with one hand. "I can't hide my feelings from you. Honestly, with Doug on death's door, I know we won't have any more crunch family circles debating how to handle him. I never want to lead another family council like those of the past few years. I look forward to clan gatherings as peaceful and festive occasions."

"Hmm, you told me Jon and Jeremy are still tight-lipped about Doug, but you seem to be more open to the subject."

"Hey, I've had three decades more experience in juggling a wide range of emotions. I'm glad they had their farewell session with him, to resolve any future guilt feelings."

"And you—has Father Whitmore given you absolution?"

"That's a complex issue. You may recall I had problems forgiving my father, but eventually got over that problem, thanks to Saint Harriet. Doug is a little more ambiguous. When I saw how miserable he was, my hate turned to pity. Jon taught me that pity is just feeling sorry for someone. Jeremy showed Jon the meaning of love, reaching out to someone you don't like. I admit, my attitude toward Doug is more pity than Christian love."

"You're an excellent example of do-it-yourself psychoanalysis. Hmm, but you don't see your relationship to Doug through Christian love."

"No, I've worked out what ... well, I can't call it a philosophy of life, but maybe a narrative of life. I call it my destiny — something I didn't choose but had to accept. Meeting Doug was happenstance. But it set the course of my entire life. That meeting at Pappy's Pizza Parlor with Doug—we called him the devil—gave me the twins, who defined my reason for existence. Even during the decades when we were separated, and I didn't live *with* them, I still lived *for* them. Jeremy and Jon became my twin destiny."

"So you can't see Doug as totally negative."

"No, otherwise there would be no twins."

Scott rubbed his chin. "And you call that your destiny."

"Yes, mixed in with serendipity. By that I mean things happened that I had no knowledge of, no control over. Your curiosity led you to do detective work on Jeremy and Jon, documenting them as identical twins. Think of all the circumstances that might have intervened. You might have been too busy and never gone to Canton and verified their identity, in which case they wouldn't know today they had a twin. And there's no reason they had to look me up. They might have just gone on with their lives. I'm glad they tried to find me, and with your help, did locate me. All of these circumstances are like links in a fragile chain, and if one link were missing, you and I wouldn't be here today."

"Scary, isn't it?"

"Yes, and one not so serendipitous link in this chain is when Father Whitmore helped me move past forgiving Dad, and forced me to think of Doug. He recognized Doug as unfinished business. That's where you entered the picture, doing the detective work locating Doug."

Faith laughed. "I thought I had forgotten and got past Doug, but Father Whitmore realized that I needed to be honest and face him. You helped me see him in Peoria, and I became unhinged. That's why I call Doug the Devil Déjà vu. He re-emerged from my past. And let's face it, if it weren't for that second encounter with Doug, I wouldn't have met you."

"You're right."

"Fortunately, you didn't give up on me after my Peoria meltdown."

"I had never met someone like you, and couldn't give you up."

"And you helped forge the family circle. Jeremy claims I'm the founder of Mothers and Kids, but you're the founding figure of our family. I don't want to say 'patriarch,' that sounds too macho, but it's true, you hold the clan together, and the grandkids worship you."

"Well, you started talking about the Mothers and Kids Foundation becoming a family business, and I guess I'm the odd man out."

"Not for long, I hope. Jon was right; we need more male staff members at the Foundation. He initiated storytelling and will volunteer once a week. I hope you can find one morning a week and lead play time. I admit I have done the best I could, imitating and improvising from what I saw you do with our grandkids. But you can do a much better job. And you can show the youngsters that father figures can be fun figures."

"You know I'm an incorrigible ham and would love to do that."

They sat in silence for a few minutes. A very bright shooting star lit up the sky and the lake.

Faith bolted upright in her lounger. "You know, Mark Twain was born when Halley's Comet appeared and died the next time it showed up. I wonder if this shooting star means that Doug passed away. If so, it is a sign of the end of the devil déjà vu.

ACKNOWLEDGMENTS

I would like to thank those who read early drafts of this novel, especially Caroline McCullagh.

I would also like to thank my publisher, Rick Lakin, at iCrew Digital Publishing, and DJ Rogers of Justwritedesign.com for finishing the cover.

PRAISE FOR H. BYRON EARHART

For No Pizza in Heaven

In *No Pizza in Heaven*, H. Byron Earhart uses his vast knowledge of comparative religion to craft a compelling study of how belief can both destroy and heal.

—*Richard Lederer, best-selling author of books about language and history*

For Faith Finds Forgiveness

Faith's quest for forgiveness is matched only by her professional expertise which becomes a part of her spiritual journey. This journey is especially challenging when she faces decisions about the twins' father. The reader is drawn convincingly into her struggle and the conflicting emotions that result after she takes action. Faith's saga examines religious beliefs, soul-searching, and the power of understanding and compromise when finding common ground. This is a thought-provoking read that leaves one fully satisfied.

J.T.

For Meeting the Devil

Growing up in the 50's I remember my mother going next door to have coffee with Betty. Betty and mother would share the ups and downs and little ordinary details of their lives. Years later when Betty passed away my mother shared with me the details of her friendship with Betty. They were ordinary women. They did not blast dragons from the sky or hack zombies or machine gun terrorist hordes. They were not prostitutes or princesses draped in diamonds.

This book is about one woman sharing with the reader the ups and downs of her life without machine guns or magic. There isn't blood and guts oozing from the pages. We share with her hope for better times. We don't want her to lose her moral compass. This book is sharing life with a friend. It is warm, satisfying, and a pleasure to read.

—*Sara Allen, Attorney*

For Devil Déjà Vu

After devouring the first three books of the Twin Trilogy, my wife and I couldn't wait for a fourth book to appear on the scene. We weren't disappointed! The Devil Deja Vu is another terrific read that we both thoroughly enjoyed. Now we're hoping to see a fifth book in the series to be published soon.

ABOUT H. BYRON EARHART

H. Byron Earhart, born in central Illinois, attended Knox College, and received a doctorate in History of Religions from the University of Chicago and was awarded a grant as a Fulbright Scholar. He began writing fiction as a teenager, but as a professor at Western Michigan University, published books on religion, especially religion in Japan. After retiring to San Diego, he returned to his early love of writing fiction. *The Devil Déjà Vu* is Book Four of The Twin Destiny Series.

Visit his websites at <u>byronearhartauthor.com</u> and <u>byronearhart.com</u>